Insatiable Love

Insatiable Love

Latoya Chandler

www.urbanbooks.net

Urban Books, LLC
300 Farmingdale Road, NY-Route 109
Farmingdale, NY 11735

ISBN 13: 978-1-64556-247-4
ISBN 10: 1-64556-247-6

First Mass Market Printing October 2021
First Trade Paperback Printing March 2021
Printed in the United States of America

10 9 8 7 6 5 4 3 2 1

*This is a work of fiction. Any references or similarities
to actual events, real people, living or dead, or to real
locales are intended to give the novel a sense of reality.
Any similarity in other names, characters, places, and
incidents is entirely coincidental.*

Distributed by Kensington Publishing Corp.
Submit Orders to:
Customer Service
400 Hahn Road
Westminster, MD 21157-4627
Phone: 1-800-733-3000
Fax: 1-800-659-2436

CHAPTER 1

LATAVIA'S GETTING MARRIED

I can't control the stream of tears escaping my eyes as I admire myself in the mirror. This is the happiest day of my life and the best off that I have ever been. However, I feel like something is missing. *Maybe it's just wedding-day jitters*, I think before swallowing back the anxiety creeping up my throat. There is no way I can have my Prince Charming waiting too long. Oh yes, I, Latavia Watkins, am about to walk down the aisle in one of the baddest gowns money can buy. Thanks to my bestie and wedding planner, Nariah. I pretty much told her what I wanted, gave her a budget to work with, and she made my dreams a reality. It's still unbelievable that in approximately forty-five minutes, I will become Mrs. Darnell Maxwell Carter. It's crazy because, in all actuality, it feels as if we just met.

I become lost in my thoughts and begin reminiscing about just how Darnell and my relationship began. No one would ever believe that we met only a year and a half ago, on a dating website of all places. Hell, I was there, and I still don't believe it. What started off as a hobby, or a way for me to pass time at work, turned into something bigger. Six feet, three inches of dark chocolate–covered muscles had me intrigued. When he smiled, I was instantly infatuated and knew I had to meet this god on earth face-to-face. It wasn't just his looks that had me going; it was his conversation too. Darnell knew exactly what to say, when to say it, and how to say it. Then, on top of all that, he listened to me. He didn't just hear me. He actually listened, and it all just seemed too good to be true.

Despite the nervous tension that I was battling, I made up my mind, stepped outside my comfort zone, and agreed to finally meet him in person. I figured, after all, that since we had been chatting and getting to know one another via text messaging, picture mail, and countless hours of phone conversations for a little over six months, it was time to meet. Once we agreed upon a face-to-face introduction, I requested that he meet me at a lingerie store in Queens Center Mall. It was a neutral location and was close by for both of us since we both lived in Queens. The mall was approximately thirty minutes away from both of us. I suggested a bra and panty store because we had never spoken about sex. I needed to make sure he wasn't a punk when it came to maneuvering his way around all this goodness and mercy that God had so graciously blessed me with.

Who would have thought that it would turn out to be the best first date that I had ever had in my life? I ended up modeling every single item for him in my heels, per his request. So, not only did we end up shopping, but once his eyes beheld all this flawlessly crafted edible arrangement, he wanted to run his pockets in the worst way, and I kindly accepted. I am what you would call beauty and brains, and I happen to be thick on all the right places, or thickums, if you let Darnell tell it. No, I'm not the perfect Coke bottle–shaped female, but I know how to capture a man's attention. Hence, when he pulled out his credit card for lotions, body spray, bras, and underwear, I let him have it his way.

I snap out of my moment of reminiscing when Nariah walks into my dressing room.

"You have twenty minutes to dry your eyes, get your makeup refreshed, and get your ass ready to walk down that damn aisle! I have worked entirely too hard for you to make me look bad," she snaps before smiling.

I have to laugh at her crazy butt, because her utterance sounded like something I would say to her. That's one of the reasons why we are as thick as thieves to this day: we are so much alike.

It takes me all of ten minutes to reapply the makeup I've ruined with my tears, and before I know it, it's showtime.

"Well, this is it," I say aloud to myself as I take one last look in the mirror at the snow-white, floor-length gown that is accented with crystals. It hugs my frame seductively yet tastefully. "There's no turning back now." As soon as the words part my lips, I become nervous and hesitant. I quickly ignore the nagging feeling and regain my composure. I assume it comes with the territory of wedding-day jitters.

I'm so glad I listened to my heart and not my panicking mind, especially once the double doors of the church open. The sound of the acoustic guitar playing "Here Comes the Bride" gives me my cue. Moments later, I lock eyes with my Prince Charming, who stands smiling at the end of the aisle. A lone tear escapes his eye and rolls slowly down his face before he wipes it away. As I stand in my designated spot, I know I am making the right decision. However, that doesn't stop my nerves from going into overdrive, causing me to squeeze Nariah's hand even tighter.

Nariah is the only person in my life that is fit to give me away and walk me down the aisle. She is a wedding planner by trade, my bestie for life, and the only family that I acknowledge. The closer we get to the end of the aisle, the more I panic and tighten my grip. Although I am squeezing the life out of her hand, Nariah turns to me and gives me a warm smile. Which assures me that, as she stated earlier, Darnell is the best thing that has ever happened to me. Despite all that I've been through throughout my life, it is evident right now that everything has been and is working together for my good, as evidenced by the prize that presently awaits me.

The rest of the wedding ceremony goes by in a blur, and before I know it, Pastor Foreman is pronouncing us husband and wife. Darnell pulls me into his arms, and I am finally able to slob my husband down. Oh yes, today is a good day.

Words cannot begin to express my feelings for this man. He is undoubtedly a gift from God, specially handcrafted just for me. Darnell loves me past my hurts, pains, and insecurities—well, at least the ones he knows about. The way I see it, we all have a past buried in the back of our mind, a past that is off limits for discussion and something we would prefer to keep hidden and take to our graves. I am quite sure he has a few skeletons of his own that he purposely hasn't mentioned. To put it another way, things are beautiful just the way they are. That's neither here nor there, because no matter what he or I may have gone through, he makes sure to keep a smile on my beautiful face and ensures I stay happy no matter what.

He does just that and then some. For instance, since our three-week honeymoon cruise to Europe, I have been to Hawaii, France, Italy, and the Bahamas, and these trips included shopping sprees. All the places I'd seen on television, dreamed and read about, my beloved made a reality for me. However, I don't love him just for the material things; I love him because he genuinely loves me. He taught me what love is and how to love not only him but also myself.

Let's not forget about his sex game. Good Lord, that man has my body free on demand; whatever he wants me to do, say, or explore, his wish is my command. Every time we intertwine our flesh, it's like the very first time we examined one another's bodies. Speaking of the first time, it happens to have happened the night we met, during our first date. If I'm not mistaken, I was trying on some lingerie in the dressing room in keeping with his request, and seeing the bulge in his pants let me know I was doing a fantastic job. Anyway, as I tried on bras for Darnell, he wanted to purchase each item I touched or looked at, along with a few other things.

I become lost in thought as I recall what we did next.

"How do you feel about going to happy hour to have a few drinks and appetizers?" he asks as we exit the store.

"I would love that," I reply, blushing and grinning like a Cheshire cat.

"Cool. We can take my car, if you don't mind."

"Lead the way, handsome," I reply seductively.

Mahoney's Bar and Grill must know that this is our first date and that I want to leave a lasting impression. Our drinks are on steroids, strong as all hell. I, no doubt, drink entirely too much and am feeling myself, which, of course, leads to me being very frisky. My hands have a mind of their own, and they want to touch, caress, and grope Darnell's bulging manhood, and they do just that.

"I'm sorry. I know it's not ladylike, and while my brainbox is saying, 'Stop! No,' my eyes and hands are saying, 'Oh yes,'" I joke.

When I feel his manhood at full attention, my mouth begins to water. I want to see, feel, and taste all that thickness being held hostage in the jean shorts he is wearing. Darnell must have read my mind and has plans of his own. The look he gives me would have made my panties soaking wet if I had any on. He stares into my eyes with a dirty, lustful grin on his face as he grabs that mouthwatering bump in his pants. Without removing his eyes from mine, he gives me a head nod toward the door.

"I think we're done here, little lady," he says, helping me to my feet.

I quickly follow his lead and get my hot tail up out of my seat. Then I grab my purse and proceed to exit the building. Looking over my shoulder, I can see Darnell is right behind me, practically on top of my four-and-a-half-inch pumps. As we approach the car, Darnell grabs me by my hair and pulls me to him. The back of my head rests on his chest as he lifts my skirt, then allows his hands to travel the pathway to my love garden. When he reaches his desired destination, my hot juices begin to drip on the two fingers he uses to dance around my juice box. He is now able to feel just how turned on I am.

"Damn, baby. All this is for Daddy?" he asks inquisitively.

I can see this has turned him on to the eleventh power. Darnell slowly begins removing his fingers from my hot box, allowing my nectar to drip down from his fingers onto my inner thigh. He wastes no time in slowly and seductively devouring the secretions left behind on each of his fingers, one by one. I learned a long time ago that there ain't no fun if Mama can't get any, so I join him. I lick my juices off with him, stealing kisses when our lips connect. That is something I have never done, and to my surprise, I instantly become addicted. I am fascinated with the way I taste, and he enjoys it just as much as I do.

"You taste so good, baby. I can imagine how good it's going to feel when I slide up in that."

"I love the way your mouth feels, Darnell," I moan.

He allows his hands to have a free-for-all and roam all over my body. Then, without notice, he lifts me off the ground and gently places me in a sitting position on the hood of the car.

"Relax while I tame that cat," he instructs as he proceeds to spread my legs wide enough to get a good look at my honey bun. From the looks of it, he must like what he sees. He goes into beast mode before sliding me down to the edge of the car. Darnell drops to his knees, goes headfirst, and licks and sucks all over my sweetness, as if it is his first and last meal. He allows his tongue to penetrate me, as if it is his manhood. Then he switches between stabbing his tongue in and out of my canal to using the tip of his tongue to dance across my clit to a tune only he can hear. I love every minute of it. Within a matter of minutes, my legs begin to shiver, and then I experience my very first orgasm at the age of twenty-nine.

"Oh, my goodness! What are you doing to me?" I wail in pleasure.

"Treating you like a lady," he replies, increasing the speed of his tongue lashing.

It is one thing for a man to make you cum, but an orgasm, my friend, is, and I quote, "a whole new world." In my entire existence, I have never, and I mean never, had a man take his time to please me the way Darnell has. To top it off, it has taken place on the hood of a damn car. That alone has me open like 7-Eleven. He doesn't give me any time to recover from that mind-blowing orgasm before he forcefully yet gently slides me off the car.

"Bend over and grab your ankles," he instructs with the same authority an officer of the law would use when arresting someone.

I do as I am told, and he lets his masculinity find its way home, entering me with a quick thrust, then explores every inch of my walls. I match his rhythm and throw my ass back at him. I am testing him to see if he can catch all this good loving I'm pitching to make him feel as good as he is making me feel. Just when I feel him tensing up, I ease away from him and push him up against the truck.

"My turn," I utter enticingly, sliding to my knees and locking eyes with his before demolishing all nine and a half inches of him. I gag a little. However, I am far from a punk. I take me time and relax my throat. Slowly, I take all of him into my warm mouth, like a real champion on a mission to accomplish the task at hand. I professionally lick, spit, slurp, suck, and deep-throat that thick chocolate beef stick, as if I am getting paid for my services, until his knees begin to buckle. Once he commences to shuddering, I suck even harder and allow him to explode in my mouth, releasing all his burnt-sienna babies down my throat.

"Damn, girl! What are you trying to do? Make a brother wife you up?" he inquires, slightly out of breath.

"Just giving you what you gave me, to let you know all of this is real," I retort.

By the time we regain our composure, I happen to look over to my left, and that's when I notice we have an audience.

"Darnell, I think someone's watching us. Look over there." Embarrassed, I point in the direction of the Peeping Tom.

"He has company, and from the looks of it, he's not paying us one bit of attention."

Getting a better look, I realize the gentleman watching us isn't alone. He has a female companion on her knees, and she is taking him to the same place from whence Darnell and I have just returned. That turns us on even more, and before I know it, I am being picked back up and tossed into Darnell's truck.

"Where are you taking me?" I ask.

"You will find out soon enough," he shoots back, fastening his seat belt.

Thirty minutes later, we pull up to a two-story hi-ranch home. Being that it is now pitch dark out, I am unable to get a good look at the house or the neighborhood. I don't have my glasses on or my contacts in, so I really can't see a thing. That's what I get for trying to be cute and grown up. I assume this is his home, because he uses the remote atop his visor to open the garage door before pulling in. After he exits the vehicle, Darnell makes sure to grab all the bags before he proceeds to walk to the other side and open the car door for me. Darnell can't get the door to the house open fast enough between fumbling with the keys and trying to feel me up at the same time.

"You need a little help there, buddy?" I say, clowning.

"I got this. You're the one who's going to need help," he threatens as the door swings open.

As soon as his hands are free, he makes sure they find their rightful place back under my skirt, in search of my well-manicured garden of love.

"Can you please give me a tour before you make another mess?" I taunt, admiring his stylishly decorated home.

"The grand tour will come much later, little lady. Right now, I need another show. I want to see just how hard you can get me before this bulldozer tears your walls back down."

"Your wish is my command."

"In between modeling everything in these bags—from the lotions to the sprays—I want them juicy lips on this dick, and make sure you leave them heels on. Don't hold back, either, because I'm going to tear that wet ass up."

His words only make my camel toe do a backflip.

CHAPTER 2

DARNELL'S FIRST DATE

Well, the day is finally here for me to meet ole girl. I can't believe I've been dealing with her for six months straight and have yet to physically lay these hazel eyes or these ass-palming hands on her. *Yeah, I'm slipping*, I think. I hope and pray her ass looks like it does in them damn pictures. I would have no problem leaving her right up in that store, and that's my word. I'm shocked she wants to meet up at Victoria's Secret; she's probably a real live freak, with her nasty ass. I have to laugh at that one. Honestly, her wanting to meet me there, of all places, has me rock hard just from the thought of it alone.

This is too good to be true.

"Lord, I need a favor. Please let Latavia be all she displayed in those damn pictures—well, not the first one she sent. You know the picture she sent the first time I requested one? The one of Lil Jon? She got me good with that and grabbed a brother's attention at the same time. That was different, with her crazy ass."

Yo, why am I smiling? This shit is bugged out. My bad!

"God, please forgive me for cursing. She's got a brother a little nervous. Amen!"

I know you're probably wondering why a distinguished gentleman like myself would have to resort to online dating when I have to wear a full-body condom to stay protected from all the trim shoved in my face on the regular. I'm not saying I'm one of those *GQ* dudes, but I clean up nicely if you ask me. I stand before you—a six-three, dark-skinned man with the complexion of dark chocolate milk, an average muscular build, and brown eyes. I keep my head shaved bald, my face always freshly shaven, and my goatee on point. You can call me King Ding-a-ling, and I'll leave it at that. Yes, I'm blessed: my dick game is unmeasured, and I'm a blessing to the ladies. If Latavia plays her cards right tonight, she will receive some of the blessings.

Unfortunately for my ex-fiancée, Nicole, I'm a police officer, and I have a knack for reading people. She started acting brand new, spending countless hours on her phone and the computer. Which she, of course, covered up with work. But I know a lie when I hear and see one. Which led me to hack into her email, and I saw a bunch of websites she was a member of. With my newfound knowledge, I did the next best thing. As the old saying goes, "If you can't beat them, join them." Because I don't chase. Darnell replaces them.

Hence, that's how I ended up on the dating website Plenty of Dates over a year ago and became a regular on it, until I met Latavia. She doesn't need to know all of that, though. Real talk: I don't know what it is, but there's something about this woman that does me dirty, and the craziest thing is I haven't even met her in person. Latavia is under this strange belief that this online thing is as new to me as it is to her. And the long hours I put in on the job prevents me from meeting new women, as well as being the primary reason that I've been a bachelor for the past two years. We are going to leave it that way too.

I make sure to arrive a half hour early at the mall in order to peep her out ahead of time when she gets out of her car. She said she drives a 2000 white, four-door Audi A6. With that fact in mind, I park in the back, by the entrance/exit closest to Victoria's Secret, so I can watch the cars coming in and out and spot her. I know one thing: if she isn't the five-four, brown-skinned, big-booty cutie from the pictures, I'm ghost. I am quickly torn from my thoughts when I see her walking into the mall.

By the time I get out of my car and head through the doors, I have lost track of her.

"Are you looking for someone?" she asks as she taps me on my shoulder.

Of course it is Latavia; I should have known. You could locate that smile of hers anywhere—well, I could. That beam has turned me on since the first time I saw a picture of her. Now, as we stand face-to-face, it's putting a brother in a choke hold. Damn, she got me good, but I will get her ass back. Since she wanted to meet in this lingerie store, I'm going to have her try on some shit, if she can, and have her give me a show. I hope she's oiled the fuck up and down, because it's on. If I like what I see, shit, she can have whatever she wants up in there, along with what's being contained in these here boxer briefs.

"I believe what I was looking for has found me," I reply.

Damn, she looks even better in person! I think. *Thank you, God. I owe you one*, I silently pray.

From the moment I lay eyes on this woman, my one-eyed monster is on swole, and once we enter that store and I see her in the bra and panties she is trying on, it has me defeated. I want to bend her sexy ass over one of these racks and give her some deep, long strokes. I'm going to play it cool, though.

"What's next on the agenda?" I ask as we leave the store, bags in hand.

"I left that part up to you," she retorts.

As we approach the parking lot, I offer to take her to happy hour. We need to get as far away from this mall as we possibly can. I can't take it anymore. Shit, I'm trying my best to be the perfect gentleman the old lady raised me to be. But thickums has me turning against everything I believe in and has me trying to hide my joint. It's hard as fuck right now. Latavia is just too damn sexy, from her personality to her beautiful round ass. I can't believe no one has snatched her ass up by now.

Both of us are feeling nice after a couple of rounds. I can see ole girl is feeling it, because she keeps trying to touch my shit, and he is responding excitingly to it. I know she wants me as much as I want her. As soon as we hit the parking lot, and I slide my hand under her skirt, and my stomach growls. This freak doesn't have any panties on. Her nappy dugout is soaking wet, just the way I like it. I have to taste her.

I put her on the hood of the car and start with small kisses to her inner thigh, which is the sniff test: got to make sure her shit is right. Latavia passes my test, and I begin feasting on my newfound treasure. Her flavor is as good as she looks. I start by gently pinching her pussy lips together with my thumb and my index finger as I French-kiss her lips as if it is her mouth, and then I allow my tongue to trace the words *This is my pussy now* across her clit.

After opening her legs wider, I allow my lips, chin, and nose to circle slowly all over her goodie basket for that extra effect. In other words, I bury my face in that shit. I stick my tongue in and out of her wetness. And quicken the pace until her back begins to arch. Now that she's right where I want her, I pause for a few seconds, placing my wet, sweltering tongue on her clit gently and leaving it there, allowing the muscles in my tongue to twitch now and then. Penetrating her with my index and middle fingers while my tongue does its job causes Latavia to climax all over my face. Yes, I'm good at what I do! Just call me Mr. Pussy, because I handle that shit.

CHAPTER 3

NARIAH'S SECRET

I am so happy for my girl Tae. You know her as Latavia, but most of us call her Tae or Tavia for short. Fortunately, she is blessed to be able to meet and marry the man of her dreams. I can honestly say that in all the years I've known her, she has never been this happy and bubbly. Actually, she used to be Bitter Betty, another nickname I gave her. All jokes aside, I know her bitterness was the result of the horribly terrifying things she witnessed and experienced from such a tender age. Tae has endured more than any one person should have to in a lifetime. But as we can see, the good outweighs the bad. God gave her someone to love her unconditionally, while teaching her how to trust and love, and all he had to do was love her.

Isn't that some shit?

Her happiness is evident. My girl looked absolutely beautiful on her wedding day. The entire wedding ceremony was tastefully and elegantly put together. For starters, her attire was a gorgeous classically styled silk gown with a touch of crystals strategically placed throughout, all the way down to and through the detachable four-foot train. She also had a matching tiara that was crafted perfectly to accentuate the details of the gown. The ceremony was held at our childhood church, Greater Bethel, and the reception was about fifteen minutes away, in the ballroom of the Marriot Marquis Hotel, located in Midtown Manhattan. The food was fantastic: the best all-you-can-eat buffet selection of hors d'oeuvres, along with top-of-the line wines and cognac, which spelled out Latavia and Darnell. All the tables were decorated with the same beautiful silk white material as Tae's gown, with a splash of the same crystals. I tell you, from the table settings to the chairs, everything was decorated beautifully, and I would like to personally thank the person responsible for making my girl's day a day to remember.

Wait a minute! That person would be me, so please allow me to introduce myself. My name is Na-to-the-Riah. I know, I'm cracking myself up, but seriously, I wouldn't have had it any other way. I would do anything for my girl to make her happy, and I mean it.

CHAPTER 4

LATAVIA'S SLEEPING SICKNESS

Darnell is leaving today to go on his annual made-man getaway with his boys from the force, and I am sick to my stomach about it. This yearly vacation is when all the fellas go away together without their significant others for an entire week and a half. They start off going to New Orleans for three days, and then they take a seven-day cruise. Translation: I will be alone for ten days. I will need the good Lord to give me another dose of strength to get through this. I do relish the opportunity for my husband to get away. He deserves it. And it affords me a chance to miss him even more. But at the same time, I'm not too fond of this yearly ritual. Darnell takes my mind off my past and helps stop the nightmares. So, I am dreading the idea of being home alone in this house and our bed.

Since tonight is officially the first night that I will be alone, I put a call in to Nariah, asking her to come over and have a girls' weekend with me. She agrees to a divas' slumber party but says she will have to come over later on tonight or first thing in the morning. She has a hot date with some new guy she says she met at one of our events. So at the moment, it is me, a DVD, wine, and some popcorn.

Earlier today I picked up a few movies while shopping at Walmart, and naturally, I'm having a hard time making up my mind about which movie I want to watch first. It looks like the decision process will be random: the first film my hands touch will be the movie of the hour or two. The selection happens to be *Precious*. I have heard so much about this one but have never had the chance to see it. I am so geeked finally to see this movie; however, due to my negligence, halfway through it, my stomach turns into knots, and I'm crying hysterically. Why didn't I read the synopsis for this damn movie beforehand? Had I read it, I would never have picked this film, or even purchased it, for that matter.

Through my tears, I try to take my mind off everything and decide to try a different movie. A comedy, perhaps, will afford me the opportunity to clear my mind and will prevent me from falling asleep with this mess on my brain and having yet another nightmare.

Yes, that's what I will do, I think as I rummage through Darnell's duffel bag of bootleg movies until *Laugh at My Pain* catches my attention.

"I can't believe my husband! Darnell, the police officer, buys bootleg movies. I guess he doesn't know it's illegal," I joke.

This comedy show takes me from crying hysterically and falling into an acute bout of post-traumatic stress to laughing uncontrollably. However, as I drift off to sleep, it doesn't prevent the nightmares from recurring.

Maybe if I wrap myself up real tight in my blanket, he won't come into my room when Mom goes to sleep. Why does Mommy sleep like the bears we learn about in school? If she was up, I wouldn't be so scared, and he wouldn't come into my room. I'm getting so sleepy, but

I'm scared to close my eyes. My sleep makes him come in here and do those bad things to me that I see him do to Mommy. I don't know why Mom likes that stuff. It hurts, and it makes me bleed down there.

God, please *make him stop! Why would he want to hurt me? He's supposed to love me. Oh my God, here he comes. I'm so scared. I tried to apologize to him for walking in the room on him and Mommy, but he wouldn't listen. He's taking the covers off me. He's touching my boom-boom. He's hurting me again. "Please stop! Please stop!" I try to scream, but he's covering my mouth.* I hate him! *Mom said* hate *is such a bad word, but so is hurting me! I'm too afraid to tell Mom he keeps doing these things to me.*

"Tae, wake up. Everything is all right. I'm here!" Nariah yells, shaking me awake. Once again, her perfect timing saves the day.

"Thank you so much for being there for me, Nae. It's like you always know when to show up," I tell her.

"Girl, you are like my sister, and I would do anything for you! You don't have to thank me. I'm just glad I came when I did. I hate that these dreams are still haunting you. Have you considered going back to counseling? You were doing so well for a while. Do you know what caused them to return? Or better yet, when did they return?"

Embarrassed and unable to look at her, I reply, "Well, I was watching the movie *Precious*—"

Before I can complete my sentence, Nae cuts me off, screaming, "Are you crazy? Why did you watch that movie? That is the reason I told you we didn't need to see it when you recommended it when it first came out! Did you not see the previews to the movie, Tae?"

I have to think. Honestly, I don't remember seeing the previews. I just recall hearing people say Monique was a mean and horrible mother in the movie, but she played the hell out of her role. When I inform Nariah I haven't seen the previews, she hugs me and escorts me into the kitchen. I have some leftover pizza in the refrigerator, so we reheat it and grab a bottle of Merlot to help us relax as she excitingly fills me in on her date with her new mystery man.

CHAPTER 5

DARNELL'S ONE-NIGHT STAND

I have so much on my mind. I am desperately in need of this getaway with my boys. I just need time to myself—to relax, drink, and have a cigar—without thinking about anything. I hate leaving Latavia. She fronts, acting like she's happy to have me out of the house, but her eyes tell a whole other story. Thank God she has Nariah; that woman holds Latavia down almost as well as I do. If I didn't know better, I'd swear they were fucking, but I guess they just have a bond nobody else can understand or relate to.

It's insane how we live in such a small world. Shit was crazy the night Latavia had her dinner party and introduced me to her girl Nariah—who just happened to be Rakeiya. At least that's the name she gave me when we met on the online dating site. I remember that shit like it was yesterday. Latavia planned the little get-together after we had been dating for about nine months. She thought it was time I met her peoples. Due to the tragic passing of her parents in a car accident, she doesn't have any family other than her aunt and her close friend Nariah, whom she also calls her sister. Latavia said we couldn't go any further until I met Nariah.

However, there was a stipulation: I had to bring one of my boys with me. Of course, I brought my brother from another mother, my boy Bernard, but you can call him Nard. We work on the force together and have been partners since graduating from the academy about ten years ago. Nard has my back, and I have his. He had just ended a three-year relationship with this big-booty freak who had gotten him open, then had played the shit out his ass. I would have choked her up if it had been me. I don't play that shit. However, I did think this little meet and greet would work well for him, from what Latavia had told me about her girl.

Latavia and her homegirl were still in the kitchen, putting the final touches on dinner, when we arrived, and they instructed us to make ourselves comfortable in the living room until dinner was ready. Twenty minutes later, Latavia let us know it was almost time to eat.

"Welcome to Tae and Nae's Lobster. We will be bringing Red Lobster our way," she announced, entering the living room.

I chuckled at my baby girl's little corny-ass joke. She was a fake-ass comedian, but I loved her ass. She'd got a brother all caught up, like I was Usher in this bitch.

Once dinner was done and ready to be served, Latavia called me and Nard into the dining area and told us to have a seat at the table. Then the girls walked out of the kitchen, carrying shrimp scampi, along with their version of those garlic-and-cheese biscuits they serve at nasty-ass Red Lobster. I was too zoned out, admiring how good Latavia looked in her damn jeans, to even notice Nariah. Yo, when she finally caught my attention, I thought I was being punked. If Ashton brought his skinny ass out, I was fucking him up.

"Darnell, this is my best friend and sister, Nariah. Nariah, this is my love, Darnell," Latavia said, introducing us.

"It's a pleasure to finally meet you, Darnell. I've heard so many amazing things about you," Nariah said, staring me dead in my eyes.

"Likewise. By the way, this is my boy Nard," I responded.

I really couldn't believe that shit! Latavia's homegirl was playing it off cool, shaking my hand as if she was actually meeting me for the first time. I played along. But I couldn't wait for Latavia to go into the bathroom or something; this was some bugged-out shit.

Latavia, of course, had one too many drinks, as usual. I will have to check her on it. I don't do that drunken shit; that's a complete turnoff for me. I hate to see a woman who's intoxicated more than she's sober. However, I have to say it happened right on time that evening and made it easy for me to get a chance to holler at her girl. Nard thought this shit was the funniest thing he'd ever witnessed after I discreetly filled him in on what was going on. I know I didn't find a damn thing funny.

After escorting Latavia upstairs to her room and getting her settled in bed—butt-ass naked, of course, so she would be good and ready for Daddy when I got back up there to do my duty to please that booty—I walked back downstairs. To my surprise, but really not so much of a surprise, Nard had Nariah assuming the muthafuckin' position—bent over the couch. That nasty-ass chick was on some other shit, and that's my word. I knew Nard was on some rebound stick-and-move shit, but I was a little caught off guard, considering we usually didn't eat after each other, but it was what it was.

I knew one thing for sure: that bitch Nariah was far from the person Latavia had described her to be. She was the same ho I'd met online, that's for sure. I hated to interrupt their formal yet informal introduction, but I needed to get to the bottom of that mess. There was no way in hell I was going to allow that mishap to interfere with what I had going on with Latavia, especially not at the hands of that nasty-ass ho.

"Excuse me," I interrupted, then cleared my throat, startling Nard and Nariah when they finally realized I was standing there.

Nard was more embarrassed than anything, but that woman just smirked and said, "My bad."

"You're good. I just want to know what the fuck is going on," I said.

I didn't care that they hadn't got themselves together yet, either; that shit had nothing to do with me.

"I had no idea Tae was talking about 'Black' from the dating site, considering it appears we gave each other false names and clearly erroneous personalities. Well, mine was the truth, other than the name I gave you," she smirked.

Not allowing me a chance to get a word in, she continued her spiel. She advised me that the night we'd hooked up meant absolutely nothing to her, which I could see was the case.

"We both wanted to bust a nut and got just that," she reiterated.

I stood there like a deer in the headlights. I couldn't believe that woman! She was on a whole other level with hers. I was just relieved she wanted to leave well enough alone. One thing for sure, as she had said, was all I'd been interested in that night was to bust off—nothing more and nothing less. So it was better we ended this conversation.

CHAPTER 6

TAE'S UNCOMPROMISING POSITION

Darnell has been gone for two days now, and it feels more like a month. I know one thing: I never should have taken a week off from work, like I had somewhere to go. Honestly, I had hoped Darnell would make an exception this one time and allow me tag along with him and the boys, but that didn't happen. I don't understand why not, considering they are always at the house with me on any other day, so there really isn't that big of a difference, just a change of scenery, but there was no convincing Darnell of that.

Nariah is out with her new, mysterious lover boy, whom she appears to be falling for. She usually keeps them around for about two weeks tops before she discards them like yesterday's trash. She has said a man's favorite saying is, "There's no pussy like new pussy," and in her eyes, there's no dick better than the sweet taste and feel of a new dick. Hopefully, the right man will come along and change her mind. Until that day comes, she's said, "It's a dog-eat-dog world, and she's humping and dumping." I, on the other hand, cannot wrap my mind or my legs around that many men coming in and out of my life, my kitty kat, and my mouth, if, like

Nariah says, "they're working with a monster." I am so good on that, so she can have all that action all by herself.

It never fails. Once again, I am having yet another sleepless night, and to top it off, I'm all out of melatonin. Looks like I am going to have to take this opportunity to get out of the house and make a quick run to the twenty-four-hour Duane Reade since I've been cooped up here all day. I'm not trying to impress anyone, but I refuse to step out of the house with a scarf on my head or looking crazy, so a pair of leggings paired with an oversized sweater and my black-and-gray UGGs will do just fine. Since my hair is in braids, all I have to do is remove my scarf and I'm good to go, though I will have to put it right back on when I get back in the fifteen or so minutes it takes to get to the store and back.

As I observe myself in the mirror, it dawns on me that no matter what I put on, without a shadow of a doubt, I always look good. I can walk out of this house with a garbage bag on and still turn heads. Yes, I am conceited, and I have a reason. I have never felt this good about myself or my life. It feels good to finally love and admire the beautiful, intelligent woman I see looking back at me in the mirror. On that note, let me make this run so I can get back here to do nothing. Thank God the weather isn't too cold and I'm not forced to wear a jacket, because I hate wearing them. They are so unnecessary.

Just my luck, Duane Reade is all out of melatonin, and I don't know what to look for as a substitute, and to make matters worse, the pharmacists are off the clock at this time of night. While I destroy what's left of the shelf as I look for a sleep aid to cure my insomnia, I hear a male voice reciting my entire government name prior to my marriage to Darnell.

"Latavia Watkins!" the male voice yells.

When I look up, I almost die and come right back. I haven't seen this man in years—Mr. Braxton Kirkland, also known as BK for short.

"Hello there," I reply uneasily. I haven't a clue why the hell I'm all nervous and feeling like the same teenage schoolgirl I was when he and I were back in the ninth grade.

BK and I stand in the middle of the aisle and catch up on lost time for about forty-five minutes. I am able to learn he is newly divorced, hasn't been with his wife for the past two and a half years, and doesn't have any children. He also makes mention of meeting someone a few months ago while out of town on business, someone with whom he has been kicking it. BK makes sure to include the fact that the relationship isn't serious yet, but this woman might be a keeper.

Whatever that means, I think.

Finally, we say our goodbyes and exchange numbers— and before you go minding my business once again, yes, I did inform him I was married to the love of my life, Darnell. Unfortunately, that didn't staunch the pool that is forming in my panties. *What the hell is going on*? I think. I do not understand where this feeling is coming from or why. The last time I recall seeing or speaking to BK was in the tenth grade, the time I almost gave him my virginity. In my heart, I was still a virgin at the time, because I had never willingly given myself to a man.

BK was able only to crown my love canal with his shotgun's head before I pushed him off me, crying hysterically, because I was scared to death of the pain. I didn't think it would be as painful as it usually was, because that time I'd wanted it, but I was proven wrong.

He angrily called me a tease and said he wanted nothing else to do with me. Devastated by his behavior after all I had withstood at a man's hands, I developed an ingrown hatred for all men. At that point in my life, it was clear to me that the men I loved wanted either to hurt me with their man parts, break my heart, or do a little of both.

On my drive home, I wonder how long it has been since the last time I saw BK. He looks the same, just sexier. Darnell must have known my thoughts were not my own, I think, as my BlackBerry goes off just then, interrupting me before my mind goes to a place it has no business going. There's an alert informing me of a new incoming text message. I assume it is my beloved Darnell, but to my surprise, it is BK.

The text message reads: You looked exquisite this evening, and time has been good to you. Please don't go missing in action on me again, and please do me the honor of staying in touch to catch up on lost time.

I reply, I would love that.

I am now smiling from ear to ear. Why? My panties are completely soaking wet. How? As my mind begins to recap how good that man looks at an even six feet tall, with his caramel complexion, dimples, the waves on his head that would make a nation seasick, and a body that looks like he spends a lot of time in the gym and needs me as his new workout buddy or personal weight bench.

I don't know what has come over me. I pull my car over to the side of the road, put my hazards on, and put my car in park. I can't fight this feeling any longer or wait until I get home. After I recline my seat, I permit my hands and mind to stray as I close my eyes and suck on my fingers to get them moist so I can trace my erect nipples with the tips of them, imagining they are the tip of BK's tongue. My other hand locates and explores my love garden, searching for the pearl switch to release my hidden waterfall. As I sink deeper into my thoughts, my fingers become BK's fingers, and he is playing my pearl like it is a piano. I love the sounds of his fingers playing in my treasure chest. As I reach a much-needed and anticipated climax, a tap on my window startles me, almost fast-forwarding me straight to heaven.

"Mrs. Carter, is everything okay?" Officer Martinez questions.

Placing my seat back up and opening my eyes, I can see the flashing lights behind me and Officer Martinez standing at the driver-side window of my car. *Oh shit, this can't be happening!* I hurriedly pull my sweater down to cover my exposed flesh, and out of reflex, I lick my juices off my fingers. I can't allow them to just dry up and go to waste.

"Yes, I'm fine, Officer Martinez," I reply after letting the window down.

"Good. I was patrolling the area when I noticed your car, and pulled over to make sure everything was all right with you," he explains.

"Thank you. I'm fine. I just had to stop to put in a call to order some Chinese food, so it's ready by the time I get to my side of town," I lie.

"I understand, Mrs. Carter."

"Thank you again, Officer Martinez. I haven't eaten all day and need some food before taking my medicine," I say, exaggerating, as I lift up my Duane Reade bag to make my lie look and sound good. He's a cop like Darnell. They are always investigating something, on and off duty, so I have to make this look and sound good.

"Enjoy the rest of your evening, Mrs. Carter," he says before walking back to his patrol car.

Pulling off, completely mortified, I have to thank and praise God, from whom all blessings flow, for petitioning Darnell to have limo tints installed on these windows; otherwise, Officer Martinez would have gotten a glimpse of me tearing my clit up, thanks to BK.

The thought of Darnell hits me like a ton of bricks, changing my entire mood from horny to upset, ashamed, guilty, and paranoid all at the same time. He would kill me if he knew I'd allowed another man to bring me to a climax and I'd touched myself. Yes, that's right. He'd kill me for touching myself; you heard me right. Darnell feels that I don't have a need to touch myself or use toys, because I have a man to satisfy my every need, along with the needs I didn't even know I had. He said touching myself and using vibrators is just as bad as cheating on him. His toy is my toy, it's battery free, and I can use it whenever and wherever my little heart desires.

I honestly don't know what just came over me, but it stops here. I love my husband way too much to be doing some mess like this or to violate the vows we made before God, our family, and friends.

CHAPTER 7

ORALLY YOURS, NARIAH

I hate knowing that Tae is still having them damn nightmares as a result of what that bastard did to her. I'm genuinely shocked she didn't kill his nasty ass. That situation alone is one of the reasons why I don't trust a man as far as I can throw him. I treat them the way they need to be treated, and that's like a quick piece of dick. The only thing they are good for is giving me an orgasm, when they can get that shit right. I don't need a man to take care of me. I am self-sufficient. Some people would say I'm selfish, but I don't give a fuck. I do me.

With my lifestyle, I really don't want or need kids in my life; that's why it wasn't that hard for me to terminate my pregnancy after my one-night stand with Black's ass. I know one thing is certain: the man Tae married is nowhere near the guy I met online. This made the whole situation that much easier to overlook and enabled me to act as if it had never happened. In actuality, it never did; plus, his dick game wasn't that good in the first place, to boot.

I have been dealing with this guy Walter for almost six months now. Of course, I still have my other shorties, including Nard, whom I fuck with from time to time when I'm bored. Nard's ass was open from the time I hiked up my skirt, bent over the sofa, and told him to come stick his chocolate bar in this warm, sweet pussy so I could make that shit melt. That was funny as hell, especially when Darnell walked down the stairs. Nard almost passed out mid-stroke. Just thinking about it to this day still makes me laugh. It doesn't really matter, because he is just a fuck, like they all are. I need variety, like both Baskin-Robbins and a bag of Lays' potato chips. I can't have just one. Dick doesn't have a face. It just has a purpose, which is to beat this cat into a coma and, if it's any good, give me multiple orgasms.

Walter is a bit older than I am, but he has the energy and the body of a thirty-year-old, and my man is taming this kitten like no other, so I have to keep his old ass around and on my to-do list. I ran into Walter six months ago, while I was across town, looking at properties, as Tae and I were looking to expand Elite Glamour Events, which specializes in taking special occasions and making lifetime memories that your guests will discuss for years to come. We are doing very well, so the expansion will be another notch on our belt. The new location works to my advantage because Walter lives out that way, and so does this other cutie I met at Dunkin' Donuts last week. I ended up giving that little cutie the honor and the privilege of eating my poison right up in that piece too.

That afternoon was quite comical and couldn't have happened at a better time. There I was, sitting in a back-corner booth, putting together quotes on my laptop, having my daily caramel iced latte fix, when I suddenly felt someone's eyes piercing right through me. I looked up and this five-foot-seven, thick, dark-skinned, choco-late-macchiato chick was staring at me like she wanted to take a bite out of crime. You know good and damn well I made it easy for her and stood up, closed my laptop, and placed it in my briefcase, all without taking my eyes off Miss Mahogany. That bitch looked good enough to eat. One thing I like is a thick, dark-skinned chick and a thick, light-skinned dick—yes, Lord, the best of both worlds. I could see right then I had to make sure I introduced her to Walter; he would adore her ass.

After walking over to the area where Miss Mahogany was sitting, I introduced myself as Honey, then sat down and made myself comfortable. "I taste sweeter than I look," I kindly informed her.

Skipping the formalities, Miss Mahogany did exactly what I expected her to do: she slid down to her knees under the table and lifted my skirt up. Thank God I rarely wear panties and keep a dress on for easy access. You never know when an opportunity may arise, so I have to stay prepared. Miss Mahogany found what she was looking for and didn't waste any time licking and slurping on my clit, hitting every spot like she knew how to please a ho. That tongue ring she had in her wet mouth needed to be locked the fuck up, because it was taking me to places that have *got* to be illegal. I loved every minute of that shit; it gave my hot box so much life, causing me to rush her jaws in a matter of minutes.

I was so glad Dunkin' Donuts was unusually empty that day and we had a seat far in the back. That taste test felt too good to be trying to stop, go get a room, or even move. God knew I needed that; I had way too much pent-up stress. Miss Mahogany finished her meal and wiped her mouth like a real lady should after making a mess of herself.

"Make sure you give me a call sooner or later so we can pick up where we left off," I instructed, slipping her my business card across the table as I prepared to be on my way to see Walter's old ass. That shit had made me even hornier, and now I needed some long dick from the back. That is why I have to make it my business to get Mahogany and Walter to meet; being with both of them together would have me squirting all over the place.

Oh yes, it's on!

CHAPTER 8

TAE'S HURTING INSIDE

Mommy has to do a double today at work and won't be home until tomorrow night, which means she is going to leave me here with him. I should just run into traffic; that way I'll be able to be at the hospital with my mommy and away from him. I hate him so much.

For five years now, I have been going through this, and my mommy doesn't even realize it. I am older, and my body is filling out faster than that of most girls my age. It causes me to get a lot of attention from the boys my age, and I dislike it. I hate my body even more. I try to hide it by wearing larger clothes, but that just seems to draw more attention. Now that I am fifteen, he makes me do things to him that make me throw up, but I have to swallow my vomit. If I don't, he beats me and puts his man part in my butt. That is the worst feeling I have ever felt in my life! He really has to be gay. Why would a man want to do that? I hate him so much, but I hate my life even more. What did I do to deserve this? Why can't I be normal, like my friends?

I should run away, but where would I go? If I do and get caught, I will be in even bigger trouble, so I opt out and take what appears to be the longest walk home from school that I have ever done. When I reach the house and unlock the door, I see this pervert sitting on the couch, with no clothes on, his dirty, long man part hanging out. I try to run to my bedroom and lock the door, but I'm not fast enough. He grabs me by my hair and slams me onto the couch.

"Don't move until I tell you to, little bitch," he spits as he walks over to the television and turns on a DVD. With his back still turned to me and his hairy butt cheeks facing me, he demands, "Remove all your clothing, and then sit right back down!"

Scared half to death, I close my eyes and obey, holding back my tears. I know tears will make my punishment that much more severe. I flinch out of reflex when he finally sits down next to me. I'm afraid of what he's going to do to me. He makes me sit there and watch people on TV having sex as he moves my hand up and down on his nasty pole.

"You had better be paying attention to everything on that DVD, because your job is to do the same exact thing to me that the woman did in the DVD," he instructs as he stops the DVD.

I would rather die than do that to him, and I guess today will be that day. I am not doing all that nasty stuff to him. Why doesn't he let Mommy do this stuff to him? Why do I have to do it? Out of nowhere, he slaps me so hard, I fall to the floor; then he yanks me back up by my hair onto my knees. Now I am face-to-face with his nasty man part.

"Open your mouth wide and do every single thing you saw on the television, cunt!"

I do as I was told until I see he has his eyes closed. Then I bite down on that nasty thing as hard as I can. That makes him scream so loud that it scares me. He punches me in the side of my head so hard that I fall back onto the floor. The last thing I remember is him punching me in the stomach over and over until I pass out.

"Damn it, another dream!" I cry. This one was a lot longer than they usually are, and I am so sick of all of it. "Why do they continue to haunt and torture me?" I ask myself aloud.

I was awakened by the vibrating of my BlackBerry, but I ignore it. My bed is soaking wet, as if I have had an accident on myself. I touch my panties just to see if I did. I am embarrassed when I realize my grown ass done had a nightmare and pissed on myself like I am ten years old. That's when he started feeling over my body, and he did that for years, until I turned fifteen. I don't want to think about it any longer. I have to do something else; I can't allow myself to become depressed again.

One thing I can say is I am happy Darnell is still away right now. I probably would have jumped out the window if he was lying next to me in bed and I peed on myself. I get up, remove the linens from the bed, and stuff them into a garbage bag to throw away. I don't want to see those sheets ever again. How the heck am I going to be able to clean this mattress without leaving a stain or destroying it with bleach? I don't want the damage to be noticeable if and when Darnell changes the sheets.

Instead of driving myself crazy, I'm going to do the next best thing and call Sleepy's to see if I can purchase the same mattress, have it delivered today, and have them remove the old one. I am overjoyed when the sales manager says that it won't be a problem at all, that they can deliver it before the close of business today. Darnell returns from his vacation tomorrow, so I need to make sure everything is in place. I don't want anything to interfere with the festivities I have planned for him. I miss my baby, and I am so glad BK hasn't texted or called me since the night I ran into him. I was really tripping that day.

While putting my bedroom back in order, I remember my phone had gone off and retrieve it from the night-stand. I'm alerted to an incoming text message, which has me shaken and frozen for what seems like an eternity. Damn, I thought about this man, and his fine behind must have sensed it!

The text message is from BK. **Is it possible for you to sneak away and meet me for coffee tonight, around 6:00 p.m.? I could really use a friend right about now.**

I know I have no business whatsoever going to meet BK for coffee or anything else, but he is a friend in need, so I really don't have a choice. What if it were me and I needed someone to talk to? I am a firm believer that you reap what you sow, so I try my best to sow good seeds in every situation to reap the benefits. When I agreed to meet with BK, I asked him to meet me at the Dunkin' Donuts across town, near Elite Glamour Events Too, so that afterward I can go check on the property to see how things are coming along. Since I will be over that way, I can kill two birds with one stone. Darnell isn't scheduled to be back until tomorrow, around noon, so I have enough time to talk to BK, check on our new store, and get back home to get things situated for the romantic evening I have planned for my baby.

When I pull up to Dunkin' Donuts, I become con-sumed with so many emotions before I can even step out of the car. I don't know what to feel or what not to feel, but I know one thing is for sure: I am suddenly hornier than I have ever been in my entire life. I have no idea what it is, but the thought of BK alone sends my hot pocket into distress, like a broken pipe in need of a plumbing job. But I know I am not here for that. I have a man who loves me, and I am not about to ruin what I have for anyone.

As soon as I step out of the car, my cell phone goes off. I immediately think it is Darnell, but it is Nariah. I'm sure she's just checking on me, so I send her to voicemail. I will give her a call to catch up with her later, after I leave here. BK is sitting at a booth in the back, and I spot him as soon as I walk in. His sexy chiseled caramel cheekbones, mesmerizing warm brown eyes, bright white teeth, smile, and fine ass have my mind going in all the wrong directions. Damn, I am a sucker for a man with bright eyes and white teeth. And those broad shoulders exude masculinity, like he could pick you up, throw you up against the wall, and put his entire back into it. I love his well-manicured nails, along with those soft, enticing, well-shaped, kissable, pudding-eating lips.

Damn! What is going on with me? I am bugging out! I have a husband at home. Why do I have to keep convincing myself of that, as if I don't know this already?

The shit just got real! I can smell BK from the door. I have no idea what the hell kind of cologne he has on. It has to be named Come Suck This Dick and Let Me Beat That Twat Up, because that's what rushes through my mind before I can even get comfortable. I have to regain my composure.

"Hello," I say, throwing myself onto the seat to sit my hot tail down.

BK stands up and says, "A brother hasn't seen you in forever. The least you can do is give me a hug."

Really? This dude is pushing his luck. Talking and hugging are two different damn things! I think.

"Speak your mind. I have a few errands to run!" I snap.

That slaps the smile clean off his face. I am proud of myself. I am doing well, and I feel good about it, until this ninja decides to apologize for breaking my heart because I wouldn't give him my virginity.

"I was wrong and wish I had put my pride in my pocket and sat on that shit. I married the wrong woman and missed out on you—my true love," he confesses.

Yes, I died instantly and have yet to come back. Why would he do this to me? He knows I am married! I hate him for this; he is playing dirty. I refuse to allow him to see me sweat.

"An apology is unnecessary, although I appreciate it, but that was twenty-three years ago. We have all grown up and moved on from there. Everything happens for a reason."

Just when I thought I'd made it through the storm and the rain, BK gets out of his seat and sits on my side of the booth, right next to me.

Why? Why, Lord? Why?

As he sits down, he stares me in my eyes and says, "You are still as beautiful as you were in the ninth grade."

Oh God, I have just died again. He must know it, because he decides to take it upon himself to give me mouth-to-mouth. Well . . . I sort of . . . kind of . . . initiate it. I fall right into his trap. I begin to slob him all the way down and right back up with so much passion. Out of nowhere, my hand decides to cop a feel of his manhood. I snatch it back real fast, hoping he doesn't realize what

I've done. I'm wrong. Of course, when I pull my hand back, he stops kissing me and starts laughing. I am now confused and would love to know what the hell is so funny. I instantly catch an attitude, and BK picks up on it.

"You still look cute when you get mad," he taunts.

I shake my head; he is getting on my nerves, thinking he knows me.

"Please inform me as to what's so funny?"

He tauntingly replies, "You are! You are still scared of this dick!"

Oh word! I say to myself.

"Please know, sweetheart"—I look him up and down—"I am no longer that little girl from the ninth grade. I am a grown-ass woman."

"That's what your mouth says," he replies.

I lose all my home training at this point and scribble the address to Glamour Events Too, which is two blocks away, and then I get up, kindly say, "I can show you better than I can tell you," and leave, with him right behind me.

I don't know what I can possibly be thinking. I can't do this. I'm going to tell BK I've changed my mind as soon as we get to Elite. It is only five minutes away from Dunkin' Donuts, but the drive there seems to take more like five hours. I think I've just developed a newfound hate for Dunkin' Donuts. Starbucks it is from here on out.

Why did I let him kiss me? What is happening to me? Never in a million years would I have imagined I would be struggling with something like this. Darnell is an amazing man, and even more astonishing to me, he caters to every inch of my body. So why in the world am I feeling up the next man?

When I pull up to Elite, I notice a light on in one of the upstairs offices, but there aren't any cars parked in the lot, so I assume Nariah or one of the contractors left the light on. Or am I turning into Darnell? The thought of him has my stomach in knots, and I'm beginning to feel sick. This alone is a clear indication I can't do this. As I slowly and nervously exit the car, BK pulls up and parks behind me.

Damn, this man is fine as hell, and looking at him, I know right then and there I am making the right decision. I have to show him I'm not that scared little girl anymore. Why is he grinning from ear to ear? He's making me blush. He has on a fitted brown Yankees T-shirt, blue-denim Levi's jeans, a green-and-brown Levi's hoodie, and some beef and broccoli Timberlands. Let's not forget the Come Suck This Dick and Let Me Beat That Twat Up cologne. That completes him and all his sexiness. If I had a penis, it would be rock hard, and I would bang the dog poop out of him.

Damn! Am I turning into Nariah? I guess it is true what they say: birds of a feather flock together. Whatever it is, BK is driving it up out of me.

BK walks into Elite like he is part owner or something: he turns on the lights, takes my keys and purse, removes my jacket and throws it on the floor. That right there turns me on, and my nipples get hard. If he was close enough and my blouse was off, I am sure I would poke his eye out. I love it when a man takes charge, but I have a point to prove. I go to grab at his pants, but he pushes my hands away and starts tongue-kissing my bottom lip nice and slow. He gently sucks on it and uses the tip of his tongue to play with it, as if it's my clit. It's driving me completely insane, so I go to grab at his pants again. He pushes my hands to my sides and holds them there. Now I'm confused, and I don't understand. What is the problem? I take it he wants to run the show, but I am wrong once again.

BK looks into my eyes and says, "I want to make sure you're ready for this. I am what they would call blessed, and not every woman can handle me, baby girl."

I look at him like he has completely lost his mind and proceed to unbuckle his belt, unbutton his pants, pull his zipper down. I allow his pants to drop to his ankles. He doesn't have on boxers or briefs, so his penis drops down, seemingly to the floor. In complete awe, I fall back, land in a sitting position on the floor. Sitting there and staring at *it*, I wait for him to turn into Denzel Washington's character in the movie *Training Day* and start yelling, "King Kong ain't got nothing on me!" This is the biggest piece of manhood I have ever seen in my entire life. He should be on exhibit somewhere or in *The Guinness Book of World Records*.

This is unheard of. There's no way it can be real! I have to touch it, feel it inside me, and see if I can fit all of it in my mouth. I honestly can't find the words to explain what this beautiful masterpiece looks like, but it is fat, probably a baseball bat's width, and that includes the mushroom head. It looks like a mushroom too. And the whole thing curves slightly to the left and ends right above his knees. If curiosity doesn't kill this cat, his dick damn sure will.

CHAPTER 9

BRAXTON KIRKLAND'S LUCK

What the fuck just happened? Before I ran into Tavia, I had been looking for her for three years, without any luck. I am so glad I just so happened to run out of condoms and had to make that quick stop at Duane Reade. I had purposely moved back to New York to find Tavia after things went sour with my soon-to-be ex-wife. And look what just happened.

A year back, I ran into Nariah's dick-sucking ass, but she refused to give me Tavia's number and to tell me anything about her other than she was a happily married woman. *Bitch!* Who the fuck asked you all that bullshit? Her nasty, trifling ass was still on her shit, talking about I could be a real man and finish what I'd started with Tavia on her, because she was the closest I was going to get to Tavia. She was completely unavailable and off limits. Being the gentleman I am, I let her dome me off real quick, busted in her mouth, and kept it moving. She can play that hard shit with the next man.

Nariah is a dime, and she knows it. She's just fucked up in the head. I already wifed up a head case, and there is no way in hell I am going to get sidetracked by another one. *Nariah, I'm good!* I don't get why she is the way she is. The bitch is fine as hell and could probably pull any man she wanted, as long as they don't get to know how her scheming ass gets down. Nariah is a five-foot-nine redbone with legs for days. She's real slim, with no ass at all, but those big-ass titties make up for that, along with those sexy-ass gray eyes of hers.

When she polished me off, I had to close my eyes and act like it was Tavia, just to get my shit hard. When I opened them and saw Nariah's face, I skeeted in her mouth and bounced. I'm a great man. I just have a low tolerance for bitches that play hard on some tough shit. Get out of here with all that "trying to be a big boy" shit and know your role!

Enough about that ho! Tavia is the true love of my life, and I fucked that shit up over some pussy. It wasn't like I wasn't already getting any on the low; I was just so on a mission to be the first one to pop her cherry that I let my pride get in the way and lost her ass for some willing bipolar pussy—the same pussy I was stuck with for twenty years. I married Sharon right out of high school, when she turned up pregnant. Because of my upbringing, I felt it was the right thing to do. Unfortunately, six months into the pregnancy, she lost the baby, and that shit ate the both of us up real bad.

I never loved Sharon, but I stayed because I felt sorry for her. Yes, I have a goddamn heart! I gave her ass time to get her shit together and get back on track after the loss of our child, so we could go our separate ways, but that shit never happened. Every time I was ready to bounce, she had one tragedy after another, so I was stuck with the bitch. Yes, she is a bitch! While I was married to her, I was faithful to her stank pussy–smelling ass. One day I got in from work, tired as fuck, and this bitch had the next man up in the crib. I started to peel both their wigs back, but I used it as the perfect opportunity to get the fuck out.

Sharon is convinced that I drove her to it and that I'd never loved her, because she could never match my precious Latavia. *Bitch, I did not drive you to another man's dick! If that's the case, your rotten-smelling pussy should have drop-kicked me into some other pussy. Please save that shit for the next man!* But she is motherfucking right about one thing: she is not and can never be my baby, Tavia! I just hope Tavia's dude, Mr. Police Officer Darnell, is up for a fight. I'm not giving up this time—not unless I'm six feet deep, my dude. I put that shit on everything I love. The way I see it, I ain't got shit to lose, but you do, muthafucka.

I knew it! I knew it! I fucking knew it! You can't tell me I don't know good pussy when I see that shit. I must have had this unique gift from birth. That's why I was so tight when Tavia wouldn't come up out of them panties and let me beat it up right when we were freshmen in high school. But she knew what she was missing; that's why I just finished beating that wet shit the fuck up. When I am done with her ass, she won't even remember Officer Bitch Ass. My shit is on point, and she is falling right into the palms of this man's hands, so I can slap it, flip it, and rub it the fuck down. Shit is going better than I thought it would, especially since I didn't have to fuck anybody up, including Officer Bitch Boy. I know one thing is for sure: one way or another, Tavia will be mine! Fuck what you heard!

That shit went down perfectly, if I do say so myself. To top it off, she initiated that shit. She knew what it was from the gate, when she gave me those digits. All I had to do was make the phone call. Damn, my dick is crazy hard from my just thinking about that shit! We met at Dunkin' Donuts, and I purposely got there a little early so I could see that gushy shit walk in the door. I knew she would be leaking just looking at a brother. I also knew she would be late. That's just Tavia— late all the damn time. Ain't shit changed.

She was looking nervous as fuck while sitting across from me, but the way she kissed and sucked on my lips when I sat next to her showed me just how much she was missing me. I knew from there it was on. The funny shit about it was when she tried to cop a feel and felt how big my man is, she didn't flinch or sweat it at all. I played along and teased her about it, knowing good and well her ass would catch an attitude. That was all part of the plan. When we got to her job, I didn't waste any time in letting her know just how blessed I am, but again, she didn't sweat that shit one bit and put this fat dick in her mouth. Yo, her head game is on point! She swallowed and gargled all my seeds like a muthafuckin' professional. That shit right there turned me to into the Incredible Hulk, and I went into beast mode and smashed that pussy the fuck up.

I started off by pushing her legs all the way back, so she was lying on the desk, with her lower back off it. She was lying on the top part of her back, her neck, and her head as I laced her pussy with extremely quick jabs right down the middle for about two minutes. I pulled out real quick, teasing that pussy and making her beg for more; then I shoved my dick in her while I played with her pussy and squeezed on her nipples, driving that pussy insane. When I felt she'd had enough, I slid back inside her and fucked her hard with slow grinds to allow her to try to catch up and match my strokes. She must have started doing them Kegel things bitches be talking about while I was in her, because her pussy started gripping my dick like it was in a choke hold, causing me to bust hard all up in her shit. I hope she's on the pill; if not, she, no doubt, just got knocked the fuck up.

Baby girl must have had her Wheaties today. She was trying to take a brother the fuck out. After that good nut I just finished busting in her, she got on her knees and gave me the best head this big dick–carrying man could ask for. I knew right then and there that Tavia is still in love, because a brother like me regards good dick sucking as the highest form of expressing your love. Her ass showed me just how fucking much in love she is too.

"Lie down on the desk," she instructed.

"It's your world, little mama. I'm just a squirrel trying to give you another nut."

She took my dick in her hand and stared at it like she was worshipping the very essence of this fat dick. Tavia started cupping my balls with one hand and using her tongue to lick up, down, and all around, like I was a fucking Blow Pop. When she got to the underside of my dick, she put her lips together and started sucking real soft in that area. That fucked my head up real good. Then she did some fly shit and put my dick in her mouth without tightening her lips, then moved her head in a circle, like the big hand on a fucking clock or something, causing my shit to float all around in her mouth.

It seemed like she did that shit forever, until she decided to switch the game up and use her tongue to find the underside of my balls. She then rested her wet tongue on my balls before she licked up and down to the tip of my dick, using both of her hands. It looked like she was trying to wring my shit out, like it was a rag or something, and that shit felt so fucking good. I can't even explain that shit, but it had me harder than I have ever been.

Tavia knew she had me fucked up and decided to go in for the kill. She slid my dick slowly all the way into her mouth, twisting her head from side to side as she deep-throated my shit and making sure her tongue stayed in contact with the ridge where the head of my dick meets the shaft. She then switched between doing that and moving her hands up and down the shaft of my dick. Fuck that. I couldn't take it anymore. I grabbed her by her braids and shoved my dick all the way down her throat, to the point where it felt like her throat or tonsils were playing with my dick. Before I knew it, I was busting in her mouth once again.

CHAPTER 10

DARNELL, AKA RONNIE ROMANCE

It feels so good to be back at home; I missed the hell out of my wife. I have been horny as a hell since we boarded the plane. You would think I didn't get any of that sugar hole from my wife before I left home, but I did. Latavia just better be ready to spread-eagle. I'm about to live up in that sweet stuff of hers. Don't get me wrong—I did enjoy my time away with the fellas, but that shit will make you miss your woman in the worst way. It got to the point where I was dreaming about that shit. That woman has me sprung. I would never have thought I would get caught slipping like this. I guess it happens to the best of us when you have yourself a good woman and real love.

When I get to the house, I rush inside, trying to get to my baby, taking two steps at a time. I really missed the hell out of Latavia. To my surprise, when I get to our bedroom, the bed is still made, and it looks like she ain't been nowhere near it. Where is she? Wait, let me relax. She is probably out with Nariah, considering she can't go too long being in this house alone. I have never been the jealous type, but I will really fuck something up over that woman.

Since Latavia's not home yet, I will take this as an opportunity to plan a romantic evening to show her just how much I missed her sexy ass. I order two dozen long-stem roses, to be delivered to the house before five, along with a bucket of rose petals. The florist said they now sell the petals by the bucket, so I'm about to make it do what it do and put them shits everywhere. I'm just not cleaning that mess up tomorrow. I'll hire a little cleaning company and have them get the place back together to give my baby a break.

Next on my list is to change the sheets and put the silk ones on that Latavia usually throws on when she plans this type of evening for me. Yes, a brother does pay attention to all that shit, but I have something better up my sleeve for her tonight. As I remove the sheets, I notice the mattress looks unfamiliar and practically new. The burn mark that was on the mattress on my side of the bed from the night I fell asleep with a cigar in my hand isn't there. I know I am probably tripping and in cop mode, as Latavia would say, so I'm going to chill on that for right now.

I switch gears and continue putting my romantic evening in motion. I carefully remove all the furniture from the living room and place it in the dining room so I can set up a picnic area in its place for a romantic floor picnic. Just call me Ronnie Muthafuckin' Romance tonight. I'm about to romance the shit out of my beautiful wife. Since I know Latavia is fascinated with candles and they relax her, I'm going to take all those little shits out of the china cabinet and set them up all around the living-room floor, including around the blanket, but not too close. I'm not trying to be Fire Marshal Bill in this piece.

Once the rose petals arrive, I will sprinkle them all over the floor, from the entrance up to our bedroom, and I'll scatter some atop the bathwater I will have run

and have waiting for her. I'm going to take the rose petals and spell "I love you" on the bed with them, and I'll
have a bottle of Merlot, along with two wineglasses, on
the nightstand. Guess I'll have a drink of that nasty shit
with my baby tonight, but after that, it's Hennessy for
me. I can't drink that weak crap for too long. I don't have
enough time to cook, so I'm having dinner prepared at
our favorite restaurant, Teddy's, and it will arrive at our
door within the next hour. I had them prepare two lobster tails, a couple of steaks and potatoes, and a Caesar
salad—got to make sure my baby gets her roughage in.

Now that everything is set up and pretty much in
place, all I have to do is light the candles when I hear her
pull up. In the meantime, I'll take a shower and put on
my Yacht Man cologne. Latavia loves the smell of that
shit. She says the smell turns her on, and I need her to
be turned on high tonight. Sleep isn't in our near future
tonight. When she walks in the door, I will have on a bow
tie and silk boxers, with the leftover roses in my hand to
give to her.

I know I told Latavia I wouldn't be home until the
morning, because I wanted to surprise her, but she hasn't
texted or called me, and it's going on 8:00 p.m. right now.
Guess I'll have to call over to Nariah's place and ask her
to send my wife home without letting her know I'm back.
When I call, Nariah answers on the second ring.

"Nariah, this is Darnell," I state before she cuts me off.

"I know who this is."

"Well, is my wife with you?"

"Ummm . . . yeah, she is, D. We're at the movies right
now. What's up?" she questions a little hesitantly.

I give her a rundown of how I want to make this work,
and she says she will send Latavia straight home after

the show. I have to pull the phone away from my face and look at it. I don't have her cell phone number, and I called her house phone, given that it is programmed into our home phone. I'm going to assume she has her calls forwarded to her cell and not stress it.

"Good looking out," I reply before ending the call.

Well, two and a half muthafuckin' hours later, the food is cold, those little bullshit candles have done burned out, and my wife has yet to call me or walk through this damn door!

CHAPTER 11

NOSY NARIAH

I played hooky from work today and decided to plan a little freak fest with Walter. I asked him to meet me at Glamour Events Too around seven this evening and to wear a suit and tie. He has no idea what I'm up to, but I want to do some role-playing and play the naughty real estate agent. My desk was delivered today, perfect timing for me to set up my little scene. I love role-playing. I think I will set up the camcorder while I'm at it and record my stellar performance. Lights! Camera! Action!

Walter is running late, as usual, and just when I start to cop an attitude, I hear his car pull up. I parked my car around the corner so I could get into my role, and if Walter plays his part, it will be the perfect ending for both of us. When I look out the window, I am shocked and disappointed at the same time. It isn't Walter out there. It's Tae. What the hell is she doing here? She's supposed to be home, getting things ready for Darnell's return.

At the thought of Darnell, my cell rings, and it's Tae's house phone number, which means Darnell is back, and he's looking for her, as usual. I have my home phone calls forwarded to my cell phone, because I'm never home, and I am also awaiting an urgent call. After I lie to Darnell, telling him we're at the movies, he ends the call.

I call Tae's phone, so she won't come inside and ruin my evening, but she sends me to voicemail.

Oh, my God! Wait a minute! Who the fuck is this guy getting out of the car behind her? That's BK's ass! I say to myself. How the hell did he find her? She better not be up to no good. Before I forget, let me text Walter to tell him not to come, because Elite is occupied at the present time, and I will make it up to him.

I ease my way downstairs and hide in the far office space, with the lights off, to be nosy. I feel as if I am being sucker punched in the stomach when I see BK kissing Tae and her kissing him back. Why would she do this to Darnell? Why would she do this to me? Doesn't she know I got rid of my baby so she could be happy? Doesn't she know that because I terminated my pregnancy when I was thirteen weeks along, it caused me to have complications? Now I am unable to have children. I might say I'm not ready for children, but had Tae not met Darnell and got with him, I would have kept my child and raised him by myself. You'd best believe I am going to get into Tae's ass when this little rendezvous of hers is over. I can't believe her. Honestly, I never thought she even had it in her timid ass.

When BK stops Tae from grabbing his cock, and she tries it again, regardless of her being immediately blinded by that elephant trunk he calls a dick, I just know right then and there she is going to run for cover. She does the complete opposite and handles that shit like a real bitch. That shit turns me the fuck on. Since I am already nude under my trench coat, I do myself the honors and get in on the action. I please myself as I watch these two fuck their brains out. I am mad as hell, but the sight of BK's tool and the way Tae takes him in her mouth, with tears coming out her eyes and all, makes my pussy wet instantly. She deep-throats that thang! Shit, I can't even deep-throat his ass, and I'm supposed to be a professional!

I wait for BK to leave and do not make my presence known. While Tae is in the bathroom, freshening up, I go and hide in her car. When she gets her happy, cheating ass in this car, she will be in for a rude awakening; my ass will be sitting right here, waiting.

Tae gets in the car and pulls off. When I feel the car stop, I know we are at the traffic light, so I sit up and say, "What the fuck is wrong with you, Tae?"

She screams at the top of her lungs, holding her chest. I guess I scared the shit out of her. When she calms down a little, she asks me, "What in God's name are you doing in my car, and how the hell did you get here?"

I respond, "No! The million-dollar question is, what the fuck were you doing with BK?"

She proceeds to pull the car over as a tear falls from her eye. I have zero remorse for her; she knew what the fuck she was doing. I tell her to save the crocodile tears for someone else. Tae tries to explain that I don't understand, and I kindly inform her she is wrong. BK is just using her, and all he wants is for a bitch to suck his dick. That's when the shit hits the fan.

"How the fuck do you know what he wants, Nariah? I talked to him. He explained to me and apologized. He feels he was wrong, and he never should have let me go. He's never stopped loving me. You know good and goddamn well I am not the one to be with random men like that. I have been with only three men in my life, and that includes BK. That isn't how I roll. That's what *you* do. You're the one who will fuck any and everybody!"

"Is that right?" I ask. "Let me bring you back down to size, sweetheart. I do what the fuck I want to do. I am a grown-ass woman, and since you must know, the reason I know for a fact that's all BK wants is that last year he had me do the same thing you just finished doing to him. That's right. Slobbing his knob—"

Before I can finish my sentence, Tae punches me in the face.

"You stupid bitch!" I yell.

"I got your stupid bitch, you tramp!" she yells.

Then she grabs me by my hair, pulls me out of the car, and starts whaling on me, landing punch after punch. I'm able to get ahold of her braids, and I pull them with my left hand and punch her with my right until she stops hitting me. We end up letting each other loose at the same time.

That's when Tae gets all dramatic, talking about, "I can't believe you! You're supposed to be my sister."

I say, "Yeah, the sister you just called a slut!"

"Well, the truth hurts," she replies in her defense.

"I got your tramp, bitch, and for truth's sake and the record, you have been with four men, not three, you cunt! Did you forget about fucking your father for all those years?"

CHAPTER 12

TAE'S MONSTER

When I open my eyes, I look around the room in fear because I don't know where I am, until I realize I am lying in a hospital bed. My mother is standing over me, praying and crying. The last thing I remember is my father—the man who's supposed to be the first man I ever loved, who's supposed to love and protect me, who's supposed be the rock I depend on when everything else confuses or scares me—hitting me until I can't breathe and everything goes dark.

He is no father to me. He is a monster who does things to my body and my head. He makes me think bad things about myself and everyone else. Starting from when I was ten years old. He told my mother I came home from school with all the bruises on my face, arms, and neck. He claimed that before I passed out, I told him I was jumped by some kids on my way home. I didn't get to see who it was, because they came out of nowhere and started hitting me, and then a couple walking past pulled them off me.

As my mother repeats the lie to me, I cry even harder. I don't understand why this is happening to me. Why does he hate me so much? Am I that bad? Mommy kisses me on my forehead and promises me she won't rest until she *finds whoever did this to me and* they will pay*! I glance over to my right and see the fake tears running down the monster's face and him trying to look like he cares and is upset by what happened to me—when he's the one who did it.*

I start screaming at the top of my lungs, and that's when Mommy gets on the bed with me and pulls me closer to her and apologizes that she wasn't there for me as tears rain down from her face.

"Tae, baby, you had a miscarriage, and I need you to be honest with me. How long have you known you were pregnant?" Mommy questions.

Right then and there, I begin to throw up all over Mommy's chest and the arm I was lying on. Before I can respond, the monster cuts me off and says, "Princess Tae, we aren't upset with you, but when I find out who the young man is who got you pregnant, I am going to hurt him badly."

I just look at him and cry even harder, then bury my face in the same spot on my mommy's chest and arm I just finished vomiting on. Not only did he do all these things to me, along with making me do all those embarrassing things to him, but he also put a baby in me and killed it. Right now I wish I was dead, with my baby.

After being released from the hospital, I have to take it easy and can't return to school for six weeks. I'm provided a home tutor. Mommy takes off from work to take care of me and, little does she know, protect me from the monster. Daddy spends more time out of the house; he says he is taking on another shift at work so Mommy can stay home with me. I love it when he isn't in the house, and I start to feel like a normal fifteen-year-old girl. After a while, my daddy starts to act like a father to me again and not the monster.

Maybe God didn't forget about me. Maybe He does love me, after all. I am feeling much better, fully recovered. My mom and dad have been great, and now I can go back to school. Since Mommy changed her hours at work, she is now home when I get in from school. She says I am no longer allowed to walk home by myself, and she picks me up from school.

CHAPTER 13

DARNELL HATES THE TRUTH

Latavia must have lost her mind. I have been calling and texting her, and she's never picked up or returned any of my calls or texts. I even called Nariah's trifling ass back, and she sent me straight to voicemail. I know one thing: Latavia's ass had better be unconscious or something, because I will kill her ass. Let me calm the hell down. I know I will lose my mind if something has happened to that woman. I have been driving around for a half hour now, looking everywhere, and Latavia is nowhere to be found. Now that I think about it, she's probably over at Elite Too, getting it situated before their grand opening. There really is no other place she can be. On that note, I make a quick U-turn to head in that direction.

I am in complete shock and mad as fuck when I pull up to the traffic light down the block from Elite Glamour Events Too. Latavia and Nariah's ghetto asses are thumping right down the street from their place of business. I would expect that behavior from Nariah, but definitely not from Latavia.

"What the hell is going on?" I say aloud to myself. I have to sit here for a minute; I can't believe this crazy shit. Even though Latavia is spanking Nariah's ass, I have to break this mess up. So I hop out, but before I can get close enough to intervene, they let each other go, and that gutter rat hits my baby below the belt. I don't know if I'm more shocked by what she says or the reason she says it. Nariah yells in anger, calling Latavia out of her name and accusing her of sleeping with her own father for years. At this point, it looks like Latavia sees red. Before I can grab hold of her, she goes on some WWF shit and rushes Nariah's ass, picks her up, and slams her to the ground. Latavia straight power-drives her, then goes straight to stomping her out. Damn, my baby is a beast! I think I just fell in love all over again. That shit makes me hard, but I have to snatch Rocky up real quick and put her in the truck before she hurts that poor girl too bad.

I am silent as I drive home, with Latavia crying hysterically. We will have to get her car tomorrow; I just have to get her out of here for now. I have no idea how Nariah's ass is getting home. I didn't see her car, and honestly, I really don't give a damn. Although I have a million questions, I don't even know what to say to Latavia. At least now I know why she couldn't answer my calls or text messages. Tyson's ass was in the ring, putting in that work. I have to laugh to myself at that one. That shit was crazy as hell, but I will give her time to calm down.

Until we walk into the house, I forget all about the romantic evening I had planned. As soon as Latavia sees the house, her eyes light up like flying saucers, and she starts to cry uncontrollably and apologize.

"I'm so sorry, Darnell. What have I done? Please forgive me. I love you so much! I will never do anything like that again."

"Baby, it's okay. You've done nothing wrong. Please try to calm down," I reply, trying to comfort her.

Our vows said "For better or for worse," and I don't think it can get any worse than this. I feel horrible right now for my baby. She's taking all of this so hard. She starts off blaming herself, like she was somehow responsible for what happened to her with her dad. Now looking at the evening I had planned, it looks like she is blaming herself for that—as if any of this is her fault.

"You have no reason to apologize, Latavia. You didn't do anything wrong," I reassure her, leading her by the hand upstairs.

I run her a bubble bath before undressing her. I relight the candles I already have in the bathroom, and place the bottle of Merlot and a glass on the counter next to the sink for her, trying to make it as easy for her as possible. Right about now, I know she needs a drink—or the whole bottle—after all this shit. God knows I damn sure do. While she is unwinding in the bathroom, I go back downstairs to try to clean up the aftermath of our ruined romantic evening.

After two hours in the bathroom, Latavia comes down the stairs to join me on the sofa. Her tear-stained face upsets me so much; I hate that I can't fix it and make it better for her.

"How was your bath, baby?"

"Not bad," she whispers.

Sitting beside me, she rests her head on my chest as she relives some of the most horrific experiences anyone should ever have to go through. Listening to her clears up so many things—like her fear of being home alone. The excessive drinking. Her always feeling judged and rejected and, most importantly, not wanting to have children. I am all man and don't have an ounce of bitch in me, but I can't help the tears that stubbornly refuse to stay hidden as I sit there in silence, listening to my baby relive her very own horror story.

"Babe, I hope you don't hate me. I knew the day would come when I would have to be open and honest with you about my past. Although I'd hoped and prayed it wouldn't. Just know I love you with everything in me. All I wanted to do was leave my past where it belongs—and that's in the past. But since you heard what Nariah said, I don't want to leave you in the dark any more than I already have," she confesses, looking down toward the floor as fresh tears continue to stream out of her now-swollen eyes and run down her scared, hurt, and yet still so beautiful face.

"Take your time, baby. You don't have to talk now if you don't feel like it. I'm here. I am not going anywhere."

"Thank you, Darnell, but it's time to get this out in the open. My life growing up was so horrific that I usually tell people my parents died in a car accident. "My mother—well, Mommy is what I usually called her—worked as a nurse practitioner, and she usually worked the overnight shift. She also worked a lot of overtime. If and when she wasn't in school, before she overdosed on the pain medicine, they said she had been stealing oxycodone from her job. I personally don't believe it was true, but, anyway, on my tenth birthday, Mommy planned the best party for me at the roller rink.

"All my friends were there from school, including Nariah. She lived two blocks over from me while we were growing up. We found out one day while walking home together from school how close we lived to one another, which happened to be the same day we became sister friends. Well, anyway, on the day of my birthday party, like clockwork, Mommy was called into work and had to leave before the party even started. I was so upset because her job or school always kept her away from the house. When she was home, all she did was sleep. She tried to make up for it with gifts and occasional Mommy-daughter days out. Mommy always did it real big for my birthday. My father kind of rushed things along because he didn't want to be left there with all my friends and their parents. He said Mommy was the hostess, not him.

"After the party concluded, Mommy returned home for a few hours, but she had to go back to work for her regular shift. My parents went to their bedroom, and I happily ran to mine to open up the rest of my birthday presents. The last gift I opened happened to be from my mommy and the monster—I mean my father—and it was a brand-new cell phone. I was so excited because none of my friends had one, and we all wanted one so bad. In my excitement, I ran straight into my parents' room to thank them, and they were in the middle of having sex.

"I can remember all of it like it was yesterday. My father very angrily yelled at me to go to my room and not come out until told otherwise. Mommy, on the other hand, was completely embarrassed, as was I. She didn't say a word. I apologized, ran to my room, and cried. I heard them arguing and Mommy reassuring him that they could finish where they'd left off. He didn't want to hear any of it at all.

"That turned out to be the worst birthday of my life, and I have hated my birthday ever since. About an hour or so later, after Mommy had left to go back to work, the monster walked into my room. He was firecracker mad, yelling and screaming at me. 'Since you don't know how to knock on doors and didn't allow me to get my medicine, your grown ass will be punished and taught a lesson,' he threatened.

"He wasn't wearing a shirt, just his khaki pants with a brown belt. As he began to remove his belt, I automatically assumed I was going to get a spanking on my birthday. I began to cry uncontrollably.

"The monster—or my father to most—grabbed me by my hair and barked, 'Shut the fuck up! You should have cried before you walked into our bedroom!'

"That was when the abuse began. He snatched all my clothes off me like he didn't know me and he wasn't my father. He had this cold look in his eyes as he threw me back onto my bed and made me lie facedown before he forced himself into me. It felt like I was being ripped apart. I bled for an entire week because of it. When Mommy eventually saw the bloodstained sheets, she thought it was the result of me getting my period for the first time. I just hid my face from her out of embarrassment. How could I tell my mommy that my dad—the man who was supposed to love and protect me—had raped his daughter and only child? I was so afraid, and I've always thought it was all my fault."

At this point, after reliving those horrendous events, Latavia becomes even more frantic and asks if we can finish talking about this in the morning. This is a lot for her to deal with all at once. I agree with her and just hold her as those damn stubborn tears continue to race down my face. This is a lot for both of us, and I'm sure I won't be prepared for the rest of this sick nightmare. I am so vexed right now. If her father isn't deceased already, I will find the coward and blow his brains out.

CHAPTER 14

NARD CAN'T FEEL

I can't believe, even after all these years, I'm still running behind Nariah's mean ass. From the first day I met her, I wanted to fuck her. It's just a little unfortunate she smashed my boy D. It didn't mean anything to either of them. On that note, we will continue to govern ourselves accordingly and act like the shit never happened. Honestly, I wasn't going to mess with her at first, but when she lifted that skirt, exposing her clean-shaven man cave, what was a brother supposed to do? Exactly what I did—jump in and jump out—and I have been jumping in and out of her shit ever since. I gave her pussy the "man cave" nickname because after a bad day or night on the job, that's where I like to hide out.

Ever since things went sour with my ex-girl, I've been on tour, sticking and moving from hole to hole. I tried the nice-guy routine, and that got me nowhere. It blew the fuck up in my face, so with that, I'm on a mission to blow up all pussy far and near. You would be surprised what a female will do to avoid getting into trouble—I'm a cop—or just to be with you because she thinks you're a good catch. Of course, I play along, get what I want, and bounce.

As for Nariah, I deal with her on a regular. We have an understanding, with no strings attached. The only problem is I crave her pussy on the regular. When she goes missing, I tend to be on some bitch shit, blowing her phone up and coincidentally—or should I say purposely?—running into her. Which, without question, propels her to see me and run me the wet stuff I can't seem to get enough of.

I thought when D caught me dicking Nariah down, he was going to be in his feelings, but he brushed that shit off—as he should have. Tae, on the other hand, has his ass strung the fuck out. He stays paranoid, thinking stupid shit and being in his feelings on a regular. That's my man, a hundred grand and all, but he needs to go back to the dude I met ten years ago at the academy and get the bitch up and out of him.

It has gotten even worse since all that went down between his wife and Nariah. Shit, I told him bitches fight all the time; that's just what they do. Then he wanted to play Mr. Tough Guy, talking about if I refer to his wife as a bitch again, we're going to have a problem. He has me fucked up; ain't shit between us but air and muthafuckin' opportunity. Partner or no partner, if the opportunity presents itself, I will lay his monkey ass out. Now he's on some shit, talking about I need to be careful around Nariah because she's a coldhearted bitch. She's going to do me like she did Tae, and she's ten times worse than my ex. Well, excuse the fuck out of me, Dr. Muthafuckin' Phil. I see it's okay for him to refer to a female as a bitch as long as it's not his darling Latavia. What he needs to be doing is worrying about *her* sneaky ass, not what Nariah is doing. Oh, she ain't fooling nobody but her damn self.

While on one of my excursions to locate my man cave, which had gone missing, I went by Glamour Events Too. I saw Tae's trifling ass with some dude, whom I watched her suck and fuck. Why she was in there with him, with nothing up against the windows, is beyond me. I had no idea Nariah's ass was in there until I saw her come out of the office and get into the car. If you ask me, Tae was fucking lucky Nariah was there; Nariah actually saved her life. D would have put a bullet in her and asked me to help him cover that shit up if he had gotten there early enough to see what really went down. Latavia needs to be apologizing and thanking Nariah for that shit, if you ask me.

I am far from a snitch—at least not right now, anyway. I am going to use this little piece of information to my advantage, so Tae's ass had better get ready. It's going to be a bumpy ride! I'll lie low with it for now, but stay tuned. Shit is about to hit the fan for Mrs. Innocent, Perfect Latavia Carter.

CHAPTER 15

TAE CAN'T TAKE ANY MORE

Nariah's words and actions spoke loud and clear. She is *not* the confidant she has portrayed herself to be all these years. Now I see the real Nariah has surfaced. I really thought I knew her and could trust her with any and everything, no matter what. How could she be so heartless and mean? She swore up and down she loved me as if our mothers had taken turns giving birth to us— as if that was at all possible. Was that her demonstration of love? I mean, if there is anyone who knows firsthand the things I endured at the hands of my father, it is Nariah. How could she throw me under the bus like that? No matter how upset, mad, disappointed, or whatever she was feeling, there was no rhyme or reason whatsoever for her to take things that far.

Then, to top it off, she had the nerve to brag about sucking BK off. I am beyond hurt and devastated as a result of all of this. My mother always used to say, "Sticks and stones may break your bones, but words and names will never hurt you." Well, I beg to differ. Mom was clearly living in denial. Nariah's words cut through me like a laser beam cutting through metal, or a hot knife through butter. To dig the knife in deeper and making matters worse, Darnell heard her throw the abuse in my face. She is so lucky he pulled me off her. I would have killed her if he hadn't shown up when he did.

I slept in late and have been in this bathroom for the past forty-five minutes, unable to move or face anyone or anything on the other side of this door. Talking to Darnell for the past two days has been one of the hardest things I've ever had to do outside of the abortions, rapes, and miscarriages. Reliving the little I shared with him felt like I was experiencing the rape all over again as the words fell from my lips. Just the thought of it all causes fear and anxiety to take complete control over me, and I begin to sink down deeper in the tub, contemplating what to do next.

I might as well just get used to being in here, because there is no way I am leaving this bathroom. All I need is water, and there is plenty of it in here, I think as fresh tears stream down my face. Lost in my thoughts, I don't hear Darnell enter the bathroom.

"Good morning, baby. You're going to turn into a prune if you stay in that tub any longer," he jokes, trying to ease the tension and make me smile.

"Good morning," I reply a little above a whisper.

"I hope you found your appetite in there. I prepared breakfast for us," he informs me as he assists me out of the tub, a bath towel in hand awaiting my wet, wrinkled body.

Still unable to give him any eye contact, with my head hung low, I say, "Thank you, Darnell." Then I put my robe on some sweats and Darnell's T-shirt and follow him downstairs.

This damn man never ceases to amaze me. He has a table set by the large bay window in the living room, and it is draped with a white linen tablecloth. In the center of the table is a clear jug containing fresh lavender tulips, which happen to be my favorite flower. He even used the good china to hold the toasted sourdough bread, with cinnamon butter alongside it for dipping. This is his version of French toast. As I admire the table, I note that there are also scrambled eggs, fresh strawberries, turkey bacon, and mimosas chilled in the champagne flutes Nae purchased for us as a housewarming gift. The thought of her causes me to tear up. Darnell must have observed my emotions welling up again, and to defuse the situation, he pulls me in close to him, wraps his arms around me, and holds me tight, like he is trying to squeeze the pain away.

"Tae, I know this is hard for you, baby. I promise you if you allow it, we will get through this together. You are not alone. I am here with you and will do whatever I have to do to make things better for you," he pleads through the tears he is trying so hard to hold back.

Darnell breaks his embrace when the ringing of the doorbell startles him. "Babe, have a seat and get started on breakfast before it gets cold, while I go and get rid of whoever it is at the door."

I take a seat at the table, and as I stick my fork in the eggs, I suddenly hear Nariah screaming in the foyer.

"Get your fucking hands off me, Black! Why are you choking me?"

Wait one damn minute! Why is she calling Darnell Black? I think. *Isn't that the guy she met on the website? Oh my God! Are you kidding me!*

I fly out of my seat and race into the foyer. "How could you do this to me, Darnell?" I yell, snatching my purse off the table. I run straight out the door, with no destination in mind.

CHAPTER 16

NARIAH'S DEMONS

Usually, I wouldn't give a flying fuck if someone is angry, in his or her feelings, or not speaking to me. This is different. It's Tae I'm talking about; that girl means the world to me. I really don't understand why she's this upset. Hell, she knows me better than anyone else, so the slick shit that comes out of my mouth should be expected. Tae knows good and goddamn well I don't mean any harm by any of it. Now she calls herself angry and not speaking to me or something. All my text messages and phone calls have gone unanswered for two days now. As I leave another message, I assume she will call me back right away.

"Tae, I apologize for bothering you, and I know you are upset with me right now, but as you always say, when it comes to Glamour Events, all the personal crap between us becomes irrelevant. With that being the case, I am calling to inform you that we are now being instructed to push back the opening for Glamour Events Too because the foreman fell through the ceiling and hurt himself. We will have to see what the construction company is talking about, as I received a message saying the balance of the job has been postponed until further notice," I lie, trying to sound as sincere and convincing as I possibly can. To no avail. She is as stubborn as I am, and my calls remain unanswered.

To try to ease my mind, I call Walter, and his ass is nowhere to be found. This is really pissing me off; right about now, dick is the only thing that can take my troubles away. *It looks like this will be Nard's lucky night*, I think as I send him a text message telling him to meet me at my place in an hour and making sure to include my address, considering I've never granted him the honor or privilege of gracing my humble abode with his presence. He's lucky I am too tired to drive and am feeling a little down, or he would be running his pockets for a room.

I now have an hour to shit, shower, and change. Better yet, I'll just keep my birthday suit on; that way, we can cut the small talk and get this party started. Nard is one of those guys you love to hate. You hate him because he is too clingy, but you love him because he will dick you down by fucking your brains out, leaving you wanting and begging for more. This is the primary reason why I keep him and that sexy, mouthwatering brown dick of his in heavy rotation. Between Nard and Walter, I have been having the best sex of my life.

Like clockwork, my doorbell rings at eight on the dot; he is a very punctual man.

"Hello there, handsome," I say seductively as I open the door. I stand there for a minute. Nard doesn't look like himself. His eyes look strange, yet familiar.

"What's up?" he says coldly, brushing past me.

Now I am stuck. I don't understand what's going on. I usually have the upper hand in this situation, but tears are now pouring down my face like a waterfall.

"What the fuck is wrong with you? Who knew your ass even cried, and what the fuck are you crying for, anyway?" Nard asks harshly.

I can't even respond. My words are caught in my throat, and all I can do is cry. Standing there, staring at him, I can't move, as the strong stench of Scotch whiskey paralyzes me. Out of nowhere, I begin to have an out-of-body experience, and the past flashes before my eyes.

"Hello, Mother," I say to my mom as I enter the house after school.

"How are you doing, baby girl?" she replies.

"I'm good. Going to get my homework done before Dad comes home. Hoping we can have a good night tonight," I reply nervously.

"No matter what, baby girl, just remember I love you, and I would never do anything to hurt you. You understand me?" my mom says.

"Yes, Mom, I know. Why are you saying this? You're scaring me."

Mother doesn't have to answer. As I stand in front of her, I can see the fear in her eyes as the smell of Scotch whiskey infiltrates my nostrils. I turn to greet my father, but he angrily brushes past me and goes straight to my mother, lands punch after punch, sending her toppling to the floor, knocking a tooth out of her mouth. Using his legs, he pins her down, trying to prevent her from moving freely. Mother is able to wiggle her arm and extend her hand to try to block the punches, but he is too quick and much stronger than her. He twists her arm behind her back forcefully with all his might to the point where I can hear her bones cracking as she screams out in excruciating pain.

I want to run over to help Mother, but I am frozen. I can't move. I try to scream for him to stop, but the words won't come out. There's blood everywhere, and Mother isn't moving anymore.

When I snap back to reality, I realize I have lost complete control of myself and my emotions. I am standing over Nard, kicking and punching him.

"You will not control me! You will not abuse me and kill me, like you did my mother. I hate men, and I hate you. I will do all you bastards the same way you did my mother," I cry as I continue to rain blows on Nard's drunken face, which looks like my father's face right now.

It looks like Nard snaps out of his drunken stupor after I whale on him for about five minutes straight. He takes his right leg and wraps it around my legs, then grabs my wrist, causing my knees to buckle. I fall down, and he pins me to the floor. I completely lose it, as this is exactly the same way my father hurt my mom, and I won't allow history to repeat itself. Nard must have heard me thinking.

"Nariah, I am going to let you loose, but promise me you will keep your hands to yourself. I am not your father! I would never hurt you intentionally. I need you to calm the fuck down. Now, get on your knees and suck this dick real good for being a bad girl!" he demands.

Hearing the words that escape his lips brings me back to the present, and I am turned on with the quickness.

"Yes, Daddy. Your wish is my command," I reply seductively.

"Shut the fuck up! Turn around and lie on your stomach," Nard says cruelly, then forcefully helps me turn over. With my face now to the floor, he takes his left knee and places it against my lower back, then seizes both of my arms and places handcuffs on my wrists. I love to role-play, so I hurriedly get into character.

"What did I do, Mr. Police Officer?" I say, trying to sound frightened, and take my mind off everything.

"What part of 'Shut the fuck up' don't you understand?" he shouts before he turns me over and shoves his dick in my mouth. It is difficult for me to get into a groove lying in the position I'm in and having him crouched over me, but I try my best to please him so he can in return please me that much more. Frustrated that his manhood keeps slipping out my mouth, Nard snatches me up by my hair into a sitting position and fucks my face with no mercy, ramming himself in and out of my mouth with so much force that I gag and vomit at the same time. This must turn the sick bastard on. He begins to ejaculate in my mouth before removing himself to release his remaining seed all over my face.

Sitting there, mortified and embarrassed, I can't control the fresh tears that cascade down my face. Nard just looks at me coldly, with a devious smirk on his face, as he removes the cuffs from my wrists.

"Thanks, Nariah. I really needed that shit after the day I had," he says, then pulls himself together and walks out the door.

"I cannot believe he humiliated me like this," I cry, pulling myself up off the floor. "There's no way I'm staying in this house alone. I have to go see and talk to Tae. I really need her right now," I say aloud to myself.

CHAPTER 17

DARNELL CAN'T WIN

"What the fuck is going on, Nariah? Why are you here?" I ask angrily.

"It doesn't matter. I need to talk to Tae right now, so please get your ugly black ass out of my face," she replies through tears.

Not giving a fuck about her or her tears—she has caused more problems in one day than any person should in a lifetime—I grab her by her neck to toss her nasty ass out of my house. She screams just as Tae walks into the foyer and heads out the front door.

"Fuck!" I say to myself, now looking in Tae's direction. I rush outside.

"It's not what you think, baby! Please let me explain," I plead as she speeds backward out of the driveway in my damn truck. "Now what the fuck am I going to do?" I ask in a panic.

This shit is crazy. Tae's car is still at Glamour Events, I think before locking eyes on Nariah's car, which is parked in front of the house. I trot over to the driver's side and see that the key is still in the ignition. *Bingo!* I jump in her car without a second thought, start the engine, and pull away. The only thing I am concerned about right now is my wife's safety. "She's in no condition to be alone or driving," I say aloud to myself, causing me to press harder on the gas pedal.

Now doing seventy-five miles an hour, I have to pump the brakes to slow down as I come to a traffic light. As I stop, I realize I've pulled up alongside Tae. I put the car in park, hop out, and proceed to walk over to the truck just as the light turns green. She speeds off. Hurriedly, I jump back in the car and hit the gas pedal. So as to prevent Tae from getting out of my sight, I increase my speed. I catch up to her and tail her.

As we reach the junction of Merrick Boulevard and Springfield, she is forced to stop at another traffic light. After slamming on the brakes to prevent myself from running into the back of her, I lose control of the car and swerve to the right. Trying to avoid a collision, I swipe an oncoming car, and this causes my car to spin out of control and flip over. That is the last thing I recall happening before everything goes black.

A few days have gone by, and I haven't heard shit from Tavia. I've shot her a couple of text messages and called a few times, but she ain't even trying to communicate with a brother. She can't be having second thoughts; that shit was too good for her to be having second thoughts all of a sudden. Truth is, I'm tired of playing Mr. Fucking Nice Guy.

Tavia belongs to me, so whatever she has going on over there with Officer Bitch Ass is about to come to a screeching halt, I think, lacing up my Timberlands. I keep them on deck just in case I gotta stomp a mutha-fucka out.

The first time I ran into baby girl at Duane Reade, I followed her home. I've been keeping a close watch, making sure this clown is treating her right until I come in and take my rightful place. Little does she know, Daddy will be coming to the rescue real soon. The way she was throwing that pussy at me displayed just how unhappy she is with homeboy. Instead of wasting any more time, I've decided to head over to the love nest to see why my baby ain't reaching out to her first love.

As soon as I turn down her street, a truck comes flying out of her driveway, almost backing into my car. I quickly maneuver to my left to avoid a collision, and off to the right, I see Officer Dick Ass running toward the truck, yelling something, but I can't make out what he's saying. The look on his face tell me exactly what is going on: my baby girl has decided to leave his bitch ass and come home to Daddy. With that, I put my car in drive and head in the same direction as Tavia.

Shit went from zero to a hundred real quick, and I am lying low to scope shit out when I see dude's ass come flying down the road. He loses control of his car, hits Tavia's car, and swerves every which way before he smashes into my shit and flips his car the fuck over. He is on some *Action Jackson* movie–type shit. I can't believe any of it, but this is playing out lovely right before my very eyes. Thank God, my car has only minor damage and I am able to be on my way. The way things look, Tavia will be crying in Daddy's arms in no time. Damn, God answered a brother's prayer! It looks like the non-driving police officer will be out of the picture for good.

CHAPTER 18

NARD'S JAMMED UP

Today is a horrible-ass day on the job. D's ass didn't come in. He's home, trying to fix things with his simple-ass wife. I am now stuck with this clown who is afraid to walk on the same side of the street as the civilians. Somebody please tell me how the fuck he is a cop with a gun but is scared to walk down the goddamn street.

"Officer Cooper, why are you walking in the middle of the street?" I ask, walking in his direction. When I lock eyes with him, I can see fear in his eyes. I grab my gun, then turn around slowly to see what has him shaken. I see two people yelling and running toward us, and one of them has something in his hand that resembles the Glock forty-caliber handguns we carry.

"Drop your weapon!" I yell as the armed suspect runs in our direction. He doesn't comply. "Please drop your weapon!" I shout again before letting off two shots, hitting the armed suspect in the arm and the leg.

I didn't realize until after shooting that the armed suspect was actually a twelve-year-old boy with a toy gun. He was playing cops and robbers with his friends, and he was so caught up in his make-believe street chase that he didn't hear or see me and Cooper, according to one of the witnesses. All I want to know is, why the hell are these kids out playing at nine in the morning on a school day? Now I'm jammed up. My commanding officer has placed me on modified duty until the investigation is concluded.

CHAPTER 19

LATAVIA'S NAGGING PAST

I can't believe Darnell had the audacity to come chase me in Nariah's ho mobile. He flew down the road in that piece of shit, like a bat out of hell, and ran right into me. The crazy thing about it is I could see him in my rearview mirror as he swerved from left to right, trying to avoid a collision, but to no avail. Without warning, before I could react, he smacked into the back of the truck, pushing me into oncoming traffic, causing the airbags to deploy right in my face. Thank God I had my seat belt on! I am so furious right now I could scream. The paramedics are insisting I allow them to escort me to the emergency room to get checked out due to the impact, although I feel just fine. I give in and lie down on a stretcher.

Clearly, Darnell and Nariah have me confused. *I am so tired of playing Miss Goody Two-Shoes, having everyone take my kindness for weakness*, I think angrily as I lie on the stretcher. Darnell looks pretty banged up; they had to use the Jaws of Life to remove him from the car. I pray he is all right. I can't take any more heartache. I've had more than enough. Growing up, Mommy always said, "God won't put any more on us than we can bear." I wonder if she really knew what she was talking about, because I am at my breaking point.

The paramedics transport me to the hospital, and after a full examination, I learn that I was eight weeks pregnant and had a miscarriage. I am hurt and in shock; I didn't see or feel any blood or discharge. Which is mind blowing, because after my forced abortions, I was informed that there was a 99.9 percent chance that I wouldn't be able to conceive or carry a child to full term.

"I have the worst freaking luck! The two people I loved the most have betrayed me and killed my unborn child!" I scream through my tears before snatching the IV out my arm, tossing it, and jumping out of the bed. I start tossing and throwing any and everything within arms' reach. Suddenly I feel dizzy and can't keep my balance. While the room spins around me, my eyes become heavy, and then everything around me darkens.

It has been three months that Mommy's been picking me and Nariah, my new bestie, up after school every single day. Now that her hours have changed, she's around a lot more, and my father has been a real father to me, *I think as we wait for her. I smile.*

"She's never this late," Nae says, looking at her watch.

"I don't know what can be taking her so long," I reply dryly, and then I notice my father's car pull up. When it comes to a full stop, we both climb in the backseat.

"Hey, princess and Nariah. Mom was called in to do some overtime, so look who got stuck picking your lazy behinds up," he says jokingly. "Honestly, both of you are too damn old to be getting picked up from school every day. Your grown asses need to start walking home instead of wasting gas," he spits.

Neither Nariah nor I reply. We both know if we do, he will take his anger out on me. I've recently shared with her the horrible things he's done to me over the past few years. She is fully aware of how this could play out. Remaining quiet until we reach our desired destination is really our only option. Happy that it's Friday and that Nae is sleeping over for the weekend, we excitedly jump out of the car as soon as he parks and run straight upstairs to my room.

"I'd better not hear none of that loud-ass music up there, either," Daddy yells before I slam my door shut, ignoring his complaints.

We polish each other's nails and talk for hours, catching up on the latest music videos on BET.

"I'm starving, Tae. Do you have any snacks in this place to eat?" Nariah says after a while.

"I have no idea. Let's go downstairs and check." In our own little world, we never notice my father on the sofa until we reach the bottom of the steps.

"Who the fuck told your nosy little asses to come down here without making sure it was okay with me?" my father scolds, zipping his pants before turning off that nasty mess he's always watching.

Embarrassed and no longer hungry, Nariah and I run back upstairs as fast as we can, trying our hardest to get as far away from him as we can.

"Not so fast, hot asses. I know exactly what you be doing up here in this room with the door closed. I'm not stupid," he says sarcastically when he reaches my room. "Since you ruined my happy hour, you'll have to make it up to me. You both know good and well what will happen to Latavia if you disobey me." A smirk creeps across his face. "Nariah, take off all your clothes, and, Latavia, you will do what I instruct you to do," he says, removing his jeans.

Nariah and I close our tear-filled eyes as my father, the monster, forces me to kiss and touch my best friend in every forbidden place Mommy said was off limits until marriage. Once he reaches a climax, he throws two fifty-dollar bills at us and leaves the room.

"Nariah, I am so sorry. Please forgive me. Please don't hate me! I never meant for you to get dragged into this crazy mess. I'm begging you, please don't tell anyone about this ever! He will be mad at me if anyone finds out," I plead.

"Tae, you don't have to apologize, and you have nothing to worry about. We will get that bastard. Sooner or later, he will pay!" she cries.

Sweating and full of anxiety, with my heart racing a mile a minute, I begin to panic, completely unaware of my surroundings, until I locked eyes with BK.

"You all right, baby girl? That must have been a hell of a nightmare you were having. Don't worry. Big daddy's here now to make it all better," he says. "The nurses came in while you were asleep. They have to keep you a couple more days for observation, but all you have to do is say the word and I will get you out of this hellhole," he says, consoling me.

"I can't stay here. I don't want to see any of them. I hate them. Please get me out of here," I whimper.

CHAPTER 20

NARIAH'S CHOCOLATE DELIGHT

The past four days have been emotionally draining. Nard and Black, I mean Darnell's ugly ass, will pay for their actions—trust and believe that shit. I don't know when and how. And it may cost them a little, or it may cost them a lot, but it *will* cost them. There's no way in hell I'm going to allow either of them to get away with how they've disrespected me. Now that I think about it, I haven't heard from any of them since Tae's ass ran off all dramatic into the sunset, with Darnell running after her funky ass. I'm sick of all of them muthafuckas right about now. They have me so fucked up in the head that I've been in the house, drinking and depressed, for the past three days. No phone, television, car, or company. Just me and Jack Daniel's.

"Walter's been missing for a few days now. I have no idea what's crawled up his old ass," I say aloud to myself as I wait for my cell phone to power back up. Purposely, I ignore all my missed calls, text messages, and voicemails. I just can't deal with any of the bullshit right now. I am on a mission, in search of that one person who has the skills and talent to satisfy my yearning sweet tooth. After locating my problem solver, I send a brief text message requesting some company. I can use an ear to get all this shit off my chest, plus a mind-blowing orgasm to take my stress away.

Before retiring to my bath, which awaits me, I make sure to leave the front door unlocked for my guest. The last thing I want is to do is interrupt my bath to open the door. I retreat to the bathroom and test the bathwater with my forefinger. *The water is nice and hot, just the way I like it*, I think, admiring the scene I've created. Candles and rose petals adorned the bathroom. I disrobe, step into the tub, and sink down into the water. *I refuse to wait for anyone else to be good to me when I can be good to myself*, I think, closing my eyes as I lie back on my bath pillow, trying to allow the stresses of the past few days to evacuate my mind.

Minutes later, feeling someone standing over me, I open my eyes to a Kool-Aid smile invading my vision. Lost in my thoughts, I never even heard Mahogany bring her sexy, thick ass in the house. I can't stop smiling as I admire my hot lover for the night.

"Good evening, sweetness. I'm overjoyed you remembered my number. However, you can't keep doing me like this. Mama has a problem when she has to go too long without tasting her sweetness," my chocolate delight announces, seductively removing her clothes to join me in my bath.

After climbing in behind me, she pulls me closer to her so my head can rest on those perky double Ds. While she bathes me, I unload my woes from the past few days on her, and it feels good to get it off my chest. Mahogany has become a good friend since our Dunkin' Donuts meet and greet. She is an excellent listener and is nonjudgmental. I can talk to her about any and everything, and I have done just that—more so than I ever have with Tae. Mahogany and I just have a different kind of connection.

About twenty minutes later, Mahogany rises from the water and steps out of the tub. "Let Mama take your troubles away, sweetness," she says, extending her hand to assist me out of the once scalding-hot bath.

Mahogany must have been a magician in her former life, because she works magic with that long, thick tongue of hers and those soft, gentle hands. She is a masseuse by profession and owns one of the best spas in the area. It's located near Queens, on the border of the Island, which partly explains how I ended up running into her a couple of days after our first meeting. Tae and I were having our monthly divas' day, and we decided we were in need of a massage after being referred to Massage Envy. Guess who happened to be my masseuse for the day because she was short staffed? My Mahogany chocolate drop. She had no idea, but I was really feeling her.

"Sweetness, whatever it is that's occupying your mind, I need you to release it, so you can enjoy what Mama has in store for you," she says, jolting me from my reminiscence.

As we enter my bedroom, I am blown away. She's come with her own personal bag of tricks. There are tea-light candles and purple rose petals (my favorite color) scattered around the room, and soft music is playing in the background. The music is actually sounds from nature or maybe ambient noises. Whatever it is, it is hypnotizing. My emotions are now all over the place. *No one has ever done anything like this for me*, I think as tears threaten to run down my face.

"When in God's name did you do this?" I ask as I lie down on the bed.

"All I need you to do is trust me and relax. I know what you need and deserve, and I am going to give you just that," she replies before placing soft, delicate kisses on my forehead.

Mahogany starts out with light, long strokes from my head to my toes before turning me over and having me lie facedown. After positioning herself behind my head, she kneads the muscles in my shoulders and neck by using her thumb and forefingers, and this turns me on like crazy. As she massages my wrists, fingers, ears, back, and neck, she relaxes my mind, body, and soul. She then allows her succulent lips to trade places with her fingers, and she kisses, licks, and nibbles every neglected region of my body, sending chills up and down my spine. I am on the verge of reaching euphoria as she allows her mouth to massage my honey love, licking my swollen clitoris and the surrounding area teasingly and, most important, pleasingly. Mahogany makes out with my box, slipping her snake-like tongue in and out, as if it were her manhood. I can't hold back any longer. She senses it, accelerates her pace, and soon drives me straight to my intended destination of orgasmic pleasure, causing my body to tremble violently.

CHAPTER 21

BERNARD'S DAY FROM HELL

"Can this fucking day get any fouler?" I ask myself out loud. Now I can't find my phone; the last place I recall having it was at O'Neill's, before I headed over to Nariah's place. Speaking of Nariah, that chick was on some extra shit tonight. I'm not sure what her pops did to her and her mother, but that bitch needs to be in a straitjacket. She blacked out for a minute on a brother. If her pussy wasn't first class, I would drop her paranoid-schizophrenic ass like a bad habit. Quiet as it's kept, the problem is she's my drug of choice. Nonetheless, she might consider taking up permanent residence at a psychiatric facility.

Retracing my steps, I return to O'Neill's in hopes of finding my phone. However, I find melancholy instead, and it embraces me with open arms as soon as I step out of the car.

"Hey there, comrade. I'm sorry to hear about your partner," Officer Martinez says solemnly when he and I practically collide right inside the door to O'Neill's.

"I'm sorry, Martinez. My partner? What are you talking about?" I question.

"You didn't hear about Carter? It's all over the news."

"No, I haven't been watching the fucking news and haven't heard shit! Now spit it out and tell me what the fuck happened!" I bark irritably as fear overwhelms me.

"Maybe you should have a seat," he suggests.

"No, maybe *you* need to sit the fuck down and tell me. I am really getting tired of playing games!"

"Carter was in a severe car accident early this evening, and he is now in Winthrop Hospital, in critical condition."

Before Martinez can utter another word, I bolt out the door, race into the parking lot, and search for my car. "Where did I park? Is this happening right now?" I ask myself. Relief consumes me, as opposed to frustration, when Martinez pulls up alongside me. He must be on some *Knight Rider* or superhero-type shit out this bitch, since he just magically appears.

"Good looking out," I say as I jump in the car.

"No problem, my man," he replies.

"Did you move my car on purpose or something? You showed up out of nowhere, like a Power Ranger," I say, and we erupt in laughter. I am trying to defuse the situation and calm down in order to brace myself for whatever it is I have to face at the hospital.

I'm not sure if time stands still on our ride over to the hospital, but it feels as if I have just gotten in the car, and now we are pulling up to the emergency entrance. When we get inside, I notice most of our fellow officers from the Seventh Precinct in attendance, but I don't want to see any of them. I just need to make sure my boy D is good.

"Good evening, Officer Peterson," the nurse says as I approach the nurses' station. She knows me and D very well. Being cops, you encounter your fair share of injuries, especially working at the NYPD.

"Good evening," I reply.

"Your partner is still in surgery. The doctor will be out to speak to you and Mrs. Carter immediately following surgery," she informs me.

"Thank you," I reply.

Now that I think about it, where the hell is Tae? I think, scanning the waiting area in hopes of seeing her. She's probably a mess right now, so it might be a good thing if I don't see her right now. I can't deal with her and this at the same time. I have to get myself together. I'm in no shape to console anyone right now.

Looking at my watch, I realize I've been sitting in the waiting area for two and a half hours. Panic starts to set in, but I know I have to remain calm for D. "He needs me right now," I say in a low whisper, trying to encourage myself. I begin to calm down when I notice a surgeon in scrubs walking in my direction.

"Officer Peterson?" the surgeon asks, his voice trembling slightly.

"Yes?" I reply, springing to my feet.

"I'm sorry we have to meet under these circumstances," he says apologetically.

"No problem. How is he?"

"As you are aware, Officer Carter had to undergo emergency surgery due to bleeding in his brain. The gash to his head from the airbags deploying caused trauma and bleeding. The surgery went well. However, I must inform you that these types of injuries are severe and can be life-threatening."

"So what are you saying, Doc?" I ask, unable to fight back my tears.

"What I am saying is, miraculously, there wasn't a large amount of bleeding. Therefore, we were able to drain the blood and control the bleeding. This means there's a possibility Officer Carter will make a full recovery and walk out of this unharmed. On the other hand, with bleeding to the brain, oxygen-rich blood is prevented from flowing to the brain tissue, causing additional swelling and pressure. Although the operation assisted with alleviating some of this pressure, there is still some pressure and swelling present. Right now, we have to allow the swelling to subside and his injuries to heal before taking any further steps. Officer Carter will be monitored around the clock, and we will make sure you and Mrs. Carter are kept apprised of his progress."

"So how long could this take?" I ask through tears.

"It's hard to say, honestly. Brain swelling can cause you to be unconscious for a week, a few days, or months," he replies.

"Thank you, Doc," I say, shaking his hand, weeping on the inside.

He nods, then turns and slowly walks away.

Hold the fuck up! They've mentioned Latavia twice, and I have been here for hours and haven't seen her. Was she in the car with him? I ask myself as I walk back over to the nurses' station.

"Excuse me, was Officer Carter in the car with his wife when he had the accident?" I question one of the nurses.

"No, she wasn't in the car with him. However, she was involved in the accident, as well, and she was admitted," the nurse informs me.

This shit just went from bad to worse.

CHAPTER 22

BK TO THE RESCUE!

When I get to the hospital, there are more police officers than a brother can handle at one time. Not that I am riding dirty or am on the run or anything, but being around that much law enforcement will make anyone a little nervous. I'm just going to play it cool and peep shit out, so I know what my next move is. Now is not the time to get caught out there slipping and getting locked the fuck up for trying to salvage what's rightfully mine.

I take a seat in the waiting area, with my back turned to the entire NYPD. Moments later I can hear all the commotion going on when this officer, who I assume is Tae's husband's partner, arrives.

"We are here for you if you need us, Officer," a couple of his fellow officers say simultaneously.

Everyone begins catering to that muthafucka's every move and word, acting all sympathetic and shit. The only other thing I can make out from the noise is that homeboy got fucked up real bad in the car accident and he is now in surgery. In other words, that was my cue to go console my baby girl.

"She's sleeping like a baby," I say softly to myself as I enter the room and catch sight of her.

As I proceed to walk to the other side of the room, I can hear her talking in her sleep. I can't see her face, since she is lying on her side, with her back facing the door.

"I'm so sorry, Nariah. Please forgive me," she pleads.

A few seconds later, I get close enough to see her beautiful but frightened face, and it's drenched with sweat. It looks like she's crying too, and I can't take seeing that shit at all. I go to wake her up, and her eyes pop open, scaring a brother half to death. She looks right past me, around the room, like she is lost or has mentally left the building.

She doesn't look good at all. This isn't the beautiful woman I was with just a couple of days ago. My baby looks like she's lost a hundred pounds. Her face looks mad ashy or maybe pale; I guess that's the right word. All I know is I don't like any of this shit, and it ends today.

I start thinking to myself that I honestly don't know how, but I have to get her to see things my way and get her the fuck out of here unnoticed. Before I can even process shit, I am lying to Tae, telling her the nurse said they have to keep her here for a couple of days for observation. She falls right into big papa's hands, practically begging me to get her away from everything and everyone.

After making sure the coast is clear and Tavia is dressed, we casually walk out of the hospital hand in hand. I gave her my hoodie and fitted Yankees cap to try to disguise her so she can walk out unnoticed. I'm not going to front: she looks good as fuck with that shit on. I want to beat it up on sight, but now is not the time for that.

I can see the pain on Tavia's face with each movement she makes. Lucky for her, I keep ibuprofen in my glove box. No one likes to be in pain. I for damn sure don't, and

I've been having these killer headaches that are a bitch and a half. I guess I need to carry my lazy ass to the eye doctor and holla at some frames for these bad eyes of mine. Until then, ibuprofen it is, and it works out because I can help ease my baby girl's pain too.

Tavia sleeps for the hour-and-a-half ride to my crib in Connecticut. I refuse to bring her to that little-ass apartment I am staying in, in the Bronx. That place is just to hold me over until I snatch up what belongs to me. Considering I'm good now and Tavia's with me, I really don't have any use for it any longer. However, you never know, so I will chill on that thought.

"How long have I been asleep, and where are we going?" my sleeping beauty asks when we reach my Connecticut crib.

"We are home, baby girl. Home, sweet home," I reply, grinning like some schoolboy.

"Is that right?" she questions.

"Yes, it is." We both get out of the car and head inside. "Now grab my hand so I can show you around, if you're up to it," I tell her.

"Can I get a rain check?" she asks. "I just want to take a nice hot bath and have a nice, relaxing stiff drink," she says, a forced smile on her face.

Without saying another word, I escort her to the master bath, hand her clean face and bath towels. Then I am on my way to fetch some wine for the lady and some cognac for myself. I don't know what's in store for me tonight, but a brother will be prepared, no matter what.

CHAPTER 23

LATAVIA'S ON THE RUN

This bath is what I need right now, I say to myself. I need to try to relax my mind. Everything in my life is upside down and out of control. Darnell is a lying bastard. Nariah is a sneaky, backstabbing, slut bucket. I am so sick of crying. I hate my life right now. The only good thing I have going right now is BK. He has always been a man of perfect timing. To think I was stupid enough to believe Darnell was the perfect man. Boy, did he have me fooled. It's okay. No love lost. They say the best way to get over someone is to get under someone new. Guess who's about to go to the underworld to find out just how true that saying is—especially now that the bleeding has stopped?

If things go the way I'm hoping they will, I will just leave my past where it is—dead to me—and start over with BK's fine self. I smile as I think about BK's fine tail. Thinking about that man forces me to cut my bath short. *Where is he?* I think as I step out of the tub. I dry off quickly, wrap the towel around, and walk right into him as I exit the bathroom.

"Damn, baby girl. I'm sorry. I didn't even see you. Now you have Hennessy all over that sexy body of yours," he says apologetically, then licks his thick, cunt-eating lips.

CHAPTER 24

WHO'S THAT LADY?

I am a firm believer that there is most definitely a thin line between love and hate. I love Braxton with the same intense passion with which I despise Latavia. She was doing well, was living happily ever after with the man of her dreams. She even had a glow. From the outside looking in, she had it all—the house, the car, and a man who loved the smell of her funky drawers. Why would you mess that up? Simple bitches wouldn't know a good thing if it slapped them in the face. Fortunately enough for Latavia, she won't have to wait very long. Reality is about to pimp-slap her silly ass into a coma right next to her husband. She couldn't enjoy what she had. She had to disrupt what I had and mess with what's mine, and I, Sharon Kirkland, also known as Mahogany, refuse to sit back and allow that to happen.

Braxton loves me! I am not concerned about what anyone else says or how they feel about the situation, either. His pride and ego just have him all messed up in the head, so that he thinks he's still in love with Latavia. When, in actuality, he never really loved her. If he loved *her* so much, he never would have put a ring on *my* finger. Now he calls himself filing for divorce. I ain't signing a thing. When we said our vows before God and our family, we said, "Until death do us part." As you can see, both of us still have blood running warm through our veins. In other words, the only way out of this marriage is a his or her body bag.

Yes, I was the rebound in high school, because his precious Latavia wouldn't give him any. That was over twenty years ago. He married me, not her. Quiet as it's kept, he was and is my first and only. When Braxton caught me in bed with Mark, it wasn't what he thought it was. It was staged to make him jealous. The only thing Mark did was taste my honey bun, and he couldn't even get that right. I know it was childish of me, but I was left with no other choice.

The heartache from us losing two babies caused me to fall into a serious bout of depression. This put a wedge in our relationship and, most importantly, our sex life. When we did have sex, it was always in the dark. Braxton also wanted it only from the back. That cut me to the core. It was emotionless. I assumed he didn't want to look at me.

It wasn't like that in the beginning. If I wasn't so caught up with being the perfect wife and being better than Latavia, I would have two beautiful children and my husband at home. But no, she had to flood my man's thoughts. This is all her fault, and she will pay!

Since high school, I have never let Latavia out of my sight. I was especially vigilant when Braxton and I got married. He was obsessed with popping all the virgins' cherries he could in our early years. I knew this when we first got together. The other girls didn't give him head and couldn't handle that enormous delicacy of a dick he has. I made sure to be different and give him what they didn't and couldn't. I knew from first sight he was mine. So, you see, our loss had him reminiscing about everything he missed out on. Latavia is just on his to-do list because he lost out on bursting her rotten cherry.

Braxton and I are soul mates, and Latavia is just a distraction. Our turmoil has his thinking all screwed up. He can't think straight. He has always loved me and always will. He's just thinking with the wrong head. The crazy thing about it is, little does he know, he was never going to be able to take her virginity in the first place. The way Nariah tells it, her father was smashing it long before my beloved came into the picture. Clearly, it's obvious that he is delusional and can't see past his penis. That's understandable. Have you seen *the size* of that thing? But that's why God created Eve and women. We are here to be helpmates to our men, and I'm going to help my mate see the truth—one way or the other.

CHAPTER 25

NARIAH'S DISAPPEARING ACT

Being in this house for the past five days straight has me a bit claustrophobic. Maybe I should go check on Elite. Tae probably thinks I'm crazy. I just haven't felt like being bothered with anything or anyone after my chocolate fix. My television and phone have been off for a week now. The only entertainment I have had is Jack Daniel's, my iPod, and sleep. I have barely eaten anything, now that I think about it. This must be what depression feels like, and I am so over it right about now. Turning on the television, I decide to watch News 12 to try to get reacquainted with the real world, which I've been shutting out and hiding from.

"Breaking news. Off-duty police officer Darnell Carter remains in critical but stable condition after the tragic accident that almost took his life. We'll have more on this tragic story as it unfolds. Tune in at six p.m. tonight for more coverage," the newscaster reports.

"Wait a minute! What in the world did she just say?" I ask myself out loud. "Why didn't anyone call me? Is Tae all right?"

A million questions flood my head as I run into my bedroom to throw some clothes on. Tears are now covering my face. I can't believe I've been sitting in this damn house all this time and my Tae could be lying up somewhere, fighting for her life. I need to get myself together and head over to the hospital. No matter if it's her or Darnell who is hurt, she's up there.

"Shit, shit, shit! Darnell has my keys and my damn car!" I scream.

I really can't believe no one bothered to contact me about my car in all these days. Most importantly, I am shocked about Darnell and/or Tae being in an accident. It sounds serious, given the way the newscaster spoke about it. I just hope Tae isn't still in her feelings. Upon powering up my phone to try to get some answers before I lose my mind, I am alerted that I have a gazillion missed calls and voicemail messages. It looks like I decided to go missing in action at the wrong time. Hell, Tae knows where I live, so if she couldn't get through on the phone . . . Scrolling through my missed calls, I suddenly realize zero of them are from Tae. The majority of them are from unknown numbers, except for the ones from Nard. I have no idea who these people are who have been calling me.

"You have one message whose retention time is about to expire. You have thirty-five new messages. You have nine saved messages," my phone tells me. "First new message . . ."

"Nariah Westbrook, this is Detective Torres from the Seventh Precinct. It is urgent that you return this call. I can be reached at 917-555-2000. Thank you," a woman says.

"What in God's name is going in?" I cry.

Knock, knock, knock!

"Who is it?" I yell as I head to the front door. I swing the door open and find two police detectives.

"Good afternoon, ma'am. We're looking to speak with a Nariah Westbrook. I am Detective Torres, and this is Detective Griffin," one of them says as they present their badges.

"I'm Nariah. Please come in," I reply, then move to the side to allow them entrance.

They step inside and gaze around the living room.

"Please excuse the mess and have a seat. If you don't mind, please tell me why you're here," I say nervously.

"Do you know Officer Darnell Carter, ma'am?" Detective Torres asks.

"Yes! Why? What happened? He's my best friend's husband. Is she okay? Is he okay?" I frantically ask.

"Ma'am, Officer Carter was in a severe car accident earlier this week in a car that is registered in your name. Are you aware of this?" he asks accusingly.

I reply through tears, explaining to the detectives what took place on Saturday at Darnell and Tae's place. I also advise them that because of our falling-out, I have been cooped up in this house alone for the past five days and turned on my phone and television just moments before their arrival.

"Mrs. or Ms. Westbrook?" Detective Torres questions.

"Ms.," I reply.

Detectives Torres goes on. "Are you aware that the brake line on your car was cut and all the brake fluid leaked out from the car, which prevented the car from stopping, causing Officer Carter to lose control of the car and almost lose his life?"

I can't even respond. I just shake my head through my tears. "How is it that my brake line was cut and Darnell almost died?"

CHAPTER 26

MAHOGANY'S BOTCHED PLANS

My plan is all botched up. Now I have to think of a plan B. Nariah and I got together the night of her and Latavia's big fight. After putting Nariah's damaged behind to sleep, I tampered with her brakes in hopes that she would get into a minor fender bender. Latavia would then come to the rescue, they would patch things up, and we would become the three amigos, allowing me a greater advantage to make my move. Well, that went downhill, and now Latavia's husband is in the hospital, fighting for his life. I have to regroup; this is all the way jacked up.

It's been a little over a week since the accident, and I am assuming they haven't traced, and can't trace, anything back to me, thank God. Because of that, I have a newfound love for Google. You can find any and everything on there. The Bible does say, "My people perish from a lack of knowledge," but not this chick. I found step-by-step instructions on how to cut a brake line. Of course, I made sure to wear rubber gloves—no fingerprints—and of course, I learned that from watching a little television as well.

It looks like I will have to keep this charade up with Nariah as well. Yes, I did say *charade*! I don't even like women, so being in a relationship with one is completely out of the question. A real woman like me loves a nice, rock-hard, thick anaconda ding-a-ling up in me, Braxton's preferably. Again, I had to resort to the internet to learn how to please another female and taste her honey love. Reading is by far fundamental. I became an overnight success and turned Nariah out like a modern-day MC Hammer—"U Can't Touch This." I have to make sure to put my all into everything I do at this point in the game if I want to bring my husband back home. I will do whatever it takes to make it happen. Latavia has no idea what she has gotten herself into or who she's messing with.

One of the greatest things out of all of this is I know the good Lord is working in my favor. He made sure Latavia and Nariah were hermits in school, and we never crossed paths. My mom used to always say God knows the ending of a situation, so I am a firm believer He made sure that happened to allow me the opportunity to use them or move both of them out of the way. One way or another, something has to give. God honors marriage, and so do I.

CHAPTER 27

BRAXTON WANTS ANSWERS!

My baby girl has been home for a little over a week now, and things have been real good. The only thing I'm not feeling are those Freddy Krueger dreams she's been having. Three nights in a row, she woke up sweating bullets, crying and fighting. Shorty scared me half to death last night, when she woke up swinging and caught me in the jaw. I didn't know what the hell had happened. When she comes to bed, we have to talk. I'm not getting any sleep with Floyd Mayweather on the other side of the bed, trying to remain the champ.

"How was your bath, baby girl?" I ask when she steps into the bedroom.

"It was good, baby. It would have been better if you had joined me," she replies seductively.

"I know what you want, little mama, but we need to chop it up first, if that's okay with you," I says as I walk over to her.

"Sure thing. What's wrong?" she says.

"That's what I need you to tell me, Tavia. You've been bugging out in your sleep, and that shit has me a little worried about you."

Tears start pouring out of her eyes, ripping my heart out of my chest. She is all choked up and can't get her words out. I don't know what she's about to say to me, but I do know there's no chance in hell she's going back to that punk. I feel bad. He's in a fucked-up position, laid up in the hospital . . . Let me stop frontin'. No, I don't feel bad! Who am I kidding? He had to get out of the way eventually. So it is what it is. Bottom line, Tavia is mine, point-blank—always has and always will be. There are no ifs, ands, or buts about it.

"BK, baby, there's a lot you don't know about me, and I don't want any more secrets between us. I'm tired of lies and secrets. So I am going to be open and honest with you, in hopes it won't change things between us or how you feel about me."

"What? Don't tell me you were born a man?" I joke.

"No, crazy." She shakes her head.

After Tavia pours her heart and soul out, trying to fill me in on what her bitch-ass pops did to her, I want to grab my Desert Eagle and fuck something up. Who the fuck does shit like that to their own blood? I have to cut her off and try to change the subject. I can't take listening to any more of this shit. She's a soldier in my eyes. Any other bitch would be all kinds of fucked up in the head or would have jumped out a window by now. Real talk, that ain't no light shit to be dealing with. I have the utmost respect for her.

"Come closer to me, little mama, and let big daddy take some of that pain away," I instruct. She take two steps toward me and stops, and I just stand next to her for a few moments, staring at her, taking in all the fine chocolate fudge in front of me. There's nothing better than a beautiful chocolate woman, especially this one.

"Baby girl, Daddy wants to see you play with that pretty cooch," I say, guiding her hand to her treasure chest.

She does as I instructed and flicks at that inflated clit of hers before she moves two, then three fingers in and out of her tunnel with her other hand. Her juices are dripping down her hand, and I can't stand here a minute more and just watch. Nope, not going to happen! This shit has my man at full attention. That's when I join her and lick that sticky milk off her fingers and steal a few deep kisses in the process. Damn, she tastes so good!

I lay her down on her back on the bed, and then I kneel between her legs, pull her toward me so we are almost touching, and spread her legs wider, granting me access to that pound cake. I rub the head of my dick up and down her opening, smearing it with her juices, before slowly sliding my pipe into her. She is so wet, it slides right on up in that shit, allowing my balls to rest on her round ass. Home, sweet home!

We start off in the missionary position, but a brother like me can't stand normal ass, so I go on to the next shit. Without taking my dick out of her, I start fucking her at every angle, until she is nice and wet. Now that she's leaking the way I like it, I kneel down a little and straddle her left leg as I turn her on her left side. Her leg is bent around the side of my waist, giving me pounding room, and I penetrate her deeper and deeper, using my fingers to play with her clit. She is on the brink of an orgasm, so I remove my dick from her, replace it with my mouth, and bury my face in her sweet pussy. I suck that shit and allow the knuckle of my index finger on my free hand to trail behind my tongue. That shit causes Tavia's body to tremble and jerk, as if she is having a seizure. I love every minute of it. As she tries to pull away from me, I chase her and that orgasm by grabbing ahold of her legs and holding her in place so she can ride the wave. Pure ecstasy! The only way I like to give it.

"Oh my God, BK! You can't keep doing me like this," she says, out of breath, before she passes out.

That's right. With one shot, I knocked her out for the rest of the night. "What's my muthafuckin' name?" I say aloud, gloating to myself.

CHAPTER 28

BERNARD'S AGENDA

Everyone knows Nariah is all kinds of fucked up, but I have a hard time believing she would deliberately cut her own brake line to get at my boy D, or at Tae, for that matter. She drove the car all the way to his place, so something ain't adding up right. I know when I spoke to her about it, she was crying and snotting all over the place—definitely was not the hard bitch she portrays herself to be, that's for sure. Honestly, I like both sides of her, but it won't stop me from putting a bullet in her if she had anything to do with this shit.

Lately, I have to remind myself I'm a police officer. With this shit right here, I've been on some homicide-executioner-type shit. I don't care who has to get hurt. All I know is someone will pay for what happened to my boy, and I put that on everything I love. However, when I think about it, I know there are some advantages to being in this position if something has to go down, so I have no worries. Being on modified duty affords me the opportunity to gather all the information I need as it comes in and before anything goes out.

I was able to run Braxton Kirkland's plates, and this allowed me to find out some information on him. His dumb ass left the parking garage with Tae, not thinking about the cameras, it appears. It just makes my job that much easier. He resides in the Bronx and is married to a Sharon Kirkland, but she has a Jersey address. Whatever fucked-up situation they have going on doesn't mean a damn thing to me. All I know is I will be paying both their asses a not so friendly visit. But not until tomorrow. Tonight my dick has an appointment with Nariah's pussy.

It appears Nariah didn't get the memo about my appointment, as she has shown up here in sweats, with swollen eyes and a grief-stricken face.

Not again, I think.

"Hey, Nard. I hope you have some news for me on Tae. I hope she's okay," she utters without taking a breath as she takes a seat on the couch.

"You know good and well I can't discuss this case with you, Nae. One, because D was in your car, and two, being that I am so close to the situation, I have to wait for answers, just like you do," I say, partially lying.

"That's just great," she says, disappointed. "What do we do now?"

"I'm glad you asked," I say, unzipping my trousers.

"You can't be serious!" she exclaims, fuming, as she rises to her feet. Then she walks out the fucking door.

"Dumb bitch!"

CHAPTER 29

NARIAH VS. KARMA

Nard must be out of his rabbit-ass mind. I can't believe he was trying to have sex when my girl is missing and his boy is fighting for his life. What kind of sick-ass mess is that? I'm not even attracted to him like that. There is only one person who can take my mind off things, and that conversation would more than likely end up with us making love.

Love? Did I just say that? Can it be I am falling for Mahogany? Now that I think about it, she has been on my mind quite often, and I love the time we spend together. It's not just a creep or something to do; I really enjoy her. She is genuine and wants only what's best for me, unlike the rest of these characters I've been dealing with.

I can use a friend tonight too. I think I'll go on ahead and give my hot cocoa mix a call. Who would have thought, the moment I finally start to really feel for or fall for someone, it would be another female? You couldn't have paid me money to make me believe I would have this type of feelings for another person—let alone a woman. The only other chick I've really kicked it with or could even tolerate being around is my girl Tae, but she is more like a sister than anything else. Other than that, I'm good on these broads, except for my mahogany weakness.

"Hey, Mahogany," I say, excited when she answers the phone.

"Hey there, sweetness. How are you? Is everything all right?" she replies.

"No, not really. I went over to Nard's house to see if he had any information on Tae, and that piece of shit thought I came over to ride his dick down the block or something."

"Wait a minute. Calm down, Nariah. Who is Nard? You've never mentioned him to me."

"My apologies. I'm just rambling on and on. Nard is Darnell's partner."

"*Partner*? So Darnell is openly gay or bisexual, and Tae is completely fine with this?"

"No," I reply, bursting out into laughter. "They are police officers, friends, and partners on the police force."

"Is that right?" she says.

"Yes, it is. Why? Do you know him or something?"

"No, I don't. I was just thinking he should have all the ins and outs of the case. So you mean to tell me he didn't give you any answers?"

"No, his nasty ass just wanted to fuck. But enough about him. I sure could use some company tonight, if you're in the mood and up for a little Nae time."

"Give me about thirty minutes and I'll be over, sweetness," she replies before disconnecting the call.

"It seems like I just hung up the phone. I can't believe it's been a half hour already," I say out loud to myself as my sugar cane walks through the door.

All this time we've been hanging out, I've never tasted her chocolate pudding. She has always been the giver, and I have been the receiver. Primarily because I don't do the licky-licky. However, tonight we will trade places. Tonight I plan on becoming a chocolatarian.

"Hey there, sunshine. Tonight it's all about you. I want to please you the same way you please me," I say before licking my lips.

"That's so sweet of you, sweetness, but I'm not in the mood tonight. Can we just talk or watch a movie? I have a lot on my mind," she replies.

This can't be karma. I walked out on Nard, and now Mahogany's turning me down. What the hell is going on with her? No one's ever turned me down before. I don't know how to handle this. Maybe I am being a little selfish. I never ask her how she's doing or what she has going on; it's always about me and my drama, day after day. So a movie it is, even though I am horny as hell. I should have taken Nard up on his offer. No, better yet, I will finally make it my business to return Walter's calls when our movie night is over. He has a lot of making up to do.

CHAPTER 30

LATAVIA IS FED UP

BK is an amazing man; he cooks, cleans, and caters to me. I mean, that man can cook his hind parts off. *They say the best way to a man's heart is through his stomach. Well, it must work for women also, because I'm hooked*, I think as I drift off to sleep.

I can't take it anymore. He has to stop doing this to me. Mommy went back to working nights, and he has been in my room every night since. I'm starting to think he is sick or has some sort of illness. I don't understand why he would want to keep doing this every night to his only daughter, *I think as fresh tears run down my face. It's to the point now where he comes in my room even while Mommy is home, asleep, and keeps his hands over my mouth or punches me in the back of my head if I try to scream or make a loud noise. The monster says I am not supposed to ever enjoy sex, so if I'm not crying to myself, he shouldn't hear a sound out of me.*

I really don't sleep at night anymore. I know as soon as the clock strikes midnight, he will be in here. It's 11:50 p.m. now. I'm hoping if I lie here and pretend to be asleep, he will change his mind and leave me alone.

"*Get your little nasty ass up and come put your mouth on me. You better make Daddy nut, and if I feel any teeth whatsoever, I'm going to hurt you,*" he threatens.

As he stands over me, forcing me to take him into my mouth, I do as instructed. Then I wait for him to get lost in it before I slide my hand underneath my pillow and grab the knife I hid there. Daddy's eyes are closed, so he is unaware of what I am about to do as my mouth is filled with his nasty manhood. I take the knife and forcefully drive it into his stomach.

"What the fuck!" he yells after letting out a loud yelp, and then he bends over, grabbing his stomach.

I take off running like a bat out of hell and dash into my mother and the monster's room, only to find it empty. "I thought she was home. Oh my God! What am I going to do?" I say out loud to myself as I begin to panic.

"What the hell are you doing in my room with no clothes on, girl, and where is your father? He will kill you if he sees you like this," my mother says sternly when she walks into the room.

The only thing I can do is tearfully point toward my room as I ease the cordless phone off their nightstand and dial 911.

CHAPTER 31

MAHOGANY HAS A PLAN

Did Nariah really think I was going to allow her to put her mouth anywhere near my hidden treasure? What I do to her is just business; she just isn't aware of it. All I need for her to do is to continue thinking she can trust me and confide in me, so she can keep running her mouth like she has diarrhea of the lips. I am just glad she didn't press the issue and went with the flow. My body belongs to Braxton and Braxton only. The Bible simply states marriage should be held in high esteem, and the marriage bed is to be undefiled, because God judges adulterers. I honor my marriage, God, and my vows, so no one will have the pleasure of enjoying me except for my husband.

I know God understands and forgives me for what I do to and with Nariah. If He didn't, I wouldn't have the access I have to her and the situation surrounding Latavia. At the end of the day, this is all about her: She refuses to leave well enough alone, so she has to pay for her sins. God judges adulterous, husband-stealing whores, and so do I, especially when she has a husband of her own.

Now I have to make it my business to find a way to get close to this Bernard person. He just might be the break I need. My only problem is Nariah. Maybe if I seduce him like I did Nariah, he will be like putty in my hands. I have to get my husband back by any means necessary.

Even though I despise another man putting his hands on me, I will do whatever it takes to get my husband back. This will be an exception to honoring the marriage bed, because in actuality I will be saving my marriage. As long as I don't enjoy it, it's not a sin.

This just might work in my favor, after all, considering most men think with their private parts, which is the reason why I have to take these drastic measures in the first place. If I know anything about a man, I know ain't no booty like new booty. I guess I'll have to sacrifice and ease my way into becoming Officer Bernard's new booty. I will also find a way to make sure the three of us are never in the same vicinity. The way I see it, he and Nariah aren't in a committed relationship, and if I've learned anything from listening to her babble, it's just sex between them. Therefore, they have no reason to discuss who they're with, screwing or not screwing. I am not too worried or concerned, anyway. I know God is on my side, and He will work all of this together for my good.

"Good evening, handsome. Is this seat taken?"

"It is now," he replies.

"Why, thank you. I'm Mahogany, and you are?"

"I'm impressed."

"Nice to meet you, impressed."

"Nice to meet you, Mahogany. What a fitting name for a sexy, mesmerizing thick, chocolate woman such as yourself."

"Why, thank you. You're not bad on the eyes yourself."

"I'm not bad on a lot things. Hopefully, I'll allow you to find out."

"Excuse me? A little cocky, don't you think?"

"No, sexy. It's confidence."

"How about you put your dick where your mouth is?"

"What?"

"I mean, I'm a visual woman. I need you to show me better than you tell me."

Just thinking about last night has my mind in overdrive. I don't know how to feel, and confusion is not of God. Let me pray!

"Are you there, God? It is me, Mahogany. Forgive me, Lord, I mean Sharon. I spend so much time in character, sometimes I forget who I am, but I know you understand. Father God, I just want to petition you to extend your grace and mercy. I have been having thoughts that are not my own since taking Bernard into my mouth. Lord, my vows said, 'For better or for worse,' but the acts I am forced to perform on Nariah and now Bernard seem to be a bit much. But like you said in your Word, you will never put any more on me than I can bear, so I will endure like a good and faithful soldier because I trust you.

"I just don't understand how I have become sexually attracted to Bernard after giving him oral pleasure, when all of this is part of the plan to restore my marriage. Is this a sign you're giving me to be intimate with him in order to win him over to get closer to him? Whatever it is, God, please lead me and direct me. I have never had sexual feelings for any other man besides my husband. I ask all these things in your Son's name, amen."

Now that that's out of the way, I will wait to see where I am directed to go from here. I have been thinking about the events of the past few days, and it just dawned on me that I haven't heard from Nariah since I turned her down the other day. That whole situation threw me back a little. After our first encounter, she stressed to me that she was the receiver when it came to women, not the giver, and if I had a problem with it, it wouldn't work for us. Currently, from the looks of things, she has a sudden glow and look in her eyes, like she is slipping and falling.

I am going to need her to stand up. That isn't part of the plan, and I can't have her interfering with the plan, hindering things when they are going so well for both of us. Nariah will soon learn that she is just a vehicle to transport me to Latavia in order to get to the real matter at hand, and that's Braxton—no ifs, ands, or buts about it. I will admit I do enjoy talking and hanging out with Nariah. Hopefully, when all is said and done, we can become friends. I think I would actually like that a lot. Right now, she is the closest thing—other than God—I have to a friend.

When I think about how everything from Nariah to Bernard has played out thus far, it confirms how much God is on my side. For instance, I had this plan in place to go to the precinct as a woman in distress, unable to determine the whereabouts of her husband, and ask for an officer named Bernard, saying he was recommended by a friend of the family. Clearly, God didn't want me to lie. As I entered the precinct, Bernard was leaving. One of his coworkers called his name and asked if they were still meeting at O'Neill's. I took that as a sign from God, knowing there can't be too many people named Bernard, and because I have God on my side in this whole situation, I knew he was the person I was looking for. With that, I made sure to get to the bar before he did, and I worked my magic. I am just caught off guard with the way I felt while giving him fellatio and afterward. However, God will direct me, so I won't meddle. I will allow Him to lead me and guide me every step of the way, as He has been doing.

CHAPTER 32

BRAXTON'S KEEPING SECRETS

Upon returning home from work, I walk into the bedroom and am disappointed to be greeted by Tavia and one of her *A Nightmare on Elm Street* dreams. This shit has got to stop! I can't stand seeing her like this, and there's nothing I can do to fix it, either. I think that's the part that eats me up the most.

"Baby girl, it's me. Calm down. You're safe with me, baby," I say, trying to console her.

"I stabbed him! I stabbed him! I couldn't take it anymore, BK! I stabbed him!" she cries.

"You stabbed who, baby girl? What are you talking about?" I question.

"My father!" she weeps.

"Would you like to talk about it?" I ask, hoping she will decline.

Tavia doesn't answer the question directly. Instead, she drops a bomb on me, just when I thought this nightmare of hers couldn't get any worse. She has to have had the worst parents on this side of the earth. Her mom was mad that she called the police after she stabbed her father. She said Tavia should have told her in the beginning, when the abuse first happened. This crazy lady told her firstborn and only child that she bet Tavia didn't tell her, because she liked it, and she also informed Tavia that she hated the sight of her face. So not only did she get raped for all those years by her pops, but she also got blamed for it right before her mother beat the brakes off her. You know she did that shit after the cops left.

I am glad I listened to her story, because I found out that her pops is still alive as far as she knows, that she just hasn't seen him since the arrest. I will make it my business to find out his whereabouts, come hell or high water, because he has to pay for what he did to my baby girl.

Before coming home, I called the hospital to check on ole boy. He is still in a coma, I'm assuming, because all they would say was that there hasn't been any change in his status. I don't think Tavia knows he's in the condition he's in. No matter how mad she is, I'm sure she would want to go and see about him, which is only right. The bad thing about it is, I ain't telling her about shit unless it has something to do with me.

CHAPTER 33

NAE'S CHANGE OF HEART

Tae is still nowhere to be found. While at the precinct yesterday, Detective Torres questioned me for several hours, and one of his questions was about whether I knew of anyone who would want to harm her. Of course I don't know of anyone at all. I know for a fact no one wants to harm her. Everyone loves Tae upon meeting her; she just has that type of personality. The second question was what really caught my attention, although I played it off. He asked if I knew of an affair or affairs she might have had or might be having. Now, as far as that goes, I do know she and BK got it on the one time; at least, I believe it was the first and only time.

What I do know is that mess is the primary cause of this whole mess. Hopefully, she didn't run off with that man. I don't care how upset or hurt she might be. For heaven's sake, her husband is in the ICU, fighting for his life. Running off with another man would be the ultimate disrespect! I can understand her being confused and upset about Darnell's and my relationship. If she had let him or me explain, instead of running out of the house, it would have been as clear as day that I don't see him in a sexual way. Nor have I been with him sexually, the way she may think. It was a one-night stand, which I told her about when it happened, and like I said before, I had no fucking clue she would end up meeting and marrying him.

If anyone should be salty, it should be me. I found out I was three and a half months pregnant the morning of the same day she had her dinner party. When it was time to meet the mystery man she was head over heels about, he turned out to be my one-night stand and the father of the unborn child I had just found out I was carrying. Being the best friend to her that I am, and avoiding all the dramatics of it all, I made it my business to terminate the pregnancy. I didn't want to hurt either of us any more than I might have been or she has been hurt; neither did I want to ruin her happiness. One thing for sure, there was no way in the world I would have been able to look at or see Darnell continuously, knowing he was the father of my child and he was building a life, and possibly a family, with my best friend.

All of this is one big mess, and it seems as if I can't win, no matter where I turn. Mahogany hasn't reached out to me since movie night, and I feel a little vexed about it. I wish she would let me in her world the way I have allowed her into mine. I am sure she will eventually. For now, I will continue my sexcapades with Walter. No one would ever understand how and why I am so attracted to him, but it's my business, so who the hell cares! Between him and Mahogany, I have never been so sexually satisfied in my life.

I wish I could mesh them together and make them one person. Walter is a male version of me in the sense that he won't do the extras. It's just sex, an outing or two, and small talk—nothing personal and no feelings involved—which is fine. All I know is I crave the orgasms he gives me. Mahogany, on the other hand, started with the same criteria, but she's wiggled her way into a soft spot in my heart, and I can't shake it. I'm not sure if she feels the same way about me, but I will make it my business to find out.

In the meantime, I am on my way to a special evening Walter has planned for us, so right now, I will get out of my moment and enjoy myself. God knows I need it.

Reminiscing about my history with Walter, I can't believe how far he and I have evolved to this day. Growing up, I detested the ground he walked on. Putting the past behind us and getting to know the man he is now have allowed me to respect him and learn that we all have a dark past. It's up to us to make changes for the better. As a child, Walter endured years of physical and sexual abuse from the woman who gave birth to him. This, in turn, taught him through the years to hate the female species and everything about women. He said he couldn't stand the sight of them; the only thing they were suitable for was to suck him off and make him ejaculate. However, his arrest led to years of psychiatric therapy, and it opened his eyes to his childhood's impact on the unspeakable things he'd done. Treatment allowed him to see the monster he was to his daughter. I do hope, when all is said and done, Tae finds it in her heart to forgive her father, so she, too, can get past those demons that are haunting her.

CHAPTER 34

BRAXTON'S PAST

Work flew by today at the job site. My pops and I went deep, opening up to each other on a lot of shit. It is crazy how we met. I was thrown into prison because of my no-sy-ass neighbors. I'd had an argument with Sharon's ass, and that bitch spat in my face, leaving me no other choice but to hem her ass up. What kind of trifling shit is that? Then she wanted to apologize, talking about our vows say "for better or for worse." I went straight left when she said that shit. Fuck that! Shit was about to get worse if she didn't get out of my face. Long story short, I was locked up behind that for four and a half months. That's when I met this older dude with so much knowledge. He took me under his wing and schooled me on some things like he was my biological pops.

From day one, we formed an undeniable bond. I felt he was the father I wasn't privileged to have. So you know after I was released, I made sure to stay in touch. I'd had Sharon send care packages, cards, letters, and everything. Now we are business partners, so I get to spend time with him every day. We have a construction company we are the proud owners of. It is legally registered under my soon-to-be ex-wife's name; however, technically, it's ours. I just have to figure out how we're going to work the business. I can't have a divorce fucking up what my pops and I have created.

While chopping it up today, he told me about this broad from his past he'd run into, and he's been kicking it with her for the past six months. I never told him about me and Sharon, and I feel real bad about it, but it's just too complicated now with Tavia in the picture. I have no idea where Sharon's crazy, Bible Scripture–quoting ass is, either.

"Son, one day I hope for you to meet this young lady. She's a sweetheart," he said.

"I would like that," I replied.

"Just try not too much. I'll forewarn you. Mother Nature sure has been good to her, if I do say so myself," he joked.

"What do you know about that, Pops?" I questioned.

"Seriously, I honestly didn't expect her to give me the time of day. I thought she hated the sight of me. There are things I did in my past to her and my family that I'm not proud of," he said, staring out the window.

"No need to explain, Pops. We are all a work in progress and have made decisions and choices we aren't proud of," I replied.

"All I want to do is make amends with the people I've hurt. It would mean a lot to me, especially to my daughter. You have a sister I want you to meet, and I know she will adore you."

"That's what's up, Pops. One day at a time we will get there," I said, hugging him.

"I will do my damnedest to make it up to her and prove to her I am a changed man," he said as a single tear escaped his eye.

CHAPTER 35

BERNARD'S TANGLED WEB

There haven't been any changes in my boy D's condition. I am not sure if that's a good or bad thing right about now. On a positive note, I was able to have him moved to St. Luke's Hospital. I trust that place a lot more than Killer Winthrop, where he was originally admitted. Also, when I was there the other day, I held his hand while talking to him, and it felt like he lightly squeezed my hand. The nurse said it's possible, and that made my day. The shit that got to me was his tear-stained face. He had dried-up tears by his eyes, and that ate away at me for a couple of days. This can't be how the story ends; my boy has to pull through.

One thing for sure, Latavia is going to make me put my foot in her ass. She hasn't been seen or heard from, and my boy is hanging on to his life by a thread. On everything I love, if D doesn't pull through, when I find her, neither will she. Whatever it was they were fighting about prior to the accident should have been obsolete as soon as shit went from left to right. He is her husband, for God's sake. These bitches these days don't know a good thing until it knocks them the fuck out. No, I am not saying this just because that's my boy. The fact is he went out of his way to do right by her. He won't even give another woman the time of day, because Latavia has his nose wide open.

After coming back from checking on D the other day, I got back to the job and went through the file Martinez had left for me. The contents of that folder fucked me up as soon as I opened it. Guess whose picture was staring back at me? Mahogany, also known as Sharon Kirkland. I knew her face looked familiar, but I couldn't place it at the time. Just my luck, the ho I'm fucking could be the prime suspect or a key suspect in all of this.

Since meeting Mahogany—or Sharon or whatever the fuck her name is—over a week or so ago, I have spent quite a bit of time with her. There is just something different about her. She is different from any other woman I have ever been with. The main thing that got me is she hasn't been with any other man other than her ex-husband. I respect that shit a lot. With that being said, she wanted me to beat it up, but I did the opposite. I slow ground the fuck out of her. It was so tight, just pulling me in, making me want to be as gentle as possible with her.

We have plans to meet for lunch today, in a few, but before I spend another second with her, I have to confront her, and she'd better be up front with me. That's my word!

"Good afternoon, handsome," she greets as I sit down across from her at Fridays.

Cutting to the chase, I slide over to her the folder that contains a picture of her and Braxton.

"Let me explain, Bernard," she petitions.

"Please do," I reply.

"Braxton and I haven't been together in years. I told you we are divorced because we are in the process of doing so," she explains.

"What I want to know is what do you know about the accident?" I question.

"Excuse me? What accident, Bernard?" she asks.

"Officer Darnell Carter's accident, the one who's married to Latavia Carter."

"I swear to you, this is the first I'm hearing of this. I have no idea what you're talking about!" she cries.

"Are you telling me the truth?" I ask.

"Yes. I have no reason to lie to you," she replies.

Lunch turns out perfectly after we get the preliminaries out of the way. She informs me that Braxton's deceased mother left him another house somewhere in Connecticut. However, she was kept in the dark as to the location or the physical address of the house.

I am almost positive that is where he and Latavia are hiding, I think.

Before leaving Fridays, I assure Sharon I will help her take that bastard for everything he has or is thinking about having. She expresses her gratitude by quenching her thirst, swallowing another round of my unborn seed in the backseat of my truck.

CHAPTER 36

LATAVIA'S ROMANTIC EVENING

I really hope Nariah and Darnell are happy with one another. How long did they plan on keeping up their little charade? I see now it was meant for me to run into BK at Duane Reade, meet up with him at Dunkin' Donuts, then allow him to have his way with me at Glamour Events Too. Had none of that taken place, I would still be in the dark about those two sneaky bastards. Thank God, I found out now, because I have my BK to go through it all with me. He said I didn't have to go back to work; he will take care of me. Right now, I need a break. I will make sure to have papers drawn up requesting that Nariah's nasty ass buy me out of the company. Oh yes, I will be contacting my attorney within the next couple of weeks to get this in motion.

In the meantime, I have a fabulous romantic evening planned for this sexy stallion of a man. Since BK has never been to Italy, I was thinking about bringing Italy to him my way. I already asked him to stop by Blockbuster on his way home and pick up *Roman Holiday*. There's plenty of wine in this place, which means the only thing left to do is to order pizza and attempt to make some gelato. Hopefully, he has the ingredients in here, considering he keeps the cupboards and refrigerator packed like a grocery store. I'm almost certain I can make it happen. If I'm correct, all I need is two cups of milk, a cup of heavy cream, egg yolks, and sugar. Now that I think about it, it can't work, because the gelato needs to freeze overnight. It looks like we will have to omit that part of the evening, settle for some pistachio Häagen-Dazs ice cream, and call it a day.

When I go to use the house phone, I am unable to dial out, which is a bit strange. "Did BK forget to pay the bill?" I ask myself out loud. Thinking about it, I realize the only time I talk to him when he's out is when he calls me. I have yet to pick up the phone to call him. I can't use my cell, either. When I ran out of the house the day of the accident, I don't recall grabbing it off the nightstand. The way it looks, I won't be needing it, anyway, considering this is a new chapter and a fresh start in my life with BK. I will talk to him about the phone and the cable too, considering that we have been getting it in a bit much with the DVDs as well. Clearly, he really wants to take my mind off things, I see.

It looks like my romantic evening won't have the gelato and now the pizza. To make matters worse, I have been sitting here planning the evening that is already here, and BK is walking through the door.

"Hey there, baby girl," he greets me, with a kiss to my forehead.

"Hey, you," I reply, blushing.

"Go upstairs and throw something on. We're going out tonight. You have been cramped up in this house long enough, baby girl," he says.

Without hesitation, I fly upstairs to find something to wear. Then I stop dead in my tracks. I don't have a stitch of clothes to wear; all my clothes are in New York. I have been walking around this house for a little over a month in BK's T-shirts.

"Here you go, baby girl. You forgot something," he says, walking up behind me. Then he hands me four brown bags.

In complete shock, I ask, "You went to Bloomingdale's and shopped for me by yourself?"

"Just take the bags. I know you, so I know you will love them," he answers, gloating.

I guess he does know me, almost better than I know myself. Everything in those bags is perfect and my size. This man is the best! I don't have to ask or say anything; he is always one step ahead of me.

CHAPTER 37

SHARON IS FALLING IN LOVE

"Dear Heavenly Father, it's me, your daughter Sharon. I come to you as humbly as I know how, but I am very confused, Lord. I don't know what part of your plan this is. Is Braxton part of your perfect will for my life? You are not the author of confusion, so I know I must have overlooked something. Lord, I say these things because at this moment, deep down in my heart, I know Braxton can't be for me, and maybe he never was. Did I want him just because he *didn't* want me?

"Bernard has shown my mind and body, in a few weeks, things I never knew existed, more than my husband showed me in the twenty years we were together. I can't fight these feelings I have. I know I love Braxton, as he was my first love, but I am no longer in love with him. Heavenly Father, please show me what you want. I can't hang on any longer. Matter of fact, I don't think you want me to. In your precious Son's name, I pray. Amen."

From the bottom of my heart, I believe all of this is God's way of showing me He has so much better in store for me. I had just been settling for whatever Braxton gave me, selling myself short like a fool for all these years. All in the name of marriage and honoring the vows that didn't honor me back. For instance, when I talk to

Bernard, he listens and actually replies without the anger and hostility in his voice I am so accustomed to. I enjoy talking to him and would love to spend every waking moment in his presence. I can be myself around him and comfortable with it as well.

Then there's the lovemaking. Lord, have mercy on my horny soul. If loving his touch, his kiss, and the very existence of his manhood is wrong, then I don't want to be right. When Bernard pleasures me, he expands his attention to my entire body: my toes, fingers, the top of my head, and everywhere else in between. He takes his time kissing, touching, and catering to every inch of my body. This is so new to me.

Braxton had been my one and only, and the only way he was able to get aroused was for me to take him into my mouth. There was no foreplay or different positions. It was lights out and from the back. Oral sex was completely out of the question with him, so when Bernard put his mouth on my honey pot, my head almost popped straight off. I recall when Braxton and I were younger, we spent countless hours kissing and fondling one another's bodies. But times have changed drastically. That was so long ago, and those activities have been nonexistent for many years now. The only way I was able to get off while with him was to use a vibrator. The sad part about it is I had accepted all of it.

I had no idea what I'd been missing—that a man can make my body feel this way, as well as make me feel so sexy just from a look. He acts like he can't get enough of me, and I love every minute of it. Every touch and kiss from Bernard sends chills up and down my spine and causes my honey bun to do victory laps all over his love muscle. Things have been so great between us that I've spent the majority of my downtime over at his place. I have pretty much moved in with him. I am here now, in some stilettos and a thong, awaiting his arrival.

After hearing his car pull up, I stand by the door and wait until I hear him approaching the threshold so I can open the door to greet him. Unfortunately, when I open the door, I feel as if I am blindsided. Nariah is standing on the other side of the door, staring at me with tear-filled eyes.

CHAPTER 38

NARIAH IS DONE

Walter has been wining and dining my socks off, treating a bitch how she's supposed to be treated. I can most definitely get into this. We spent the entire weekend together at the Radisson Hotel in Midtown Manhattan and didn't leave the room once until checkout. It was room service, mind-blowing orgasms, along with countless hours of adult conversation.

As I spent time talking and listening to Walter, I learned more and more about him. He is, in fact, a sincere man. He just has a troubled past, like the rest of us. If Tae and I can pick up the pieces of our dreadful past and make the best of it, who are we to judge and not afford Walter the same opportunity? He feels horrible for what he put his family through, plus the fact that he wasn't there for his wife, Monica, when she passed. I just hope Tae gets her ass off her high horse and forgives her father. It's only right.

Speaking of Tae, she is still missing in action. I've been trying to get in touch with Nard for the past two weeks, but he refuses to respond. I bet if I told him I want to get his dick wet, he would jump to attention. Well, he has another thing coming; that's not about to happen. I am done with his ass. What I will do is carry my happy ass over to his place. He's left me with no other choice.

While in route to Nard's, Mahogany crosses my mind. I haven't heard from her, and when I phone her, the call goes directly to her voicemail. I hope she is all right. I recall the last time I spoke to her, she said she either had a lot on her mind or a lot going on. I'm sure she just needs a little downtime, so I will grant her the space.

"Looks like I need to put that thought on hold," I say to myself in a low voice as I pull up to Nard's place. I don't see his car, but the lights inside are on, so he must be in there. I put the rental car in park and get out. Before I can knock on the door, it swings open. My stomach drops to my feet when I see Mahogany standing in front of me in her unmentionables.

"You nasty bitch!" I yell, stepping inside.

She needs to feel my pain right about now, I think, going into attack mode like a pit bull.

Not giving her a chance to explain, I start swinging like a madwoman and knock her and those cheap-ass shoes to the floor. But then super-save-a-ho Nard comes out of nowhere and yanks me up off her and throws me to the floor.

"Get your fucking hands off me, you coward!" I growl.

"Watch who you're talking to like that, and don't be coming to my house on some bullshit, Nariah! What the fuck is wrong with your ghetto ass?" he snarls back.

"The real question is, when did you start liking men, Mahogany? Before or after your face was buried in my pussy, you nasty bitch!" I snap.

"That's enough, Nariah. Get the fuck out of here, before I hurt you!" Nard demands.

He doesn't have to tell me twice. I pick my face up from the floor and carry myself outside and stomp back to the rental car. I am completely humiliated. Here I was, falling for this lying, fake-ass trick. When I mentioned Nard to her the other day, she acted like she didn't know who he was. I bet she's been fucking him all along and trying to get close to me. What does she call herself doing? Keeping her friends close and her enemies closer?

This is precisely why I don't fool with too many females besides Tae. I really need her to come to her senses—or for whatever she is doing to come to an end—and come home. I am lost without her. Everybody is on some new shit these days. The only real people I have in my corner are Walter and Tae. Fuck the rest of them!

CHAPTER 39

BERNARD IS CONFUSED

Whose car is this in front of my house? Sharon had better not have company up in my place, I think as I hop out of the car. *No shit!* As I get closer to the front door, which is wide open, these two muthafuckas—Sharon and Nae—are rolling around on the floor like mud wrestlers. *Hold up! Where the hell are Sharon's clothes? That shit is kind of sexy*, I think as I yank Nariah up off Sharon.

This woman ignores me and starts yelling at Sharon, who I'm assuming she knows only as Mahogany. That's what she keeps referring to her as. Nariah asks her when she started liking men; then she goes on, accusing Sharon of chomping on her box. I don't know if I am more turned on or upset right now, honestly. I would pay to see that shit.

"Sharon, how the fuck do you know Nariah?" I mutter. "When I asked you at Fridays if you knew anything, you denied it. Now, all of a sudden, you know Nariah and what her coochie tastes like?"

"Nard, it isn't what you think!" Sharon cries.

"Well, my dear, you better get to explaining, because right now, I feel like snapping your muthafuckin' neck."

Sharon claims that she knows of Tae from high school and that she has known throughout her marriage to

Braxton that he is in love with Tae, but she has been in denial. She said she used Nariah to get closer to Tae, but it didn't work out. The only thing she wanted was to get her husband to come back to her.

"If that's the case, what the fuck are you doing here with me?" I throw up my hands.

Through her tears, she replies, "Since I've been with you, you have shown me how a woman is supposed to be treated and that I have just been settling with Braxton."

"Don't hand me that bullshit! When I met you, I didn't show you shit! You showed me you could suck a mean dick, so cut the bull and tell me the truth, Sharon!"

"Bernard, yes, you too started out as a vehicle to get me closer to Braxton, but after being with you, I've realized I don't want him. My abandonment issues forced me to believe I needed him, being that I struggle with rejection. Why do you think I stayed with him for so long?"

"I have no fucking clue, Sharon. What I do know is you better come clean now, because if I find out you've been lying to me, you will regret the day you met me."

"I am telling you the God's honest truth, Bernard. I am not hiding anything else. I swear I've never met Darnell or seen him a day in my life, and the last time I saw Latavia in the flesh was in high school. You have to believe me," she cries.

"I need a minute to clear my head," I say, then walk out the door.

CHAPTER 40

LATAVIA IS HEATED

I am not sure what's going on, but BK has been coming home from work later and later these days. He blames it on the site they're working on and being short staffed. He must think I am Boo the Fool. When he gets in, he reeks of alcohol, and unless I am crazy, I don't know of any construction site that requires or permits alcohol.

I can tell what he's been drinking by the way he makes love to me. When he has been drinking dark liquor, he goes into beast mode and tries to tear the lining out of me. When it's the white stuff, he wants to make love. Well, if he comes in here tonight smelling like anything remotely close to alcohol, he and his fingers will become one this very evening. Things have been good, so he'd better not allow his other head to screw things up with us.

Look who decided to make his way home at two thirty in the morning.

"Where the hell have you been, BK, and why haven't I heard from you?" I yell after swinging the door open before he reaches it and can get inside.

"Tavia, calm down. We had a stressful day at the site, causing us to work late. Then we went for drinks after.

You know how it is when the boys get together for drinks, baby girl," he slurs.

"Don't *baby girl* me. You've been drinking again too!"

"Didn't I just say we went for drinks, Tae?"

"I don't care what you just said. You have been doing this too often, and I'm getting sick of it."

"Sick of what exactly? I make sure you're good, you want for nothing, and I keep that pussy leaking on the regular."

"Really, BK? Really?"

"Yes, I bet it's wet right now. Let big daddy sop it up real quick."

"Big daddy won't be doing a damn thing but sleeping on that couch."

"How're you going to put me out of my own bed?"

"Just like this," I say. I march in the bedroom, gather a blanket and pillow, march back out, and toss them at him.

He is out of his mind if thinks he's just going to come and go as he pleases—no call or anything. I'm stuck in this damn house, with no television, and I can't call out on the phone, because he says phone service costs too much and it's a waste of money. There's nothing left to do, so I've already searched the house from top to bottom, getting better acquainted with my surroundings. I did in fact learn a few new things about BK. For instance, he has the same obsession with guns as Darnell. I'm not sure why, but I see he collects them the way I collect shoes. All I know is I am not staying in this house another day until he gets me some cable, a cell phone, and fixes the house phone, or I will be in my hard hat on the construction site with him.

CHAPTER 41

BRAXTON'S REALITY

Either I am paranoid or I'm losing it. The past few weeks, I swear the same car has been down the block from the site and follows me when I leave. I've detoured and turned up and down blocks, and the same vehicle stays at least two or three cars behind me. No one knows about my mom's crib out here in Hartford, so I don't know what's going on. Don't get it twisted. I'm nobody's punk. I stay strapped. I just don't drive around with heat. Especially now that my baby girl is here, getting her mental together. She doesn't need any more chaos. Baby girl might snap, real talk.

There's this little strip joint on W. Service Road I've been hitting up before retreating to the crib to try to lie low and allow whoever this clown is who's following me to get lost. By the time I leave Mynx, it's pretty late, and I don't notice anyone in the cut. Tavia's getting on my nerves, though, with that nagging and complaining shit, talking about the only things open at three in the morning are legs. Shit, that's what I'm talking about! I been trying to get up between her legs, and she be on that bullshit. Little does she know, all I'm trying to do is make sure she's good, but she doesn't even give me a chance to explain before popping off at the gums with that rah-rah

shit. I have zero tolerance for that shit too. That's all
Sharon did sunup and sundown, and I'll be damned if I'm
about to listen to anything the least bit close to that. Tavia
is going to have to kill all that noise, word up.

As far as Sharon is concerned, my lawyer called me
yesterday to schedule a meeting with him and Sharon at
his office in order to discuss the divorce. He said she is
ready to sign everything over to me and she doesn't want
anything at all except for a divorce. Shit! This is the best
news I've heard in a minute. I'm heading my happy ass
over to his office right now to sign on the dotted line and
rid myself of that crazy-ass broad.

Once I am seated across from my lawyer in his office
at the firm Meyers & Lebowitz, I am more than ready to
get this show on the road. But Sharon hasn't arrived yet.

Of course, Sharon's slow ass is late, I think when she
finally walks through the door. *'Damn! Sharon is looking
good as hell! What the fuck has she been doing? She is
looking real good with that short Halle Berry look she's
got going. Shit, that tight-ass skirt and that little-ass
shirt with her big titties on display have my dick hard as
a muthafucka right now. I know somebody's hitting that
pussy right.*

"What's up, Sharon?" I say.

"I am well. How are you doing, Braxton? It's been a
long time," she replies as she takes a seat.

"Yes, too long. Are you sure you're ready to do this?"

"Believe it or not, I am," she says with this big-ass
smile pasted across her face.

I don't know what she's so happy about, but I do know
Sharon is looking good as fuck. She ain't never looked
this good. While I am undressing her with my eyes, she
cuts right to the chase and asks my attorney where to

sign, so she can be on her way. Because she doesn't want anything in return, it takes no time to square things away. Afterward, we shake hands like we've just met, and she just about runs out the door.

I thank my lawyer and then rush down the hallway. "Sharon," I yell. "Where are you sprinting off to, looking that good?"

She ignores me and heads out to the parking garage. I catch up to her just as she is passing the spot where I parked my truck.

"Since when have you been concerned about what I'm doing or where I'm going?" she snaps.

"You can't answer a question with a question, sweetheart."

"Sweetheart?"

"Yes, sweetheart," I say, and then I pull her close to me and shove my tongue as far down her throat as I can get it.

You know good and well she can't resist her first love, and before she can think about it, I have her thick thighs spread-eagle in the back of my Yukon. Damn, I am slipping.

She tastes too good, and her pussy is tighter than ever, I think after she's finished riding the shit out of my dick.

"Thank you, Braxton. I needed that," she says, pulling up her thong, before hopping out of the truck.

CHAPTER 42

BERNARD

I am leaving the hospital in really good spirits since my boy is coming along. He isn't completely in the clear and has a ways to go, but he is doing much better than he had been. This is just what I needed to hear with all the bull that's going on around me with the job and everything else. I don't know what to do or believe when it comes to Sharon. She's managed to wiggle her thick, round ass into that soft place where no one except my mom is supposed to be. There's just something about that woman; her energy is addicting and intoxicating. She is, in fact, a good woman all around. She just fucked around and married some joker who mishandled her and manipulated her mind.

Tonight, when I get in, I'm going to have a long talk with her to allow her another chance to come clean with anything else she might have allowed to slip her mind. I am feeling her, so she needs to be on the up-and-up, like the woman I believe she is. Being that I'm not the best cook on this side of town, on my way home, I pick up a couple of bottles of Chardonnay, a Caesar salad, since that's all she eats, and a pizza pie. That way we can eat, talk, drink, and catch a few flicks on the television. Sharon really has my nose open. She had better not fuck it up.

"Hey, Sha. You hungry?" I ask after entering the house.

"No, I'm not, handsome. Don't have much of an appetite tonight."

"Well, I picked you up a salad and some Chardonnay, if you change your mind."

"Thank you, honey. I sure could use a drink after the long day I had today."

"So how did the meeting go with the ex and his attorney?" I ask, handing her a glass of wine.

"It's done. I signed the paperwork, and now all I have to do is wait for the divorce decree," she replies solemnly.

"Are you okay?" I ask.

She proceeds to inform me that her soon-to-be ex-husband appeared to be a little hesitant with things when she asked for the paperwork. He was trying to hit on her, but she ignored him. Little does she know, I followed her over there this morning and saw him running behind her, but she ignored him, kept on walking, heading to her car. That was all I needed to see, and exactly what I wanted to happen, before I went about my day. I had to make sure she wasn't trying to run games and wasn't up to no good.

CHAPTER 43

NAE TAKES MATTERS INTO HER OWN HANDS

Bernard and the entire Seventh Precinct can kiss my entire natural-born black ass. I will hire a private investigator to locate Tae. Something is telling me she's in trouble or, God forbid, something has happened to her. No matter how upset she is with me or anyone else, I can't see her just outright abandoning her husband, knowing he is critical condition, or flat-out disregarding everything we put in to build Elite. This is so unlike her, but I will get to the bottom of it.

Walter is in complete shock when I bring him up to speed on everything. He too feels that something is wrong and that the NYPD is dragging its feet in terms of determining Tae's whereabouts. I don't bother mentioning BK to him. Now that I think about it, there's no way in hell she's with him. She wouldn't risk everything for a dick; that's something I know about Tae. She is crazy, but not that crazy.

The investigator Walter recommends asks that I allow him three weeks and assures me he will have something for me. That is a long time, but the way I see it, it's better than nothing. In the meantime, I will try not to worry and will do the one thing I learned from Mahogany—pray. I can't imagine going any further in my life without Tae by my side. This has been the longest I've been away from her or gone without talking to her in nineteen years, so right now, I feel a little lost. I think I have been spending so much more time with Walter because he is the closest thing to Tae that I have right now.

Last night Walter confessed his feelings for me, and I don't know what to say or think. I care about him a lot, but I am not in love with him. Unfortunately, right now my heart belongs to Mahogany's trifling ass. I asked him to give me some time to digest all of this, considering the circumstances and the situation surrounding our little love affair. I need Tae to understand and forgive her father; then maybe I can let my guard down and see Walter as more than just a great fuck.

If I weigh the good, the bad, the pros, and the cons, I have to admit the cons stick out like sore thumbs. He said he understood; he just wanted me to know he cares for me a lot and can see things going further with us. Why is it always the ones you want who don't want you back, and the ones you don't want who want you? Relationships and sex suck; I should take a long break from all of it. Picture that happening! I know there's no chance in hell I would make it through that successfully.

CHAPTER 44

LATAVIA'S REAL WORLD

This is the fourth text message I have sent BK's behind. He gets me a cell phone, then ignores my calls and texts. What part of the game is this? He said he had a meeting with his lawyer yesterday morning to sign his divorce papers, which was a surprise to me, and then he took all day and night to come home. He told me he was already divorced the first night I ran into him. I let that slide, along with his not mentioning to me he was divorced. He's been here with me, not her, so she is clearly out of the picture. However, he promised to take the day off today. It's going on 6:00 p.m. Where in the world is he? He said he would take the day off, take me out, and spend the entire day with me today. The day has come and gone.

I am so done playing games with him. He will not come and go as he pleases, and continue leaving me in this house. Absolutely not! That's not going to work in his favor or mine. Speaking of the devil, guess who finally decided to bring himself home? I think. I rush to the front door and swing it open.

"Wait a minute . . . *Bernard*? What are you doing here?"

Before I can get another word out, he slaps me so hard, I fly into the wall behind me.

"Don't worry about what I'm doing here," he snarls as he steps inside. "What the fuck are you doing playing house with another man when your husband is in the hospital, fighting for his fucking life?"

"What are you talking about?" I ask through tears, holding my stinging face.

The next thing I know, BK appears from out of nowhere, flies through the door, and tackles Bernard to the floor.

"My man, I know you didn't just bring your black ass into my house and put your hands on my girl!" BK shouts.

"Punk, she's married, and so are you!" Bernard says, pulling his gun out and placing the end of the barrel against BK's head. Bernard says he will ruin BK's life if he comes anywhere near me or some woman named Sharon again. At gunpoint, he forces me to grab my things and leave with him.

"Why are you still pointing that gun at me, Bernard? I am in the car and leaving with you," I cry.

"Shut the hell up! I swear, if you weren't D's wife, I would have laid your disrespectful ass out. You are a trifling little thing. You really are. How could you do this to him?"

"First of all, I had no idea he was fighting for his life. I don't even know what you're talking about, Bernard. What happened to him? Did he get hurt on the job?"

"You really expect me to believe you have no idea what's going on? Please just shut the fuck up, Latavia!"

Silently, I cry to myself as he drives wherever he's taking me. *I didn't know Darnell has been fighting for his life, or that anything had happened to him. I have no idea what's going on. How would I know if I haven't been around for a few weeks now, anyway? No, I don't wish harm on him, and I would die if something was to seriously happen to him, but things are over between the two of us. He has been messing with Nae, driving her slut wagon, and I just can't act like it didn't happen and forgive either of them for it. After I find out what's going on with him and make sure he is okay, I am going back to BK. The life I built in New York ended the moment I found out about Nae and Darnell*, I think.

Then I drift off to sleep.

CHAPTER 45

SHARON SEEKS FORGIVENESS

"Father in heaven, please forgive me, for I have sinned. I slept with Braxton directly after signing my divorce papers. When he kissed me, I lost complete control of myself, considering he hasn't kissed me in over fifteen years. That alone totally caught me off guard. Lord, I know I'm wrong, but I enjoyed every minute of it. However, it won't stop me from proceeding with the divorce. I just had to feel him inside of me one last time and show him I am not the same woman he married. Technically, we are still legally married until the divorce is finalized, so I shouldn't feel bad, because in your eyes, Father, it wasn't a sin."

My main concern right now is I have no idea how I am going to face Bernard. He should be walking through the door any minute, and the guilt of it all is gnawing at me like a bad habit. I have to pull myself together. God knows the last thing I want to do is hurt or lose Bernard. He is a great man in all aspects, and it took me, the right woman, to usher it all out of him. I refuse to allow anyone or anything to destroy what we are in the process of building. Like the Scripture says, he who finds a wife finds a good thing, and I am his good thing. Although we aren't married yet, it is evident I am who he needs in his life and vice versa. I truly thank God for my spiritual upbringing and connection with God. It allows me to see things for what they truly are and not go running back to Braxton because of the sex.

When Bernard comes home and asks if I am hungry, I wanted to yell heck, "No, I'm not hungry. I don't have an appetite, because my nerves are all over the place," but I keep my composure and play it off lovely. I tell a little white lie, using my meeting with the lawyer to cover up the truth, and it works. Favor really ain't fair, and for this I am grateful.

Bernard has me hypnotized. As soon as I sit next to him and inhale his Giorgio Armani cologne, my panties moisten. I can't allow myself to sleep with two men in the same day, but in the same sense, there's no way I can allow the mistake I made today to ruin my happiness with Bernard, either. He snaps me out of my thoughts by pulling me closer to him and allowing our lips to touch. Then he kisses me slowly and passionately with and without tongue. He allows his mouth to move to my neck, earlobes, shoulders, and upper chest, increasing my arousal for him.

Bernard pauses his kissing excursion to remove my blouse, but he leaves my brassiere in place before continuing his lip and tongue assassination of my upper body. He intensifies the kissing and caressing of my breasts through my bra, using slow rhythmic movements back and forth, stimulating my now-hardened nipples. Without removing my skirt or panties, he continues to lip-lock my now bare nipples. His hands travel under my skirt, touch the inside edge of my panties from front to back and explore my buttocks in the process, and trace back to touch and feel my wetness. At this point, I am yearning for him to enter me; he is driving me completely insane. He removes my panties, explores my inner thighs, and circles my vulva and eventually my clitoris with his wet tongue.

"Oh, my goodness, baby. Your mouth feels so good," I moan.

"You like that, sweetness?" he teases.

"No, baby, I *love* it. I need to feel you in me right now!" I say seductively.

It isn't long after that, that he takes his precious manhood and enters me. Soon I climax and have yet another earth-shattering orgasm, which he faithfully blesses me with every time he arouses my body.

"Oh my goodness, Bernard. I love you so much and the way you make me feel. Will you marry me?" I say just before the orgasm takes over my body, causing me to whimper and shake, as if I am having convulsions.

CHAPTER 46

BRAXTON'S PLOT THICKENS

This clown must be out of his mind and think I'm some kind of punk or something. I swear on everything I love, if he wasn't the law, his bitch ass would be pushing up daisies. He had the balls to come into my crib, disrespect me and my girl, and put a gun to my head. There's no way in the world I can let that shit ride, cop or no cop. Somebody has to pay, but in the meantime, I will lie low and cut all communication with baby girl, so I can catch him out there. It will be hard not seeing or talking to Tae, but I have to play this out right, being that this punk hides behind a shield. All this shit just confirmed what I suspected—someone was watching me.

Sharon's scandalous ass better not have sent homeboy to where I rest my head. The thing about it is I never let on to her exactly where my mom's crib is. Well, it's really my granny's place, but she raised me, so Moms is what she is to me. Who am I kidding? He's the law, so I know he can find shit out. Either way, I know Sharon helped him with it. This is one of the reasons why I never trusted Sharon's ass. She will do anything for some attention and a dick. From day one, she been on some "I can love you better than she can" bull, staying in competition with the next trick. I just got caught out there and married her nasty ass. She sure was looking tasty the other day at the lawyer's office, though. Just good enough to fuck the shit out of. That's all her deranged ass is good for.

What I will do is play my cards right, pay her some attention, and stay deep up in her at every given moment, so I can get close enough to peep out Officer Trigger Finger's game. She won't be able to resist her first love, so I know there won't be anything to it. You can see how easy it was for her to spread-eagle, and she ain't seen me in a long minute. I know right now I must be on some shit and bugging the fuck out, since I'm plotting a hit on one of New York City's finest, but he done fucked around and disrespected the wrong dude. Now he has to learn the hard way. Whatever happens, happens! Shit, we all got to go one way or the other, and if it's my time, then it's my time. But if I go, he's got to go too. I refuse to go out like a punk; it's not in my DNA.

CHAPTER 47

BERNARD'S MISSION ACCOMPLISHED

I can no longer tell which way is up these days. Taking off from the job the past two weeks was supposed to be pleasurable, but driving back and forth to Hartford took a toll on me. Taking a personal leave from the job was easy since I am still on desk duty for the next three weeks. I spent the majority of my time watching Braxton's every move, and I had a feeling he'd caught on at one point. He changed his routine up, making pit stops at this local strip spot. That didn't surprise me one bit, and it gave me time to get back home to take a shot of Sharon's body like a drunk.

That woman right there has a brother trying to get his romance on. The one thing standing in the way is I'm not 100 percent sure I can trust her just yet. Last night I was putting Sharon out of her misery, taking my time, melting that chocolate body of hers, causing her to cream all over the place, when she asked me to marry her.

Damn, I must have destroyed the punany, I think. It's supposed to be the other way around, but I'm sure she was just caught up in the moment. I joined her in her little role-play and replied, "Yes, I will marry you, baby doll," then unloaded another round inside her.

Now let's fast-forward to the present. After Martinez looked out, filling me in on the construction company Braxton works at, it was a piece of cake to find him after putting two and two together. The company is registered in Sharon's name, which is another thing she failed to disclose. However, we all know she ain't strapping on a hard hat unless a dick is involved. That information led me to take a leave from work, and bingo, on my first drive out there, Mr. Lover Man walked out!

I monitored his every move from that day forward, and after a week of that shit, I decided to make my move while he was at his favorite strip joint. The plan was to shut Tae's little fuck fest down, take her, and deal with him at a later date. Approaching the door, I was unsure if I wanted to be a gentleman and knock or just kick the muthafucka in. However, the door swung open before I could make up my mind.

"*Bernard*? What are you doing here?" Tae questioned.

This inconsiderate, selfish bitch! I didn't mean to call my boy D's wife out of her name, but I'd lost all respect for her, and she had the unmitigated gall to open the door with a fucking attitude when she was the one in the wrong. I just lost all my home training and tried to slap her as close to reality as I could. Caught off guard, I was then tackled to the floor by her super-save-a-ho Power Ranger; however, I was able to grab my tool going down.

"Hold on, muthafucka," I spat, withdrawing my gun. "Shut the fuck up, partner! I'll be doing all the talking from here on out. What you will do from this day forward is stay away from Latavia and Sharon if you value your life!" I threatened.

"Latavia, grab your shit and let's ride," I said, pointing my gun from her to him.

As we ride back to New York now, she's crying and acting like she doesn't know shit. If she wasn't my boy's wife, I probably would have beaten her like a dude already and knocked her fronts out.

"How the fuck are you this clueless when you was in the same accident as D?" I ask. But before she can utter a word, I say, "Shut the fuck up! What I need for you to do, Latavia, is not utter a word for the balance of this ride!"

She can try to act crazy if she wants to. I will end up excusing her from being my boy's wife and will lay her ass out. He will just have to understand, because technically, I'm doing all this shit for him. Little does Tae know, she's about to be on what I would like to call house arrest. Martinez and I will take shifts watching the house, either inside or outside. I haven't thought that far into it just yet. But this will be her living arrangement until D is good. She's been locked up in the house for the past few weeks, so she should be good and used to it by now. If she comes to her senses sooner than later, things might change, but until then, this is what it is. I'm thinking about including Sharon in on this babysitting task if she gets her shit together. I'll check with her after I drop this selfish bitch off.

CHAPTER 48

NARIAH'S PHONE CALL

"Good afternoon, Ms. Westbrook. I have some good news and some not so good news," the PI states.

"I'm listening," I reply as my stomach drops to the tips of my toes.

The private investigator originally gave me a three-to-four-week time frame, and I believe it's been only a little over two weeks now, so I am nervous as hell.

"I found Mrs. Carter's whereabouts. However, she is no longer at the same location, but I am on it," he revealed.

"What do you mean, you're on it and she's no longer at the same location? Excuse my French, mister, but I am going to need you to speak muthafuckin' English and spit it out."

"I apologize, Ms. Westbrook, and I know you're upset. I found Mrs. Carter in Hartford, but it appears she is no longer at the same location."

"*Hartford*? What the fuck?"

"If you would like, Ms. Westbrook, I can have the photographs I obtained sent to your office via courier service."

"Thank you. That would be great," I reply, and then I end the call.

What the hell is Tae doing in Hartford? Has she allowed them dreams to cause her to lose every bit of sense the good Lord gave her? Her husband is in the fucking hospital, and she's vacationing in Hartford? I think. I love my girl to death, and I am elated that she is alive and well, but I might have to fuck her up real quick and bring her back to her senses. At this point, she might need to seek long-term professional help; she is clearly out to lunch. What the hell! I have to fill Walter in on this bull crap. I wonder if Bernard is aware of this. This can't be good at all.

As usual, Walter doesn't answer his phone when I text or call. Why do I even bother with any of these jokers? We have been getting along so well too, and now he is so busy. He's going to fuck around and end up getting downgraded back to being a quick fuck when I want him to shoot my club up. He must be drinking the same shit Bernard's been drinking, but I can surely fix that shit. My motto is "Never chase. Continually replace." *Next!*

Right now, I am beyond pissed and in need of some fresh air, so I decide to go grab a bite to eat and swing by Bernard's place to apprise him of what the PI informed me about Tae. Looks like the NYPD needs to take a lesson from my little Italian investigator, considering I found Tae and they didn't. As usual, when I leave the house, before going anywhere, out of habit, I make sure to drive past Tae and Darnell's to ensure everything is good.

What the fuck! Why the hell is Mahogany's car outside my girl Tae's house? If this bitch thought I got in her ass before, she ain't seen nothing yet.

CHAPTER 49

DARNELL'S FIGHT TO SURVIVE

Can you imagine lying in a hospital bed for as long as I have, apparently dead to what's going on around you? You can hear what's going on, but you're unable to move or communicate. Well, this has been my life for over a month now, from what I've been told. Yet it feels like an eternity. The hospital staff has been great and is amazed at my progress. I have come a long way. I started off with responding to commands with eye blinking and grabbing hands, and I have progressed to now being alert and able to move around with help. I am not amazed at my recovery. I am and have always been a fighter, and I never give up easily.

Dr. Morris, my neurosurgeon, informed me that some people who have suffered the same or similar injuries have made full recoveries and are completely fine, and I should thank my higher power, because I am coming along miraculously. That thanks belongs to God alone. My mom's—or the old lady, as I like to call her—used to always say, "Little boy, all it takes is a little faith, and that faith will take you places you can only imagine going." I can hear her speaking those words to me every day, over and over, as I am lying in this bed. That same faith has me in the land of the living this day. The doc recommends I undergo extensive physical and occupational therapy, as well as psychotherapy, as the treatment necessary for my recovery process. Right now, I have been suffering from periods of confusion as well as becoming disoriented at times. The headaches have been violently brutal. However, I am determined to do whatever it takes to get back on my feet.

My greatest ambition is to be able to turn over by myself. I know if I can muster up enough strength to do so, everything else will be smooth sailing. That one desire eats away at me day in and day out. Since emerging from the coma, I have rested and tried to sleep in an uncomfortable recliner. I can't even imagine lying in that bed or any bed anytime soon. Sleep at this point is out of the question. The nurses have to sedate me intravenously or give me something to swallow to help me rest.

Memories come rushing back as I sit here, and they take me back to one of the last visits from Bernard. I can feel his hand on my hand and can hear him saying, "D, everything's going to be okay. You just have to hold on and fight. Get better. I have all the other shit under control."

Hearing the pain in his voice gave me a stronger will to fight, and I am now indebted to him. He was there for me when I know it was hard for him to do so. The one thing I don't understand is, where is my wife? Why hasn't Latavia been here to see me? I lie there day after day, waiting to feel her touch and hear her voice. No one on the hospital staff has yet to mention her since I've awakened, and for the first time in a very long time, I am afraid . . . afraid to ask.

CHAPTER 50

SHARON'S ANSWERED PRAYERS

It never ceases to amaze me, when everything is working in my favor, the devil has to throw a wrench in my happiness. Ever since I *accidentally* slept with Braxton, he has been invading my thoughts and dreams. I know one thing for sure: I'm positive I don't want him back. I am happy with Bernard; he is all the man I need. However, there is a part of me that craves Braxton's touch. Now I know, and can honestly say I understand, what Eve went through with the serpent.

Coincidentally, Braxton now knows my cell phone number, after all this time. Amazing, isn't it? He has been calling and texting me nonstop, as if we just met. I think it's quite comical, honestly, but like the old saying goes, "You never miss a good thing until it's gone," and it's evident he misses me. I can't say the feeling is mutual, because it's not. I only lust for him. There is no Scripture to justify my behavior, and right now, I'm ashamed of myself. I want both of them: Bernard forever, until death does us part, and Braxton until I get sick of him. I know the real him will show up eventually. I'll just have a little fun until then.

"Lord, in advance, I ask that you forgive me, for I know not what I do or what I'm getting myself into," I say aloud.

When I check the time, it dawns on me that Bernard is a little off schedule coming home this evening. *I wonder what's keeping him. I pray he is all right*, I think, then startle when I hear footsteps behind me.

"You're going to give me a heart attack! I didn't hear you come in," I say, turning around. I place soft, wet kisses on Bernard's lips.

"Good. I like sneaking up on you."

"Why is that?"

"Why not?" The tone of his voice changes when he adds, "I need you to do me a huge favor, baby doll."

"Whatever you need, baby."

Bernard proceeds to brief me on his task over the past two weeks. He says he found Braxton's house in Hartford, and Latavia was shacking up there with him. I am not sure if I am upset or happy right now. The ultimate kicker is when he asks me if I feel comfortable assisting in taking turns with him and Officer Martinez in keeping an eye on the little home wrecker.

A few months back, this would have been the best thing that could have happened to me, but considering I no longer want to be married to Braxton, it's not as exciting now. However, it doesn't mean I have to be nice to her. Yes, the Bible says, "Vengeance is mine," but God would not have opened this door if He didn't want me to walk on through it.

CHAPTER 51

LATAVIA AND NARIAH

I'm not sure how to feel about being back at the place I used to call home. I will say I am a little more comfortable here than I was at BK's. Not being familiar with my surroundings caused me to feel a little out of place there. It was all him and nothing that represented me. When I leave the next time, it will be for good, and I will make sure to take my belongings with me.

Bernard and Officer Martinez must be out of their minds if they think they're going to keep waving a gun to keep me locked up in this house against my will. They won't talk to me; they just wave their guns around, threatening me. There's no way I can feel free or comfortable with them taking turns sleeping on my sofa and making themselves at home in my living room. All of this is out of control, and I know Darnell's overprotective, controlling behind put them up to this. Then, to make matters worse, I've been playing phone tag with BK and sending him countless text messages. The only response I have received from him was the other day, when he claimed he needs time to clear his head, and I need to check on my husband. He believes I am confused about what I really want.

I can't believe he had the *audacity* to say something like that to me. Was I confused when I left the hospital with him or while I was having sex with him over and over again? He's the one who's confused, or he's playing games with me. To add fuel to the fire, when I went to respond to him by text, I received a return message that said, Failure to deliver. I also tried calling him after that, and the voice recording said the number I reached was no longer in service. None of this is making any sense at all. I know he's not afraid of Bernard. He has never come across as a punk, so I am extremely lost on this one. I will get to the bottom of it one way or the other.

"It sounds like they're changing shifts," I say softly to myself and laugh as I walk down the stairs. As I approach the living room, I am greeted by Bernard and some woman.

"Look, Bernard, I have played along with your little charade long enough. You will not continue to come and go out of my house as you please and keep me here against my will," I announce.

"*Your* house? *Now* you remember where the fuck you live?"

"You know what? I don't have to take this! What you're doing is against the law, making me stay here against my will, and also the way you've been pulling your gun out on me," I cry.

"The law? I *am* the law. What you're going to do is sit your tired ass down, shut the fuck up, and do as I say. Oh yeah, by the way, this is Sharon, your new babysitter."

Before anyone can respond, Nariah bolts through the door without saying a word and begins beating the dog crap out of Bernard's Sharon.

"Here we go again," Bernard seethes as he grabs Nariah off Sharon.

Without thinking twice about it, I jump on Bernard's back and punch him and scream at him to get his hands off Nariah.

"Get your hands off him, you no-good home wrecker," this Sharon person yells.

"What, bitch?" Nariah says, sneaking in another punch and sending Sharon back down to the floor.

"Hold the fuck up!" Bernard shouts at the top of his lungs, startling everyone.

"No, *you* hold the fuck up, bitch!" Nariah returns.

"Enough is enough!" Martinez interjects. "All of this has spiraled out of control. We are all adults and really need to start acting like it. Bernard, you know you and Officer Carter are like brothers to me, but I am not about to lose my badge behind any of this. The primary focus was to bring justice for Carter, and it appears that is no longer the objective. Therefore, I can no longer be a part of any of this," he says before walking out of the house.

Now all eyes are on me, like this is my fault. "Why are you all looking at me? I'm the victim here," I cry.

"You weren't the victim when you were sleeping with my husband—well, ex-husband—while your husband's in the hospital, fighting for his life," Sharon says.

"What, ho!" Nariah yells, socking her in the mouth.

After placing himself between Golden Gloves Nariah and Sharon, Bernard proceeds to inform me that the accident he feels I mysteriously forgot about was life threatening and that Darnell has been in intensive care, in a coma, fighting for his life.

"You would have known this if you weren't shacking up with Braxton," Sharon says accusingly.

"All right. I am sick of you, wench," I yell, leaping at Sharon.

"If another person swings, I'm swinging!" Bernard threatens.

"You have *got* to be kidding me!" Nariah says. She shakes her head before continuing to speak. "It all makes sense now, you trifling, pussy-eating, dick-sucking bitch! You did all of this over BK, and now you're fucking Bernard's dumb ass!"

Nariah and I take one look at each other, disregard Bernard's threat, and attack Sharon like two bats out of hell. We take it back to grade school and try to beat her like she stole our lunch money. We are so out of control, swinging at, punching, and kicking on Sharon, that Bernard really struggles to pry us off her and get us under control, until Martinez walks back in the door to assist him.

CHAPTER 52

SHARON IS HUMILIATED

"I will be pressing charges against both of you little bitches," I hiss right before Bernard drags me to his car.

Once in the car, I silently pray to myself. *Lord, please forgive me for the use of profanity. I am mortified that they repeatedly put their hands on me.*

"Bernard, why did you set me up to get assaulted like that and not arrest those hoes?" I wail.

"Sharon, right now it would be best if you didn't speak," he replies coldly.

"It would be *best*, Bernard? Now you're taking their side?" I sob.

"Woman, please, with all the extra dramatics!"

I refuse to allow anyone to keep putting their hands on me or to address me in the manner in which Bernard is now speaking to me. Braxton did his share of verbally and mentally abusing me, and I refuse to add to the list. I am too old for this mess.

"Bernard, we need to talk."

"Not right now, Sharon."

"We can't pretend none of this just happened. Do you realize what you've gotten me into, Bernard?"

He doesn't respond; he just whips the car over to the side of the road, pulls into an empty parking lot, and hits the brakes.

"What *I* got you into, Sharon? Do you hear yourself speaking? Better yet, do you even bother to think before you speak?" he asks sarcastically.

"Yes, I do, and yes, you did bring me into this mess. Had you not asked me to help you keep an eye on a grown woman, I wouldn't have all these scratches and bruises on my face, neck, and arms right now!"

"You have got to be fucking kidding me! I have been trying to be patient and show your needy ass some muthafuckin' respect, but you can't give me a minute! If you weren't so hung up on the dick you complained about not getting, you never would have had me, or any of us, for that matter. So the way I see it, your desperate ass got what you deserved! Now get the fuck out of my car, bitch!"

Bernard gets out of the car to help me out, but I won't budge, so he takes it upon himself to pick me up and sit me on the ground before returning to his car and driving off.

"Looks like he had a change of heart," I say to myself through tears when I notice his car is backing up toward me.

"You forgot your shit," he says through the open window before tossing my purse at me and peeling off.

CHAPTER 53

BRAXTON WANTS IT ALL

The last thing I want to do is ignore my baby girl Tavia, but a brother's got to do what a brother's got to do. I have to play this shit real smart so things can work out smooth as a baby's ass. Tavia is probably writing me off right about now, but I know the same way I got her to come running back to me is the same way she's going to be back with big daddy—bent over, face down, ass up, grabbing on them ankles. Everybody knows the ladies love BK; there's no denying that. However, right now, the task at hand is to get Sharon's ass caught up so she can lead me straight to that little bitch Bernard.

Just then my cell rings, and I look at the screen. "Oh shit. Speaking of Sharon, this is her calling me now," I say out loud.

I answer right away. "What's up?" I say nonchalantly.

"Braxton, he left me in a parking lot," she cries into the phone.

"Slow down. Who left you where and what?" I yell.

"Bernard did. They attacked me, and he threw me out of his car."

"Where the fuck are you? Text me the address. I am on my way."

"Sending it now, Braxton," she says before disconnecting the phone call.

This muthafucka has just signed his death warrant. He's nothing more than a coward with a badge. How the fuck is he going to put his hands on a woman, then flat out leave her in a parking lot. I see he must be one of those dudes who gets off by putting his hands on women. We'll see how much he likes to hit when I get finished with his ass.

"Hold up . . . Did she say *they*?" I ask myself as I increase my speed, pushing the pedal to the metal, trying to get to the other side of town as fast as I can.

I reach the address Sharon gave me and circle this parking lot twice in the span of five minutes, but no Sharon. *Where the hell is Sharon's ass?*

"Shit!" I yell, slamming on the brakes. I put the car in park and hop out. "Why the hell are you sitting on the ground? I could have killed your ass!" I say to Sharon.

"I'm sorry, Braxton," she whimpers, staring at the ground.

"Come on. Let's go," I say, trying to help her to her feet, but she resists. "You can't look at me, Sharon? Don't be embarrassed now. You weren't ashamed when you were fucking him!" I scold.

"Braxton, are you serious?"

When she looks up at me, I almost flip the fuck out. Her face is all scratched up, and her eye is a little puffy. *This little bitch of a man is hiding behind a badge, scratching up broads' faces? What part of the academy did he learn that shit in? He'd better not put his hands on Tae again, either*, I think, getting even madder.

"Braxton, I need to get my car, but I don't want to see Bernard's face tonight."

"Yo, fuck him. We're going to pick up your car!"

"Please, can we go in the morning? I have had enough for today."

Short of thinking twice or responding, I get her up off the ground and in the passenger seat, slide behind the wheel, and take off driving, not sure where we're headed. I'm damn sure not taking her to the Bronx with me. That's not part of the plan. Since Tavia is back here in New York, I have been staying back at my spot in the Bronx.

"You want me to get a room at the Comfort Inn?" I ask.

"Sure, that's fine. I just can't go back to Bernard's," she sobs uncontrollably.

Damn. What have I gotten myself into?

This is the side of Sharon that irks the fuck out of me. All that crying bullshit with that long-face shit is for the birds, but I know I have to play it cool. She has the means to get me closer to that punk faster than I can by myself. Don't get me wrong. I'm not a selfish bastard. I just don't have love for her like that. Pussy is one thing, but all that intimate shit with her is a negative. She ain't Tavia. No doubt, I will hold her down and not allow anyone to disrespect her by putting their hands on her. No real man puts his hands on a woman, anyway, but a real man will stomp the fuck out of a punk who does while hiding behind a badge.

CHAPTER 54

NARIAH CLEARS THE AIR

"We worked that hussy overtime," I brag, hugging Tae.

"Yes, we did. We took it back to the old school."

"I can't believe your stuck-up ass knuckled up," I say jokingly.

"Shut up, Nariah," she laughs. But then Tae quickly becomes silent and pulls away from me.

"What's wrong?" I question.

"I'm not going to sit back and allow anyone to put their hands on you—that's not how I get down—but what you and I had no longer exists," she explains.

"What? How do you throw away a friendship like ours? A sisterhood? Just like that?" I ask, disappointed.

"The day you started screwing my husband is how *you* threw it away, ho!"

"I'm not going to be too many more hoes, Tae."

"I don't think you have a choice. It's in your blood!" she says, slapping me across my face.

"Tae, if you hit me again, I am going to forget who you are and hurt you. I'm not playing with you, either."

"Nariah, get your nasty, lonely dyke ass out of my house!"

Before I land myself on the cover of *Newsday*, I escort myself out of her house. I can't believe she is still on that mess, when nothing happened. "You know what? I am tired of being nice," I say aloud to myself. I turn around and walk back into her house.

"Didn't I just ask you to leave?" she scolds.

"You know what, Tae? If you weren't so far up your own ass, you wouldn't be in the predicament you're in now. For your information, Black Hammer, the guy I met on the website, which I told you about, turned out to be Darnell, the same guy you met and introduced me to six to nine months later. I didn't want to ruin your happiness, so when I saw him at your dinner party, I left well enough alone. He meant nothing to me, and I had no intentions of ever seeing him or being with him again. You have no idea what I sacrificed for your trifling, selfish ass."

"*Sacrificed*? What could you possibly have sacrificed, other than your worn-out coochie?"

"My fucking unborn child!"

She stares at me in silence.

"Don't get quiet now, smart-ass. The evening I met Darnell, I had just found out that morning I was pregnant from my one-night stand. I was going to keep the baby and raise it by myself. However, after meeting him at your party, I knew it wasn't a good idea, so I terminated the pregnancy. Had you stuck around, instead of running off into the sunset with BK's ass, you would have known. Now who's the selfish bitch?" I say. I walk out and slam the door behind me, leaving her standing there, dumbfounded.

CHAPTER 55

BERNARD'S REVELATION

Trying to hold my boy D down has me out here caught up. Every last one of them broads is crazy, and I am done trying to be Captain Save-A-Ho. D will have to deal with Tae's sneaky ass when he's better. The only thing that Sharon can do for me right about now is put this fat mushroom head in her mouth until she can taste the sex of all my unborn seed. Nae, on the other hand, might be the only one in the camp who has kept it real from the jump.

They were really whipping Sharon's ass, and I felt a little bad for her, but she showed what she was really up to the moment she laid her eyes on Tae. Nothing but pure hate and envy in her eyes, letting us all know she was out for revenge and would stop at nothing until she got what she wanted.

Hold the fuck up! That devious little bitch thinks she's slick. She threw that ass at me to try to push me away from seeing the truth. Sharon had to have something to do with fucking with those brakes. Who else would have a reason or motive to do that shit? I have no clue what she would have gained from hurting Nariah, but now that I think about it, I bet they were together before the accident, I think, retrieving my phone from my pocket. I dial Nariah, but she doesn't pick up, so I leave a message.

"Nariah, this is Bernard. I know I'm the last person you want to hear from right now, but you're going to need to cancel all that. We need to talk ASAP!" I unload into her voicemail.

Not wasting another minute, I head straight over to Nariah's place. She'd better not be on her bullshit. I want answers so bad, it's got my shit rock hard. "This is going to be good," I say to myself as I pull up to the house at the same time Nae does.

"I am not in any mood for your shit, Nard!" she yells when we both climb out from behind the wheel.

"Nariah, I'm sorry," I say, grabbing her attention.

"You're right. You are sorry! All you no-good birth defects are," she taunts.

"I didn't come here to fight with you, Nae. I believe you didn't have anything to do with any of this. You got caught out there because of your relationship with Tae."

"*Now* you want to believe someone? You're full of shit!"

"Can we talk inside, please?" I ask.

Once inside, Nariah and I put all our cards on the table, and she confirms what my gut has been telling me. She *was* with Sharon the night before or a couple of nights prior to the accident. She said she went running to Tae's place after I upset her when she had her temper tantrum and I was forced to cuff her ass to teach her a lesson. Tears run down her face as she talks.

Damn. I thought I would escape this conversation without the waterworks, I think.

"Nard, thank you for listening. I was really sec-ond-guessing myself, everything, and everybody!" she says and sniffles.

"No need to thank me, Nariah. It's my job, and D is my boy. I will personally make sure that bitch pays for what she did!" I reply angrily.

"You look tense, Nard. Come over here and let me unclog that pipe," she says, licking her lips.

My pants are soon at my ankles. I have no clue when this freak got them down. She kisses the head of my dick, teasing me real good, getting him to stand at full attention. Shit, this feels so fucking good, the way her tongue's caressing the underside of my dick! Nariah knows how to give head like no other and will have a brother's legs buckling in a matter of minutes. She knows how to make it sloppy, so when she's sucking up and down on the shaft, it mimics the thrusting motion of pussy walls. I don't know what she is doing to me. All I know is this shit feels too good!

"You like that, Daddy?" she asks, staring into my eyes.

That's it! I can't hold back any longer. That did it! I can't even respond verbally. My seed answers her for me and goes securely down her throat.

CHAPTER 56

LATAVIA IS MOVING ON

Just when I think things can't get any worse, they do just that. "How long did Darnell and Nariah think they would be able to keep this from me?"

She was pregnant by him and walked around, pretending to be my friend, all while having an affair with Darnell. I don't even know who Darnell is anymore. He acted as if he hated the sight of Nariah, when, in actuality, he was messing with her funky butt, going half on a baby. They can have one another! All of this just confirms over and over what I said before: The life I tried to build here with the two of them no longer exists. In fact, the way things look, it never did.

I have to get as far away from these fake, backstabbing people as I possibly can. Right now, all I need to do is talk to BK so we can work things out, but first, I'm going up to that hospital to give Darnell a piece of my mind. Coma or no coma, I will let him know exactly how I feel and what I think of him before I leave here for good. *Wait a minute. How the heck am I going to get anywhere?* I wonder. None of our cars are here. Hopefully, mine is still at Glamour Events Too. I'll call a taxi to take me up there after I find my spare key.

All of this is just so heartbreaking, and now BK's obsessed, loony tunes wife wants to get in the mix of things. Her best bet is to go back to wherever she came from. It is clear as day he wants nothing to do with her. She is the least of my worries. I think she went a little overboard by sleeping with Nariah *and* Nard. They can add Darnell to the mix and become one big happy, dysfunctional family, for all I care.

I am dreading this taxi ride, but hopefully, my car is there and I can be on my way. I have no idea where I'm going, but I refuse to stay another night in that house. *Hopefully, I will be able to find or get in touch with BK*, I think, staring out the car window.

"Excuse me, sir. Change of plans," I tell the taxi driver. "Would you please follow that beige Yukon? I'll pay whatever the cost is."

Somebody must love me! What a freaking coincidence it is that I am staring out the window, thinking about BK, and he drives alongside the taxi I'm in.

"No problem, ma'am. We're on your dime," the driver replies.

If BK really wants to avoid me, he probably should have stayed in Hartford or, better yet, got a different car. We follow him for the next thirty minutes and then pull up to a brownstone in the Bronx.

"Can you sit here for about five minutes? I will be right back."

"No problem. The meter is still on."

"BK!" I yell as I exit the taxi.

"Tavia, what are you doing here? And how did you know where to find me?" he calls as he walks toward me.

"That's not important! Why did you change your number on me?"

"Look, stop following me! I told you I need time to clear my head," he scolds. He returns to his truck and leaves me standing there, watching, as he pulls off.

Embarrassed and heartbroken, I return to my awaiting taxi, to pick up where we left off and head to my original destination, Elite Too. I'm relieved to find my car right where I'd left it. I smile as we pulled up.

"That will be thirty-nine, fifty-four," the driver recites.

"Thank you and keep the change," I reply, handing him a fifty-dollar bill, before climbing out of the taxi.

I rush to my car and climb behind the wheel. "I missed you, baby," I tell my car as I put the key in the ignition. *It seems like it's been months instead of weeks since I've been behind the steering wheel of a car*, I think, shaking my head.

The drive to the hospital takes less than an hour. I literally drive from one end of the borough to the other, but thank God, I make it there safely. I park and run inside.

"Good evening. I want to know the room Darnell Carter is in," I say to the receptionist at the visitors' desk.

She searches her computer. "I'm sorry, ma'am. Darnell Carter is no longer a patient at this hospital," she informs me.

"What do you mean, he's no longer a patient?" I question the bug-eyed lady.

She looks at me over the rims of her glasses. "Again, I apologize, ma'am—"

"Mrs. Carter," I say, cutting her off, correcting her.

"Again, Mrs. Carter, our records indicate Darnell Carter is no longer a patient here."

"So can you tell me where he is? Was he discharged, or perhaps he's at a different hospital? Something?"

"I do apologize, ma'am . . . I mean Mrs. Carter, but I am not at liberty to confirm or deny if Mr. Carter's been admitted to another facility."

"Excuse me?" I ask, puzzled. "You can't confirm or deny? He's my husband!"

"I can have a manager or someone speak to you if you'd like."

"That would be great," I say sarcastically.

This has to be the craziest thing I've ever heard in my entire life. Darnell and I are still legally married, and this heifer is trying to throw some HIPPA laws and regulations in my face. I know what she's doing, as I got my CNA by attending BOCES Tech while in high school. Just thinking about this is pissing me off even more.

"Latavia?" a male voice calls behind me.

I turn to see who it is. "Hey, Officer Martinez. They called you on me?"

"No! No one called me. I just happened to see you."

"Well, can you enlighten me on what's going on and where Darnell is?" I plead.

"Let's step outside."

Once we're outside, he informs me that Nard had Darnell moved to St. Luke's because he didn't trust Winthrop and he wasn't sure who cut the brake line on Nae's car. Since he is the next of kin, in my absence, he was allowed to do this discreetly and without a hassle.

They are clearly thinking too much! Nobody cut Nae's brakes but karma, I think.

After thanking him, I run to my car, and a minute later I am en route to the other hospital like a madwoman. Thank God it's only twenty or so minutes away. I want to have closure and to get this over with as soon as possible.

CHAPTER 57

DARNELL IS HEARTBROKEN

I am unsure if it's the physical therapy, the therapist, or a mixture of both, but whatever it is, I'm not feeling any of it. The therapist comes off like he has a phobia or a disconnect with me. I'm assuming it's because he's aware I'm on the force. He's a little too aggressive with me, and the tension in the room is undeniable. Today I will lie here with my eyes shut and pretend to be asleep when they come in to take me down for therapy, which should be any minute now. I need a day off before I snap.

"Darnell, it's me, Latavia. I'm not sure if you can hear me or not," she says between sniffles.

Instead of greeting her, I decide to continue lying here with my eyes shut to hear what she has to say. *She hasn't been up here to see me this long, so this had better be good*, I think.

"I love you with everything in me, Darnell, and I really thought you were different, unlike the rest. I'm sorry you're in the hospital, but karma put you here, not me. How could you walk around all these years living a lie, pretending to love me when Nariah is who you really desired? I know all about you, Nariah, and the baby. Was this some sort of sick joke or something? I hope both of you had a real good laugh at my expense. Although I am hurt and feel betrayed, I will not allow the two of you to infringe on my happiness any longer. I am moving away with BK, the real love of my life. I hope you're happy with Nariah, now that I am really out of the picture," she cries. She places a soft kiss on my forehead, then turns to leave.

I can't move or utter a word as she speaks; I am completely frozen and stuck. It feels like I am unconscious or out again as a single tear escapes my eye. Thank God, I am all right, and not in the same condition I was a month or so ago. That could have taken a brother straight out of here. Nariah and the baby are ringing in my head like crazy. What is Latavia talking about, and what has Nae's scandalous ass started now?

After she kisses my forehead, I realize she is about to leave, and before she can make it out the door, I blurt, "What are you talking about, Latavia? A baby? I have no idea what you're talking about."

"Darnell, I am done with the lies. You fooled me once, but you will not fool me again." She bolts out of the room.

I don't have the answers for anything right now, but I do know one thing: when I find out who this BK is, he will regret the day his mama gave birth to him. My vows said, "Until death do us part." Latavia doesn't realize that when she recited those vows, she signed a check her ass can't cash. I'm not going anywhere anytime soon, and neither is she.

CHAPTER 58

SHARON UNDERSTANDS

Braxton has been so good to me these past few days. I don't know what I would have done had he not been there for me. It's just a shame that it took me to find out what love really is for him to start being supportive of me. Where was that support the twenty or so years we were married? Although I appreciate the return of the Braxton I fell in love with so many moons ago, that was then, and this is now. I am in love with Bernard, and hopefully, Braxton understands.

While we are on the subject, Bernard has yet to return any of my calls or reply to the lengthy apology text I sent him. He needs to understand I was confused back then and wanted my marriage only because it didn't want me. It was never about the marriage; I realized that once Bernard showed me how I am supposed to be treated.

I am a soldier and a warrior in God's army, and I believe in fighting the good fight of faith. I don't give up, as the battle isn't given to the weak or the strong, but to those who endure to the end. My problem was I didn't realize my marriage had ended and it was time for me to let go. I couldn't see past the hurt and pain, which is why God sent Bernard my way. Sometimes we hold on to things that God removes from our lives, but in order for us to be happy, He has to sever the ties. That's what took place when Braxton left me to pursue Latavia and when Bernard entered my life right on time—just like God. He may not come when or the way you want Him to, but He is always on time and present to help in times of trouble.

This whole time I thought this was a fight for my marriage, but it was really a fight for my freedom and happiness.

"Dear God, it's me again, your loving daughter Sharon. I want to thank you for blocking the devil's plan and sending Bernard to me. I ask for your forgiveness for pursuing something you took away from me so long ago. Thank you for opening my eyes to see the blessing that stands before me. I know Bernard is upset right now, because he needs time. I petition you on his behalf, asking you to mend his heart and send him back to my loving arms, where he belongs. Amen."

CHAPTER 59

BERNARD'S REPLACEMENT

I have been spending a lot of time at O'Neill's since Sharon's shit was blown up. I guess it goes without saying, these broads are just as sneaky as men, but I think they have one up on us, real talk. That's why I don't love them. I just fuck them, one after the other. It's better off that way. When you think you've found the right one, and you try to show her what a real man is and how she's supposed to be treated, she turns around and shits on you. No love lost, just another notch under my belt.

Nariah just finished vacuuming up my seed, and I am now in desperate need of a drink and a stogie. I love my cigars as much as I do some warm, wet poontang. *All I need at this moment is to slide up in something*, I think, on the prowl, scanning O'Neill's for my newest prey. *Bingo!*

"You forgot to leave me your name," I say.

"Excuse me, who are you? And have we met before?" she asks.

"I apologize. I thought we'd met before, unless it was in my dreams."

"You can't be serious! Did you make that line up all by yourself?"

"Sure did, and it got your attention. So what's up?"

"What do you mean, what's up?"

"Are you going to leave with me so I can take care of that gushy stuff, or are you going to continue to sit here by yourself?" I ask, getting up to leave.

"Hold on. Where are we going?"

Thirsty broads, I think before asking her, her name as we're walking out the door.

"That's not important," she tells me. "The only thing I'm concerned about is, do you have a rubber, and can back your words up with your actions and take good care of this sweet gushy stuff, as you call it?"

"The only thing that's going to be backed up is that ass when I get you to the room," I reply, opening up the car door so she can get in.

We pull up to the Comfort Inn in record time, and of course, she slurped on her newfound sucker all the way there.

"I hope that sweet stuff is as wet and sloppy as your mouth just made my dick," I say, adjusting myself to head into the spot.

As soon as we walk in, trouble greets us at the reception desk.

"Bernard, what are you doing here with her?"

"Sharon, be on your way, and stay out of mine!" I snap.

"How could you? You said you loved me!" she cries.

Before anything escalates, I usher my ride for the night closer to the desk and, displaying my badge, ask security to escort the woman who's harassing me and my guest for the evening away from us.

Security wastes no time getting Sharon's pathetic ass away from us. I make sure she is long gone before allowing the receptionist to assign us a room. I don't want any interruptions tonight. I'm about to make the bed springs sing the song of mercy.

CHAPTER 60

BRAXTON

The love I have for Tae is real, but I know she will never understand the fact that I am a man, and I don't take disrespect and threats lightly. I could let it ride, scoop her up, and be on my way, but the moment dude cocked his nine on me was when he signed his death sentence. This is not something I can just walk away from; my pride won't allow me to.

I've been sitting in my truck for a minute, trying to process all this shit. I hated walking away and shutting Tae down like that, but I don't need any distractions right now. Bad enough I'm forced to deal with Sharon's crazy ass, and I'm not 100 percent positive everything is going to pan out the way I planned it. If it doesn't, I'm willing to take an *L* if it comes down to it.

Sharon has been blowing up my phone, texting and calling, claiming she has things to do and she needs to get her car. If it was that serious, she should climb her happy ass in a cab and go get her car. She ain't fooling nobody but herself. She wants this long dick from the back and is using her car to get me over there. I will get back to her when I am good and ready. Little does she know I want to take her to her car so I can peep out where homeboy rests his head at night. That will put my plan full speed in motion.

Damn, I must have talked her ass up. Here she goes, blowing my damn line up.

"What do you want, Sharon!" I spit into the phone.

"Can you come to the hotel? He's here and had security escort me to my room."

"I'm on my way," I say, then end the call.

This muthafucka is really on some shit. He needs security, when *he's* the problem? How does that work out? He really will need security *and* a coroner when I get through with his bitch ass.

CHAPTER 61

NARIAH'S BACK WITH A VENGEANCE

I have to admit, I love sucking on Nard. The way he gets turned on and responds to my head game makes me wetter than a faucet. I had to make him bust real good, because I knew I wasn't giving him any draws. Tonight I'm meeting Walter, and I know he won't have a problem putting my kitty kat to sleep. After the week I've just had, I need to be fucked to sleep, back awake, then back to sleep again. Walter is capable of doing that and then some.

Tae really hurt my feelings, which is one of the reasons why I need a good old-fashioned dick down to the socks from Walter. They say milk does a body good, but since I'm lactose intolerant, I would have to disagree. Also, I know they are sadly mistaken. Dick does the mind, body, *and* soul good; it will take all your troubles and worries away. That's why Tae's running around, all confused, chasing and hiding in the cut with BK's sexy ass. He's torn that cherry out and has her nose wide open. I can't say I blame her; that piece he's walking around with will have you switching religions. It's just too bad he didn't let me squirt some of this Nae juice on him. He would have forgotten Tae's name, better yet, her existence.

Now, every time I think about Tae or BK, Mahogany's fraudulent ass runs across my mind. She really had me fooled. To think I was considering holding her down on some exclusive-type shit and keeping Walter on the side for when I needed to be dicked down to my socks. When all in all, she was playing me like a ColecoVision game. That is the last time I will allow someone to get that close to me. From here on out, I am having open-and-shut encounters—legs open and legs closed. If you can make me cum, you will be invited back to play in Nae's Land. If you can't, legs closed; love don't live here anymore. I tried to change, but these heathens brought it back up out of me.

CHAPTER 62

LATAVIA'S SURPRISE

He clearly has me all the way fucked up if he thinks he can just end things with me and I'm okay with it. Oh, hell to the no! Somebody done told him all the way wrong. I have risked entirely too much to be with him to be forced to sit in this car, waiting to catch him out there. I just know there's no way in the world that his horny, nympho, sex-crazed behind can go from staying waist deep in me to needing time to himself. Go somewhere with that! I refuse to accept that as the final answer. You can trust and believe I will find out on this very day.

I must really be upset, because I am cussing like I have lost every bit of my home training. I am going to need the Lord to forgive me on this one. This man has me in my feelings and ready to kill somebody. There's no way you can tell me we don't belong together. I mean, after losing touch with one another for twenty-three years, we reconnected and picked up where we left off, as if we had never skipped a beat. It will be a very sad day for him if I find out anything remotely close to the opposite of what he's telling me. If so, there will be a lot of slow singing and flower bringing, and I mean that from the bottom of my heart. He knows that when I love, I really love. There is no in between. I don't know what gray is, because my love is black and white. If he doesn't know, my dear BK is about to find out.

So I'm parked about five cars away from the apartment complex in the Bronx that I had the taxi driver follow him to. Now the wait is on, and I will sit here until he comes out. I don't care what time it is, either. *Being married to a cop comes with its advantages, I tell you that one*, I think to myself, smiling.

"Showtime. Here comes the man of the hour now," I say softly to myself when he appears. I start the car, ready to get this party started.

I follow BK to a hotel and allow him to go inside first. He goes up to the receptionist. I make sure to keep my distance and still keep track of him, but I can't hear what he is saying to her. I'm trying not to panic, but this is not turning out the way I had expected it to. When I turn to leave in order to gather my thoughts, my heart stops when I see Nae enter the hotel. She clearly doesn't recognize me in these shades and this dumb wig; she walks right past me to the receptionist's desk.

"Good evening, ma'am. Reservation for Nariah," she tells the receptionist, displaying her identification.

"Thank you, Ms. Westbrook. You have room four-six-nine," the receptionist replies, handing her the key to the room.

I exit the hotel and get inside the car to think of my next move. *Neither one of them is getting away with this*, I think as I removing the wig and shades. Then I exit the car and head back into the hotel. Since I know what room the love connection will be taking place in, I walk straight to the elevator, anxious to get to room four-six-nine. I can't believe these two, but I have a surprise for both of them. Nae is something else, giving me that damn

"Darnell is a good man" speech, telling me he doesn't deserve to be treated this way. All the while, she was screwing him behind my back. I should have known BK was next on her hit list; it appears she's obsessed with my sloppy seconds.

When I reach room four-six-nine, I knock on the door and cover the peephole so I can't be seen. When neither one of them acknowledges my knocking on the door, I knock again.

"Who the fuck is it!" Nariah yells, with her ghetto ass.

Disguising my voice, I reply, "Room service."

She repeats what I said and opens the door. When we lock eyes, she tries to close the door, but I push my way in, removing the gun I have concealed in my jacket. She immediately starts putting on a show, crying.

Through my own tears, I spit, "Don't cry now, you nasty, heartless bitch."

Looking around the room, I see that BK's lying ass is nowhere to be found, but then I notice the light coming from under the bathroom door. When the door opens, I am in complete shock and enraged and scared to death at the same time.

"I hate you," I cry, pulling the trigger and shooting until nothing else comes out of the gun. Without thinking, I let my anger gets the best of me, causing me to kill the man who had raped me from the tender age of ten.

What in God's name is he doing here in this room with Nariah's trifling ass? I think before passing out.

CHAPTER 63

BRAXTON IS FURIOUS

When Sharon called, she forgot to tell me the room number. She said she'd switched rooms because the air conditioner wasn't working, or something like that. *I don't know why she needs an air conditioner, anyway. It's not even that hot*, I think as I approach the receptionist's desk.

"Good evening, ma'am. I'm a guest of Sharon Kirkland."

"Let me phone upstairs, sir. One moment please."

"No problem," I reply, growing more impatient by the minute.

"Sharon is on the fourth floor," I say quietly to myself as I take two steps at a time up the stairs after the receptionist gives me the room number. There were too many people waiting on the elevator, and I can get there faster by taking the stairs.

"Where is he?" I spit as I barge into the room after she opens the door.

"Braxton, please calm down. He isn't in here. He's in one of these rooms, cheating on me with another woman," she cries.

"*What* did you just say?"

"He's here with another woman," she replies just before I slap fire out of her mouth, not allowing her to get another word out.

"Why are hitting me, Braxton?"

"Shut the fuck up before I kill your dumb ass. You called me over here because the next dick is with some other ho and not with you? Yo, on some real shit, you have lost your muthafuckin' mind, and I have every right to snap your fucking neck. Don't say another word, Sharon!" I growl. I lose my focus when I hear a knock at the door.

"Who is it?" I yell.

"Security, sir," a male voice replies.

I open the door to a Glock 26 nine mm staring me in the face. "Fuck! Don't cock it if you're not going to use it, playboy!" I smirk.

"Braxton, shut up! There is a gun in your face," Sharon says, weeping.

CHAPTER 64

BERNARD IS INFURIATED

"So are you going to tell me your name?" I question my mystery guest.

"If you're good to me, I will tell you my name. How about that?" she says seductively.

"It's your world. I'm just a squirrel trying to get a nut, so please feel free to bounce on it."

"You and your corny lines," she laughs. "Just sit back and relax while I put on a show for you, big papa."

I do as instructed and watch as she dances seductively before me, removing her blouse to reveal her acorn breasts. *Unfortunately, I am a breast man, so she will have to do better than this*, I think.

She must notice I'm not turned on or feeling her performance, so she straddles me, dry humps, and dances provocatively, giving me a free lap dance.

"I hope you can move like that with no pants on," I say, slapping her backside. What she lacks in the tit department, she makes up in her ass. I have to bend that over. "Make it clap," I instruct.

Acorn does as I instructed, removing her jeans.

Since she refused to give me her name, I will just call her Acorn, I joke to myself as I watch her strip down to her G-string.

"Hold up, little lady. What's that smell?" I question.

"What smell? Just relax, sexy," she replies.

There is no way I can think or relax with that foul odor in this room now, burning the hairs out of my nose. "Maybe you should run in there and shower first. The smell arrived when you took them jeans off, little lady," I say, infuriated.

"Excuse me," she replies, embarrassed.

"Yes, you are excused."

I am not trying to hurt her feelings, but she should have worked that shit out before throwing her smelly pussy at me. I am completely thrown off guard when I hear gunshots.

What the hell is going on in this place? I think, reaching for my piece. I go over to the door, slowly open it, then peek out of the room. It is pure mayhem in the hall. Guests are running every which way. I can't tell from which way the shots were fired, until I heard muffled screams.

"Acorn, or whatever your name is, call nine-one-one," I yell over my shoulder.

CHAPTER 65

NAE'S WORST NIGHTMARE

I am so anxious to see Walter, I think as I drive over to the hotel. *He is the only person who really understands me. I dig what Nard and I have, but it's nothing compared to my relationship with Walter. With age comes wisdom, and he is a wise man. If I were ever to think about settling down, he would be a prime candidate. But we all know that's not going to happen in this lifetime or the next.* I am torn from my thoughts when I arrive at my destination.

I hurry inside the hotel. "Good evening, ma'am. Reservation for Nariah," I say to the receptionist before displaying my driver's license.

"Thank you, Ms. Westbrook. You have room four-six-nine," the receptionist replies, handing me the room key.

When I walk in the room, Walter is lying on the bed, stroking himself.

"Hey there, sexy. I see you started the party without me."

"You're early," he replies.

"Is that a problem?"

"Not at all, love. I want to freshen up first, but I have something for you over on the nightstand," he says, standing to his feet.

"Let me clean that up for you. I can power wash you like no other."

"We have plenty of time for that, beautiful," he replies, then walks into the bathroom.

I walk over to the nightstand to retrieve the gift Walter left for me, and I am blown away when I open the gift bag. Inside the bag are two small boxes and a note.

I read the note.

Nae, I had a hard time deciding which one to pick, so I bought both in hopes that you would do me the honor of being my wife. Love is something that doesn't come to me easy. Therefore, I have to capture it when it arrives. Will you do me the honor of being my wife?

I stare at the note. *Is he serious? I am not in any condition to be anyone's wife. I have too many issues. However, he knows me better than anyone. He knows about all my issues, and despite them all, he still wants to marry me*, I think as tears flood my face.

Now is not the time for guests, so I will ignore the idiot with bad timing who is knocking on the door.

"Who the fuck is it!" I snarl.

"Room service."

"Room service?" I say, snatching the door open.

I have a hard time processing what is happening at this very moment, so without notice, I try to close the door on her, but she barges her ass right on in, pulling a gun out on me.

"Tae, what are you doing? It isn't worth it. Your life is more important!" I plead.

She doesn't respond. She looks around the room as if she is looking for someone or she has lost something.

"Shit!" I say as Walter exits the bathroom, wearing his birthday suit.

No other words are said before Tae tells Walter she hates him and decorates his body with bullets.

"Oh my God, Tae! What have you done!" I cry before she passes out.

CHAPTER 66

LATAVIA'S WORLDS COLLIDE

"Good evening, Mrs. Carter. You've been out for four days now. How are you feeling?" a nurse says to me.

"Where am I? And why am I here?" I ask.

"I will have Dr. Jacobs come in to talk with you."

"Why can't you tell me what's going on?" I ask as she leaves the room.

Five minutes later, Dr. Jacobs comes into the room to inform me that I am four weeks pregnant and that I passed out due to dehydration and some other nonsense. But most importantly, my baby is fine. That brings a huge smile to my face. I am going to be a mother, and I will do whatever I have to do in order to protect my child from all the abuse, hurt, and pain I have endured.

My thoughts are broken as I try to grasp what the news reporter is saying on the television.

"Homicide detective sergeant Larry Dunbar says thirty-four-year-old Darnell Carter, a fifteen-year veteran of the New York City Police Department, turned himself in following the shooting of Walter Watkins and Braxton Kirkland. He was arrested for first-degree murder and shooting with intent to kill."

Reality sets in, and the events of the past few weeks replay in my head. Tears storm down my face. I can't believe Darnell killed my father and BK. When did he get out of the coma and leave the hospital?

Hold up! I *shot my father*, I think. *Why is he covering for me? Did Nariah frame him to cover up for me?*

"What in the world is going on?" I scream through my tears.

"Mrs. Carter, please calm down, for the baby's sake, or we will have to sedate you," Dr. Jacobs informs me.

"How can I be calm when my husband is in jail and the father of my child is dead?"

"I will give you some time to gather yourself. And I'll send a nurse in to give you something to help you relax," he says before leaving the room.

"I can't believe this! I cannot believe this!" I scream at the top of my lungs.

"Believe what, you selfish bitch?" a voice says behind me.

When I turn around, Nariah is standing over me with a pistol in her hand.

"Nariah, we are sisters. What are you doing with that gun?"

"*Now* we're sisters? What was I when you almost killed me?"

"I didn't *almost* do anything! I knew *exactly* what I was doing and who I was killing when I was shooting!"

"Is that right?" she says, hitting me across the face with the butt of the gun.

"What is wrong with you?" I scream as blood oozes from my mouth.

"I hate you, Tae! You had it all—the husband and the house. To think I was happy for you and I was your ride-or-die. But no, you couldn't be happy with what you had and leave well enough alone. You had to eat your cake and have it too. Now two people are dead because of you," she cries.

"Why do you care about either of them, Nariah? I can't believe you were sleeping with my father after everything he put me through and what he made us do to one another. Have you forgotten all about that, Nariah?"

"I didn't forget anything! I forgave Walter, something you know nothing about, because you think everything is all about you. Well, you're in for a rude awakening, and you're about to go the same way you took my child and my soon-to-be husband away from me," she says, placing the gun between my eyes.

"I'm sorry, Nariah. You do what you have to do," I say, closing my eyes.

Just then, two armed police officers burst into the room. I open my eyes when I hear the commotion, and watch as they wrestle her to the floor, disarm her, and place her in handcuffs.

CHAPTER 67

BERNARD'S THE PARTNER

The crying becomes louder the closer I get to the room where all the commotion is coming from. As I get closer to the room, the cries become familiar to me, causing my heart rate to speed up a bit.

"Please, everyone, go back to your rooms! I am a policer officer!" I plead, trying to disperse the crowd.

I step inside the room. "Nariah? What happened?" I question, closing the door behind me. I observe the older gentleman who is sprawled across the floor and riddled with bullets, and then I shift my gaze to Latavia, who is passed out or dead on the floor.

"What happened here? Is Tae dead?" I question nervously.

"No!" Nariah cries. "She shot her father like a madwoman before passing out on the floor. She emptied all the bullets into his chest, Nard! He's dead!"

After grabbing Nariah's face and pulling her close to me, I calmly give her instructions, saying, "I need you to calm down. Now is not the time to panic. Latavia can't go down for this, so I need you to hold on to the gun for me, and I will take care of the rest." I kick the gun closer to her.

I turn to walk out of the room and run smack into a sweating, weak-looking man who resembles D. It *is* D, I realize.

"D, what are you doing here? How did you know . . . When did you get out of the hospital?" I quiz.

"Nard, there's no time for twenty-one questions. I had to take care of something that couldn't wait," he replies.

"What are you saying, D? Let me help you," I plead.

"It's already done, and I will have to suffer the consequences for my actions. No need for you to get any more involved than you already have been," he confesses through his tears.

"D, you're talking nonsense. We are in this together. Please tell me what you've done."

"My partner, my dear friend, and brother, you know I don't believe in divorce. It is *not* an option. I did what I had to do in order to fix my marriage," he discloses as the boys in blue flood the hall, trying to assess the situation.

CHAPTER 68

THE REVENGE OF NARIAH

Recapping what I witnessed is sucking the life out of my body. I am numb. How could Nard fix his lips to ask me to hold on to a weapon that was used in a cold-blooded murder? The murder of my future husband! Tae took everyone who truly loved me away from me, and she will pay for her hard-hearted actions. I refuse to allow her to walk away from this scot-free, like she does with everything else.

The entire police force is made up of a bunch of cowards who cover shit up, looking out for their own. They stand there and look the other way as Darnell hobbles his crippled ass out of the hotel with Nard like he didn't just kill BK. When I get done, we will be one big, happy family of cellmates, with the exception of Tae. She will be reunited with her father and BK in paradise.

I wait a few days to allow myself to mourn and have a proper burial for my love before making a guest appearance at Tae's bedside. She must have forgotten the fact that her darling husband, Darnell, gave both of us lessons at the shooting range, and I am more than happy to remind her of it. I have been playing my part, calling up to the hospital, pretending to be a concerned family member, making sure no one has beat me to the punch. Even though I am well aware they can't give me too much information, technically, all I want to know is if she's still ticking.

It feels as if I arrive at the hospital in the blink of an eye as fast as I get there. I've been listening to Keith Sweat's "How Deep Is Your Love" since my love's murder. The more I listen to the song now, the harder I press on the gas pedal. I also become more enraged by each note of Keith's begging.

Tae is about to get her Keith Sweat on in a minute, I think as I approach her room. I can hear voices in her room the closer I get, so I stand at the end of the hallway and wait for the coast to become clear. After I enter the room, of course, she is extra dramatic, with the whys and "I can't believe it," annoying the fuck out of me.

I hate her with everything in me! She had it all, and to think I stuck with her through it all, but she couldn't be happy and leave well enough alone. She caused all of this, and I am a firm believer of getting to the root of a problem and eliminating it. After saying my final words to her, I stand over her, with the gun planted right between her eyes.

"What the hell! Get off me!" I scream as two officers tackle me down to the floor.

"Ms. Westbrook, you are under arrest for the attempted murder of Latavia Carter. You have the right to remain silent. Anything you say can and will be used against you in a court of law. You have the right to an attorney. If you cannot afford an attorney, one will be provided for you. Do you understand the rights I have just read to you?" one of the officers recites as he places me in hand-cuffs.

"Attempted murder? I didn't attempt to kill anyone! She's the murderer, not me!" I scream as they lead me away.

CHAPTER 69

SHARON'S HORRIFIC DILEMMA

I've been cooped up in this hotel room for one too many days. There is but so much television one can watch, and I don't have any of my books to read. *I guess it's the perfect time to go downstairs for a glass of wine or two*, I think. *There's nothing a nice glass of Cabernet Sauvignon can't cure. That wine has been there with me through the good and the bad times dealing with Braxton.*

As I step off the elevator, my heart lights up as my eyes land on Bernard. *This has to be fate. What are the odds that he would walk into the same hotel that I am staying in at this very moment?* I think excitingly.

"Bernard!" I say, walking in his direction.

He doesn't respond, as he is currently distracted by the harlot pulling him in closer to her. Bernard totally disregards me and my feelings, not even blinking twice or looking at me.

"Excuse me, ma'am. I don't mean to be any trouble, but I am trying to enjoy my evening with my guest, and I am not in the mood for the confrontation that this woman wants to bring my way. Can you please have security or someone remove her from my presence?" he asks the receptionist, displaying his badge.

She must have some button or something to alert security, since before I can get a word out, security appears from thin air and stares me in the face. All it takes is a nod from the receptionist and they are all over me, like I am some kind of criminal or something.

"I am not a mass murderer! Get your filthy hands off me!" I demand.

"We apologize, ma'am, but are you a guest of this hotel?" the flashlight cop questions.

"Yes, I am, and this is uncalled for, sir," I state.

"We will have to ask you to leave the lobby area, ma'am. We received several complaints from fellow guests," he says.

"Several complaints? You have got to be kidding me! The only one complaining is this womanizer!"

"Ma'am, we don't need things to escalate any further and cause—"

I refuse to allow him to say another word, so I cut him off in mid-sentence. "You know what? This is ridiculous! Get your filthy hands off me. I know my way to my room, and you'd best believe this sleazy hotel hasn't heard the last of me! And you, either, Bernard!"

After retreating to my room, I cry hard. I am furious and completely mortified. The only person I can call is Braxton. I want him to get me to my car with the quickness so I can get as far away from this place as possible. I dial him, and he picks up on the second ring.

"Braxton, can you please come to the hotel? Bernard had security take me to my room for no reason," I cry, unable to get any other words out.

He hangs up the phone before I get a chance to give him the room number to my new room. I know if I call him back, he won't answer, and he more than likely will leave me up here longer. I can't afford for that to happen. There's no way in God's name I can stay another minute in the same hotel as Bernard and his tramp.

"That's record time, Braxton," I say when I open the door to let him in my hotel room.

"Where is he?" he questions.

Trying to calm down the vexed madman also known as Braxton, I assure him that Bernard isn't in the room with me, that he's in another room with his new slut.

"What did you say?" he scolds, and before I can explain, he literally slaps the spit out of my mouth.

Right now, everything is happening so fast, and before I can process what's taking place, a malnourished man who's sweating violently is standing at the door, with a gun pointed at the center of Braxton's head.

"You picked the wrong woman to have an affair with!" the man says to Braxton, still pointing the gun at him.

"Fuck! Don't cock it if you're not going to use it, playboy!," Braxton threatens. Continuing to speak, he says, "By the way, playboy, Latavia is my woman, always has been. You were just keeping her warm for big daddy."

Shots rings out in the air, and Braxton's lifeless body drops to the now bloodstained carpet.

"I apologize that you had to witness this, Miss Lady, but I take my wedding vows seriously and will honor them by any means necessary," the man, who has now been identified as Latavia's husband, says apologetically as he struggles to leave the room.

"Lord, please help me! Please help Braxton! Braxton, please hold on!" I cry, knowing it is too late, staring at the two bullets lodged in the center of his forehead.

"Bernard, why is this happening?" I ask as he enters the room.

CHAPTER 70

BERNARD'S COVER-UP

After D quickly fills me in on what he's done and informs me that Braxton is two rooms down the hall, I have him stay put in a utility closet so that he's hidden while I do what I have to. There isn't a chance in hell I'm going to let my boy go down for murder. We've worked too fucking hard to get where we are.

"Fuck that!" I say to myself as I enter the room.

Sharon asks me something.

"Sharon! What's going on?" I ask, ignoring her question.

"Latavia's husband shot him dead!"

"The first thing I need you to do for me is calm down," I instruct, closing the door behind me.

"How can I calm down, Bernard? He's dead," she whimpers.

"I understand this is hard, Sharon, but you have to take responsibility for the part you played in all of this," I say accusingly.

"What part could I have possibly played? I didn't shoot anyone!" She continues to cry.

"Sharon, do you realize none of this would have happened had you not tampered with the brake line on Nae's car? You and I both know God is not pleased by your actions, and this is the reason why all of this is playing out the way it is," I say, trying to manipulate her.

"This is not my fault, Bernard! You cannot blame me!"

"If Darnell had never gotten into that car accident, Tae wouldn't have been with Braxton, and he wouldn't be on the carpet, with part of his forehead missing!" I retort, going in for the kill.

"Oh my God! What have I done?" she sobs.

"I can help you, but I need you to do what I say exactly the way I say it."

"Whatever it is you need me to do, I will do it! I can't go to prison, Bernard!"

"Let me worry about that. How did Darnell appear to you when he came in here?"

"He looked a little spaced out to me. He didn't look well at all."

"Good. That's just what you need to say when PD comes in here for questioning."

"What about the brakes, Bernard?"

"Nae's car, Nae's problem. I have that under control. You don't know anything, you hear me?" I say, staring into her eyes.

"Yes, Bernard. I am so sorry for all of this, and I just want you to know I have never stopped loving you," she confesses.

"I love you too," I half lie. I know that in order for this to work according to plan and in D's favor, I have to be to Sharon what she needs me to be and then some, until this shit dies down.

"Sharon, when PD comes in here, tell them exactly what you saw," I instruct her.

"But, Bernard, that will get him into trouble."

"Let me take care of the rest. Your job right now is to tell them about the spaced-out, weak man who came in here, do you understand?"

"Yes, I do."

"Good. I have to leave now. I was never here, okay, Sharon?"

"Yes!"

"I will get in touch with you later. And, Sharon?"

"Yes, Bernard?"

"I love you. Everything is going to be all right," I say, trying to sound convincing.

CHAPTER 71

DARNELL'S FOR BETTER OR FOR WORSE

"Hey there, buddy. How are you feeling?" Officer Martinez greets me shortly after Latavia's words brutally attacked me.

"Not good, man, Not good," I confess.

"What can I do, man? Anything you need, name it and it's done."

"Latavia is planning to leave me for some dude named BK."

"Yeah, man, I know, and I'm sorry you had to hear it right now. Bernard tried to fix it for you, but everything went left."

"What do you mean, you know? Please tell me what the fuck is going on," I spit angrily.

The next forty-five minutes could not have been scripted or planned, and I feel as if I am being beaten repeatedly with a bag of nickels. Martinez informs me of—or should I say, "Brings me up to speed on"?—all that I missed while I was asleep.

Looks like he just woke me the fuck up.

This shit is like one of those Lifetime movies Latavia spends her Saturdays watching. From what I gather, Nariah's female lover cut the brake line on the car, the same car I jumped into to run behind my wife. *First question*, I think, *is, when did Nae's ass become a carpet muncher*? Knowing her ghetto ass, she's probably been one from the jump, which isn't important either way. What I'm really upset about is finding out that Latavia was involved in the accident and that she lost our baby in the interim.

"Do you need a moment, Officer? You've been very quiet, and there's more," Martinez says.

"I'm okay. I need to know the truth, so don't hold anything back," I reply.

I guess, like they say, you get what you ask for. He continues talking, giving it to me raw and uncut, without a condom or lubricant. Leaves nothing unanswered. The one thing Martinez says that blows my mind is that Nae's lover happens to be the wife of the man who's trying to destroy my marriage. She was out to hurt Nae in order to get close to Tae when she met Nard and fell in love. Ain't that about a bitch for you! Confusing as hell. Martinez says Nard put the pieces together with his help, and it was hard on both of them.

Now I see why Latavia never came to see me. She was playing house with this Braxton guy in Connecticut, until Nard shut that shit down. My boy is nothing to mess with; he really looked out and held me down. I know it was hard for him, and knowing him the way I do, I know he wanted to fuck Latavia up for disrespecting me and our marriage, but of course, again out of respect for me, he didn't.

"Martinez, out of everything you've shared, there is one thing that isn't adding up," I say.

"What's that?"

"Latavia mentioned something about a baby between Nae and me."

"D, you got me on that. I didn't hear about that one."

"I don't know what the hell she's talking about, but best believe I will find out."

"I'm in. I will help you with whatever it is you need, buddy."

"You've done enough, Martinez. You don't have to get any more involved than you have. I appreciate it."

"Like you said, I am already in it, Officer, and you didn't deserve any of this."

"You need to be aware that nothing's changed. Just like on the job, I believe in getting my man, and I won't rest until I've done so. We can always work out the story later," I inform him.

"Say no more. I understand," he replies, signaling he is on board.

I haven't really thought any of this out thoroughly, but I will process it after I make a quick run to the house. There's a tracking device installed on Latavia's car. I had it put on shortly after we were married. That will give us a heads-up as to her whereabouts, and we can take it from there.

Martinez assists me with getting out of the hospital unnoticed. I don't know how he does it. It's like he had it strategically planned way before I mentioned getting out of there to him. When I walk into the house, I can smell Latavia all over the place. She's wearing her favorite perfume, Angel, by Thierry Mugler. That smell arouses me every time. Latavia would spray it on the bed sheets and pillowcases, and that scent would stay with me throughout the day, no matter how much cologne I put on. This was her way of keeping the maggots away, as she would say, as well as a way for her to stay fresh on my mind when I was away from her.

I guess she should have been spraying some kind of shit to keep BK, Braxton, or whatever the fuck his name is, away. But it's not all a loss. When I get hold of him, I am going to spray him with something that will keep him away for good, I think as Martinez helps me up the stairs.

After tracking the location of Latavia's car at the Comfort Inn in Midtown, we put two and two together. Martinez makes a few phone calls, and we are now in possession of the floor and room number for Mr. Kirkland. I am fine on the ride over, but when we pull up in the back of the hotel, my heart skips a few beats.

"Are you sure you're up for this, man? You don't look too good," Martinez says.

"I don't have a choice. Until death, Martinez. Until death do us part," I reply as a single tear makes itself known. "I will take it from here. You can sit down here while I take care of this."

"No, I can't do that. I'm going in with you. I can't afford for something to go wrong or for something else to happen to you, Officer," Martinez pleads.

"You do understand, if things go wrong, you could lose everything you've worked so hard for? This is my fight, and I have to do what I have to do, Officer," I tell him.

"I understand, and like you said, we will work out the story later. Now let's go get this bastard!"

Taking the stairs to the fourth floor isn't the wisest move on my part. It takes a lot out of me, trying to climb these stairs, and I sweat like crazy.

"Let's take an elevator, man," Martinez suggests. "You're going to overexert yourself and deplete all your energy before we even get there."

"I'm fine!"

We arrive at our intended destination. I tell Martinez to stay in the stairwell, and if I am not back in ten minutes, to come looking for me.

Room four-seventy-one, I think. When I reach that room, I knock on the door.

The door opens without any acknowledgment, and I, in turn, push my way in, aiming the gun at my intended target. Looking around the room, I realize that Latavia is nowhere in sight. There is a woman here, but she isn't Latavia.

This isn't the time to be confused or caught off guard, I think.

BK, the tough guy, must be aware of my hesitation, which is on my face. He starts talking out the side of his face.

He must think I am some kind of chump, but I'm about to call his bluff.

As I pull the trigger, I silently recite, *I, Darnell Maxwell Carter, take you, Latavia Watkins, to be my lawfully wedded wife, through the good and the bad, until death do us part.*

"Oh my God! Please, sir, don't kill me!" the woman cries frantically.

I know the sound of the gunshots is going to have PD swarming all over the place in a matter of minutes, I think as I muster up as much strength as I can to get out of the room and make my way back to the stairwell.

"D, what are you doing here? How did you . . . When did you get out of the hospital?" Nard quizzes when I run smack into him.

Not wanting to involve him, since Martinez is already ten toes deep in this, I try to disregard his questions, but I know my boy like I know myself, and there's no chance in hell he's going to just let this ride.

"Let me help you fix whatever it is, D," he pleads.

"This is my problem, Nard. I've already involved Martinez when I shouldn't have," I reply.

"Where is he?"

"In the stairwell."

"Stay here in the utility closet while I handle things from here," he states, guiding me toward the closet. "I will be back in ten minutes tops. Please don't move, D," he instructs before shutting the door.

Little does he know, I can't move; I'm all out of energy. I need to rest and regain my composure before sleep completely takes over me.

CHAPTER 72

LATAVIA'S TURMOIL

I can't believe Nariah put a gun to my head, threatening to take my life over Walter—my father, *of all people*. She acts like she wasn't present back then and isn't aware of all the awful things he did to me and made me to do her. It seems like everyone I have loved or have been with—voluntarily or involuntarily—she has to have a piece of. Nariah never came across as a jealous, insecure woman, but at this point, I am beginning to second-guess that. Everyone in my life whom I've loved has betrayed and hurt me.

"Latavia, is it all right for me to come in?" Nard questions from the other side of the door, pulling me away from my thoughts.

"Sure. Why not?"

"How are you feeling?"

"Like you care, Bernard."

"What makes you think I don't care, Tae? I've risked so much for your well-being, but your selfish ass is too blind to see it."

"I'm not in the mood for your shit. I don't have the energy today."

"My bad! We all are under a lot of pressure right now, and everyone's judgment has been a little off."

"What do you mean by that?"

"Let me ask you something. Do you remember everything that happened a few days back?"

"I recall everything up until I shot my father," I whimper.

"Latavia, you didn't shoot your father. The gun you had didn't have any bullets in it. You shot blanks."

"Bernard, you're the one whose judgment is off. You have lost your mind. I am not crazy. I was there, and I know what happened."

"Listen to me, Tae. D followed you up to the hotel to try to get you away from Braxton. When he saw your father and you with the gun, he lost it. At least that's what Nariah is telling PD."

"This isn't making any sense! How in God's name did he know where I was or what Walter looked like?"

"He is a police officer, remember, Latavia?"

"But not too long ago, Nariah came in here, confirming I'd shot my father. Why would she switch it up and blame Darnell?"

"She is also the same person who was fucking your father behind your back, so put two and two together."

All I can do is sob. I am not completely confused. I remember as clear as day shooting my father; the entire incident has continually replayed in my mind ever since. Why would Darnell risk everything for me after what I've done to him? None of this is adding up.

"Did you hear anything I just said, Tae?"

"I'm sorry. I got lost in my thoughts. What did you say?"

"I can fix all of this, but I need you to tell PD your father was already on the floor, shot, when you arrived in the room."

"I am not lying, Bernard!"

"Well, suit yourself! You will be pregnant in jail for a crime you didn't commit. Do you ever think about anyone other than yourself? For once, you can do something for D and help him out, but because you didn't get the revenge on your father you wanted, you're insisting on trying to prove something to yourself by taking the blame. Have fun in prison," he says, then gathers himself to leave.

"Give me a minute, Bernard. Don't leave just yet."

CHAPTER 73

DARNELL, WHAT'S GOING ON?

"How long was I in the utility closet, when did I get out, and how did I end up back in a hospital?" I ask myself, looking around the room, confused. Trying to get my mind right before talking to anyone, I decide to take a look at the newspaper on the windowsill.

Wrong move! Guess who's in the headline?

"The preliminary hearing for the murder trial of Officer Darnell Carter, charged with the shooting death of Braxton Kirkland and Walter Watkins, is set to begin a month from today. His lawyers say he will enter an insanity plea. Court records show the defense attorney, Jerry White, plans to call forensic psychiatrist Dr. Alfred Monahan. Dr. Monahan has written a letter saying Officer Carter suffered from a brain disorder related to a head injury he incurred during a traffic accident several months back and wasn't responsible for his actions during the shootings."

What the fuck?

"Hey, partner. Glad to see you're back from your catnap," Nard jokes when he walks in.

"How did I end up back here? And *please* tell what the fuck is going on. *An insanity plea? Two murders*?"

"D, you've been admitted to South Oaks psychiatric hospital. After you passed out in the utility closet, the paramedics had you transported to the hospital, and because of your condition, you were transferred here."

"Because of *my condition*? Don't bullshit me, Nard."

"Long story short, when I went to look for Martinez in the stairwell, he was nowhere to be found—"

"He left me, and I'm being charged with the murder of a Walter Watkins. Who the fuck is he?" I ask, cutting him off.

"That's Tae's, I mean Latavia's, father. D, you mean to tell me you don't remember that, either?"

"No, I don't, and somebody had better fix this shit! I shot one person, and that was BK!"

"Listen, D, after taking care of everything, we contacted Martinez to find out what happened. He admitted to speaking with you at the hospital and filling you in from soup to nuts on everything that had gone down while you were unconscious, but he never accompanied you to the hotel."

"That's bullshit, Nard!"

"D, calm down. We reviewed the tapes from the hotel, and they show you arriving alone at the back entrance via taxi."

"What the fuck?"

CHAPTER 74

DARNELL'S FATE

Three months later . . .

"Officer Martinez, on the night in question, did you or did you not accompany Officer Carter to the Comfort Inn?" the district attorney asked.

"No, sir, I did not. I did, in fact, visit him at his bedside earlier that day, but I left alone, as the surveillance tapes indicate," Martinez answered.

"How would you describe Officer Carter's demeanor on the day in question?"

"He was spaced out. He just stared straight ahead, in a daze, as tears ran from his eyes after questioning me about the events that took place while he was in a coma after his accident. Officer Carter never looked at me, and this was completely unlike him. He always makes sure to keep eye contact when speaking to someone. This gesture and his demeanor concerned me and were the reason I refrained from discussing his wife with him any further at that time."

"Martinez, you can't be serious. You mean to tell me you're going to sit here and lie under oath and say you didn't drive me to my house, then to the hotel? I am not crazy!" I shouted.

"Order in the court! Order in the court! Officer Carter, one more outburst like that and I will have you removed from the courtroom and will hold you in contempt," Judge Clemmings scolded.

"I am so sorry you're going through this, Carter," Martinez said apologetically before being excused from the stand.

The next day an article in the *New York Post* read: *Officer Darnell Carter was found not guilty by reason of temporary insanity on Thursday, after a judge determined the ten-year veteran police officer could not understand right from wrong during the alleged attack three months prior at the Comfort Inn. New York City circuit court judge Alexander J. Clemmings said the testimony of mental health experts in particular convinced him Officer Carter did not understand what he was doing when he shot and killed Braxton Kirkland.*

On the outside looking in, I look and sound like a straight-up nutcase, and all this shit has been a bit overwhelming, to say the least. Now I'm stuck here, patiently waiting for my attorney to receive the commissioner's final deposition outlining his decision. In other words, my fate is in the hands of the commissioner, and he will determine whether or not I'm fit to continue serving as one of New York City's finest. My childhood dream could now be taken right out from under me.

Only a few things during the trial stick out in particular, like when my boy Bernard and Officer Martinez took the stand. Everything else before or after that is a complete blur. Listening to them, I began second-guessing myself and wondering if I'd finally checked out and might actually belong in this place. If I wasn't already committed or hadn't been in here the past three months, I would be looking to see where I sign up to be admitted, real talk.

"How the hell did it get to this point?" I question myself, trying to recap the entire ordeal.

When Bernard took the stand, I had to swallow all my pride and face the fact that I must have blacked out and the injuries from the accident really did a number on me. Because all I know is the incident didn't happen the way I originally said or thought it did, especially my turning myself in and admitting to shooting Latavia's father. From what I've been told now, Nae is currently being charged for his murder, along with the attempted murder of me and Latavia, and all this shit is completely and absolutely insane to me.

CHAPTER 75

LATAVIA MAKES AMENDS

First, Bernard insists I was delirious or something, and I didn't kill Walter the monster. Darnell shot him. Now Nae is in prison for his murder, as well as for attempted murder for pulling a gun on me and cutting the brake line on her car. My question is, how did she even know Darnell would get into her car? *And* why did she kill Walter, then try to blame me for it?

I have no idea what the hell is going on anymore, because none of this is adding up. I know in my heart what I did. I am not crazy. I know I blacked out after, but I can see clearly in my head what happened before I lost consciousness. I am not crazy.

Nard swears nothing was going on between Nae and Darnell. It was just the one time they hooked up off the site, and they pretty much had no intention of ever meeting or hooking up again. The one thing I do know is, if nothing happened between them two, all of this really is my fault. I have to do everything in my power to make it up to Darnell. He didn't deserve me leaving him alone in that hospital for all that time while he was hanging on to his life, and to drive the knife deeper into his back, he could now possibly lose his shield because of me. Let's not forget the fact that I'm pregnant with BK's child. How can our marriage recover from this?

Since being released from the hospital, I have been taking it easy, trying to get our place in shape as well as change things around as much as I can for when Darnell comes home. He was found not guilty by reason of temporary insanity, so he won't have to serve any jail time, *thank God.* Although I am heartbroken by the turn of events and the death of BK, I cannot turn my back on Darnell again. He is too good a man and doesn't deserve any of this. I have been a horrible wife and will do whatever it takes to try to fix things between us.

I have a piece of BK growing inside me, so I will love this child with everything in me, the way I loved BK. I guess I am going to have the best of both worlds: I will be able to love Darnell, be the wife I am supposed to be, and not have to let my love for BK go. I can love him through the baby. I am in love with my husband wholeheartedly; I just have a special love for BK. Now I hope and pray Darnell will accept this child, because I can't imagine aborting it or raising it without him by my side. We've always wanted a child; I guess this is our fate and the way the cookie crumbles, since I lost our child in the accident.

I have been in court every step of the way, supporting Darnell; his face lights up every time he sees me, which makes me feel so good. I want him to know I am here for him and I will never leave him again, no matter what. Today is the day he has to go before the Police Benevolent Association at a disciplinary hearing to hear the commissioner's response and the outcome. I have a good feeling about this, considering everything else has been going smoothly. It is our time to get our marriage back on track, with no distractions or setbacks.

"I believe the sun will shine on us today and it will be a good outcome," I say to myself as I walk into One Police Plaza.

***

"Officer Carter, how do you plead?"

"Not guilty, sir," Darnell replies.

"After an in-depth review consistent with further investigations, we have decided that termination is in order, and we ask that you hand over your shield, gun, and ID card as of thirteen hundred hours."

CHAPTER 76

NARIAH'S STORY

I feel like Ms. Sofia from *The Color Purple*. She says, "All my life I had to fight. I had to fight my daddy. I had to fight my brothers . . ." In my case, I had to watch my mother fight my daddy for her independence, and it seems that history has a way of repeating itself. I am left fighting for my freedom, just like my mama. My whole life has been nothing but a battle, one way or the other. People just don't understand me, and that's just too damn bad.

I am sick and tired of motherfuckers trying to get one over on me. I have a voice, and I will be heard, dammit! You can bet your bottom dollar on that one. I dealt with enough of the silent shit as a child; there's no chance in hell I'm going to be controlled by the system or any other human being ever again. One thing my controlling, abusive father indirectly taught me was how to manipulate people to get what I want, and you'd best believe I'm about to come out on top, literally and physically, out of this piece.

Thinking about my childhood angers me, and being that I'm in this shithole, all I do is think when I'm not burying my face in a book. My father was a bastard, and he is the primary reason why I hate men. I love what a man can do for me when it comes to me getting my rocks off; other than that, fuck all of them.

While I was growing up, my dad beat on my mom like she was a punching bag. Mom didn't have a voice, and neither did I. We couldn't speak unless he said it was okay. Only during a set time of the day and the week were we allowed to talk to him or around him while in the house. If Father caught my mother or me speaking, he would take it out on my mother, so I made it my business either to write things down and sneak them to Mom or to talk to her when he was in one of his drunken comas.

Father was an alcoholic who had a phobia of working and keeping a job. Mom worked her butt off as a house cleaner and as a nurse's aide at the same hospital Tae's mom worked at. The sad thing about it was Mom wasn't allowed to see or touch her paycheck. It was deposited directly into an account Father had given her that he had access to, and he kept the checks and the bank card. He got her one of those prepaid cards, which he put money on in order for her to get to work and keep food in the house. Of course, she had to bring every receipt to him to account for her spending.

Now that I am thinking about it, Mom was dumb as hell. I love my mother to death, but I hate her at the same time. She was too fucking weak and allowed him to abuse both of us like that. What kind of example was that for me, as her daughter? Did she expect me to grow up and become another coward's punching bag? Well, that isn't going to work out at all. That's why I make sure always to come out on top and why I am the coldhearted bitch I am today. It's also one of the reasons I stopped feeling sorry for Tae's dumb ass when it came to Walter. I did try to give her the benefit of the doubt, but at times, she reminded me so much of my weak mom that she worked every last one of my nerves.

Speaking of coming out on top, I have been in this hellhole for three months now. I'm getting tired of pleasing myself, and I'm gaining weight. I know that's from the lack of dick; too much buildup makes me put on weight. Dick is my diuretic, and I need to eliminate some of this water weight quick, fast, and in a hurry. I'm going to have to get one of these broads to slurp on my Slurpee, unless I can work my magic on one of these guards up in this piece. I've had my eye on one in particular, Officer Michaels's sexy ass, to be exact. I want and need to see what he's working with.

I know you're probably wondering why I'm not panicking and losing my mind in this place, considering I am facing a murder and attempted murder charge, as you should be. However, the dumb bastards forgot I love putting on a show, and little do they know, I had my little camcorder set up for me and Walter to make a movie, and now I have the whole thing on tape. Right now, my only problem is I don't know whom to trust, so I have to be careful with choosing an attorney and everything else. Bernard's corrupted ass pinned this shit on me, and he's supposed to be the law. We will see how far he gets with that when I finish with his punk ass.

CHAPTER 77

SHARON FINDS CLOSURE

"Lord, I'm asking you to please rest and cover Braxton's soul. I'm sorry I have been prohibited from giving him a proper burial and service. Bernard felt a service would be a bit much, considering I am unaware of any of Braxton's living family, so unfortunately, it's just me in attendance. Closed casket, of course. I couldn't bear looking at him again. I'm already having nightmares from the shooting as it is. Dear God, I am just petitioning you to cover my dear Braxton and forgive me for not seeking out any of his relatives, but you said a wife is to be submissive to her husband, and I must honor you by respecting and being obedient to my new husband."

I am proud to announce I am now Mrs. Bernard Peterson. A week or so before Darnell's trial concluded, Bernard insisted we take our relationship further, saying, "Life is too short, Sharon, and as you see, tomorrow isn't promised to us," right before dropping to his knees and asking me for my hand in marriage. This really took me by surprise, because he had been a little distant with me immediately after the shooting and had talked with me only about court and stuff relating to the case. I didn't hesitate in saying yes, as I know all of this is God's doing, giving me my heart's desires, which is one of the reasons we are just having Braxton's homegoing service—well, *I am*. Bernard is out front, in the car, waiting for me. With my hubby being a police officer, he was able, by the grace of God, to pull some strings in order for us to take our time burying Braxton the proper way.

I can't believe my dear husband is in front of this funeral parlor, honking the horn. I know Braxton isn't one of his favorite people, but he deserves a little respect, nonetheless, I think as I proceed to bid my final farewell to Braxton once and for all.

"What took you so damn long?" Bernard barks before I can even get all the way in the car.

"I was saying my goodbye, baby. Just paying my respects. You forget I was married to the man a little over twenty years, and he was my first and only love prior to you. It's only right I send him off the right way, so we can have the closure we need."

"If it's that serious, you should have got in the fucking box with him, Sharon."

"How can you be so cold, Bernard?" I cry.

"Cold, Sharon? I drove you here and waited for you, didn't I? Where in any of that am I being cold? You have yet to thank me for going out of my way for you. So, I ask, who's being cold now?"

"I apologize, and you're right, Bernard. Thank you for being supportive and going out of your way when I know this is difficult for you. Please forgive me, my love."

"That's more like it."

Lately, I've decided to choose my battles wisely by just keeping quiet before our conversations escalate into something they shouldn't. I know my husband has been under a tremendous amount of stress with everything that has taken place. He has been so worried sick about

Darnell since the accident that he rarely eats, and the shooting and the trial have made matters worse. The only thing he does faithfully is have rough sex with me and drink like a fish. What happened to the attentive, kind gentleman I met months back? Looks like I need to do what a God-fearing wife does, and that's go on a fast for my husband. He's under an enormous amount of pressure, and I don't need to add to it.

CHAPTER 78

MARTINEZ TAKES A STAND

Taking the witness stand is probably one of the hardest things I've had to do since becoming a police officer. It is a very difficult task for me to look Officer Carter in the face, knowing my testimony "can and will be used against him." This is the same man I have admired and looked up to since I began working at the Seventh Precinct. He took me, the rookie, under his wing and showed me the ropes, and I am now indebted to him because of it.

For instance, my first arrest was a drug bust, and the guy I took into custody kept taunting me. He had fifteen hundred dollars in cash on him. I knew if I stamped the money, it would take up to thirty days for him to get it back. Carter saw what was going on and pulled me to the side.

"Rookie, I know he got in your head, but what you're doing is wrong. Don't try to fuck him and end up fucking yourself in the long run," Carter advised.

I have carried those words, along with all the other advice he's given to me, for the three years I've been at the Seventh, and they have kept my nose clean.

Between the trial and my personal life, I am going to snap. I thought going to visit Carter in the hospital that day would free my racing mind from thoughts of the custody battle I'm dealing with at home. The opposite happened. That visit turned my world upside down. Carter's fate and my shield could possibly be on the line, and I have to do what's best for me. I can't allow this trial to jeopardize my being awarded full custody of my daughter.

Court is today, and I have to go before the grand jury to account for my actions after my visit with Carter.

Looking straight ahead, avoiding eye contact with my mentor, I give testimony contradicting his entire case and story, which rips my heart out of my chest. This man is already dealing with enough with the job and is suffering from a head injury, and let's not forget his head case of a wife. He surely doesn't need any of this, but I have to do what's right and can't afford for anything to happen that would jeopardize things and have my daughter removed from my home. Right now, I'm trying to have it so that her mom has to have supervised visits in order to see my precious Gabriella, thanks to that revolving door of a *chocha*, formerly known as her vagina.

Gabriella came home from school six months ago today and found her mother having a threesome with two men. What kind of mother brings that type of activity into her home? Then, to make matters worse, allows her innocent six-year-old child to witness it accidentally? Cola, the love of my life, says only a damaged soul could resort to those measures. I'm not sure if she's right or wrong; all I know is that Gabriella's mother won't have the opportunity to corrupt my baby girl. It's bad enough I had to pull some strings to get temporary custody of her as it is.

CHAPTER 79

BERNARD'S MASTER PLAN

This trial and D's, Sharon's, Latavia's, and Nariah's asses are bothering me big-time. I just know no matter what, I have to do whatever it takes to protect my boy. If Latavia had kept her trifling ass home, by his side, we wouldn't be anywhere near a courthouse now. This is all her fault! None of this would have gone down the way it did if she had just dealt with shit from the gate. But just like any other female, she allowed her emotions to run the show, instead of using the brain in that big-ass head of hers. I feel like snapping her fucking neck. She has to pay for her unfaithfulness. I don't know how just yet, but she will.

It's unfortunate Nariah got herself locked up. I didn't want things to go down the way they did. If I had allowed Latavia to take the wrap for what she did, PD might have tried to make an example out of my boy and locked his ass up. There isn't a chance in hell I'm going to allow that to happen. I wouldn't be able to live with myself if I let it play out like that. Nariah was the ram in the bush, as Sharon would say. When I asked her to hold or get rid of the gun, I had no idea D was down the hall. The way I see it, it worked out the way it was supposed to, and Nae must have needed a time-out.

Bottom line is my boy D is a good dude. I refuse to sit back any longer and allow someone to fuck him over like that. He just needs to open his eyes and close his heart so he can see Latavia for who she is. She doesn't deserve him, and now she's pregnant by the next man. D really doesn't need all this extra shit. It isn't good for his mental state. Shit, it isn't good for mine, either!

I'm quite sure you heard I ended up marrying Sharon's Bible-quoting, bipolar ass. Don't get me wrong. I was feeling her in the beginning, but she showed her ass when we got to D's place and she locked eyes on Latavia. Marrying her was merely out of a sense of obligation to my boy, so she could help with the case if need be, and testify the way I instructed her to when the time may come for her too. On another note, I have to admit I do love coming home every night to a hot meal and some warm, wet pussy. My feelings just aren't in it like that anymore, because I've lost all trust in her—well, the little I had.

CHAPTER 80

DARNELL WANTS TO WORK IT OUT

"D, you good? I was hoping they would put you on modified duty, not strip you of everything," Nard remarks.

"Nard, I don't know how to feel right now. All this shit has me looking loony tunes, and now I have nothing. Everything I've worked for is gone. The only thing they left me with is their ass to kiss."

"I'm going to hold you down, D. I got you."

"I appreciate that, man, but I have my savings, and Latavia and I are going to work things out when I get out of here."

"Just in case that goes sour, bro, I got you."

"Nard, I hear you, but Latavia and I are going to honor our vows. We've seen the worst, so now we will welcome better."

"Even with a baby on the way?"

"I haven't processed the logistics of it all. We can undergo some marriage counseling and work together once I am released. I believe we can and will work through all of it. I've lost everything I built my life around. I can't lose my heart too, man."

"Say no more, D. I support you, no matter what. I may not agree or understand, but I'm here."

"At the end of the day, what is there for you to agree or disagree about? We vowed for better or for worse, and like I said, we've seen more worse than better, so I believe it's our time."

"D, I hear you loud and clear, man. Do what you feel is best, and as your boy, no matter what, I support you."

"Thanks, man. I appreciate you," I tell him before we say our goodbyes.

I'm not sure how I am going to get through all of this with my marriage, or anything else, for that matter. When I'm released from here, what I do know is, it's worth giving it a try. Having a seed I didn't plant is a bitter pill to swallow, but I vowed for better or for worse, and I am a man of my word.

CHAPTER 81

LATAVIA'S WANTS HER MAN BACK

This is so not what I thought would happen. Those ignoramuses had expert witnesses to confirm Darnell wasn't in his right state of mind and could not be held responsible for his actions, but they disregarded all the above and robbed him of everything he put into that raggedy police force. I am so upset over this. Nonetheless, I will seek legal counsel and fight for my husband if I have to. How do they expect him to recover and live when they've robbed him of one of the most important things aside from me?

Bernard's up front talking to him now, which is a lifesaver for me, because I really don't know what to say to him anymore. All I do these days is cry, which is the only response I can muster every time I lay eyes on him. I can't ever get any words out. The confused, hurt look in his eyes, along with my own guilt, thrusts me into my very own personal cyclonic storm. Similar to a nor'easter, my emotions are a cold mass colliding with a hot mass, causing a coastal flooding of tears to rush from my eyes. I really need to try to get myself under control. Darnell needs me to be strong. I just hate what I've done to us.

Without fail, every time I look into his hazel eyes, my infidelities drop-kick me in the face.

While I was growing up, my mama used to say that love covers all and that when you really love someone, you can work through any and everything. With that in mind, I'm going to do what I have been avoiding doing—go up to the hospital to visit Darnell and have a heart-to-heart with him. The last confessional I called myself having with him was when he was unconscious and I said all those foul things based off my assumptions. Thank God he was out of it and didn't hear me. Either way, I have to clean up all this craziness and pray he allows our love to wipe the slate clean. Prayerfully, he'll learn to trust and confide in me all over again. Most importantly, he'll accept this child—our child, the one I'm now carrying. I never stopped loving Darnell. I just happened to run into my high school sweetheart and fall in lust with him all over again. Now that he's gone, it makes things a little easier for me to move past all of that and work on repairing my marriage.

Times like these, I wish Nariah's selfish, crazy ass was around and she was actually the sister and friend I perceived her to be. Deep down inside, I miss her; I miss us like crazy. I doubt we could ever go back to what we once were after all that has transpired. She was sleeping with my father, the man who violated me and stole my innocence over and over again. How do I forgive or overlook that? Let's not forget that she tried to kill me and Darnell. She's no friend; she is Lucifer himself, if you ask me.

All of this is just so demented and overwhelming, and I am so sick and tired of crying over it. No matter how much I feel hurt and betrayed by Nae, I know I have to face the music and go talk to her as well eventually. There's no way I can expect Darnell to forgive me if I hold a grudge against her and won't hear her out.

I don't know how all of this will work out, but I promised myself, after I get my home and marriage under control, I will bite the bullet and go see the person formerly known as my twin—Nariah, the backstabbing slut bucket. In the meantime, I'm heading to the psychiatric hospital to see my husband, all in the name of love.

CHAPTER 82

NARIAH MAKES A CUM BACK

"Nariah Westbrook, you've been assigned to floor duty," Officer Michaels recites as he escorts me out of my cell.

"So, what does that entail, Officer?"

"Cleaning all the floors within the facility pretty much."

"I am an excellent cleaner, some might say a professional. I'll make sure they're power washed and spotless, with the anticipated goal of having you limp at that last drop."

"Is that right?" he quizzes, stopping dead in his tracks.

Like putty in my hands. I am about to make that shit melt.

"I can definitely show you better than I can tell you, Officer," I say.

"The utility closet with the supplies you'll need is to the left, inmate."

"Once that door closes, I run the show, Officer."

"Your mouth is moving, and my dick is hard. I don't want to hear words, just moans and you chugalugging my seed. Do you think you can handle that, inmate?"

Without delay, I formally introduce myself to Officer Michaels's sexy ass by dropping to my knees. This has to be a stellar performance, because I need some dick on a regular basis, and most importantly, I'm going to use his weak ass to help me get out of this shithole.

Teasing him a little, I spend a little time kissing on his inner thigh and his pubic hair while massaging his waist and chest. Every now and then, I allow my lips to rub up against his penis gently as I move from one thigh to the other. Before taking his well-manicured, well-crafted man stick into my warm, anxious mouth, I hold it in my hand, kiss the base of his tool with my wet lips before running my tongue up and down the entire length of his shaft. As I hold it up by the base, I open my mouth wide enough to allow his manhood entrance in such a way that it barely touches the inside of my cheeks. I take him in as far back as I can before closing my mouth, and then I glide his thick penis in and out—of course, without taking my eyes off him.

"You're under my spell now. Welcome to Nae's Land," I tease with my mouth full.

Starting with slow movements, I press down on the head of his dick with the underside of my tongue and flick my tongue against it. Then I move my lips slowly and suck and slurp up and down on my newfound joystick. From the movements of his hips and the way he's grabbing my hair, I see I now have him right where I want him, so it's time to change the pace and suck with a little more gusto, all the while massaging his testicles. He's tensing up now; we all know he's about to cave in.

"You like that, Mr. Officer?" I taunt.

"Oh God, *yes*!"

"No, baby. It's Nariah. Now say my name."

Officer Michaels is clearly an amateur and should make it his business to stick to law enforcement. He is undoubtedly sprung from the tip of my tongue. I am telling you, I must be in the wrong field, and I should be giving doming lessons or something with the talent contained within these here jaws of mine. This shit should be televised—of course, for the right price, now that I'm thinking about it. My gran used to say, "Vagina and head ain't free and is the oldest profession around. Do your research." I think I'm going to have to take Gran's advice; in actuality, it's already in motion. Officer Michaels has been coming correct in making my temporary stay worth my while and very pleasant, if I do say so myself.

The things I used to take for granted, such as toothpaste, a toothbrush, mouthwash, tampons, and fast food, are considered contraband in the pen. However, my sexy Officer Michaels has made it possible for me to make sure I don't want for anything up in this piece. This is important, considering I have no one to put money on my books for me. I will admit I have learned a valuable lesson in this place, and that's to appreciate the little things in life, because all of them can be stripped from you in the twinkling of an eye. Who knew I would be ecstatic to get a damn toothbrush and fast food? I mean, a McDonald's cheeseburger, really? Especially when I barely ate fast food, to boot. Right about now that shit is like having filet mignon.

On another note, it appears as if my alluring officer is catching feelings. For instance, the last time we exchanged fluids, he wanted to be gentle and passionate. I had to get a little aggressive and tell him to work this pussy and put his back into it, and to save the lovemaking for his wife. I am assuming my words angered him, because he beat it out of the ballpark. Luckily, I am a team player; I made sure we both came in for a home run in the end. What he needs to realize is I'm not here to catch feelings. I need to get out of this place by any means necessary. I am tired of being fucked by this world and this system. I want to fuck it back, but this time I am going to get a nut in return.

CHAPTER 83

SHARON'S DILEMMA

Tonight I have the perfect evening planned for my Bernard. I cooked up his favorite dishes—steak, potatoes, lobster, shrimp, and calamari—and stocked up on his drug of choice, scotch whiskey. I say drug because he can't seem to function, converse, or be cordial to me without it. I'll make sure to have dinner set up so all he has to do is wash his hands and sit down to enjoy his meal. When he gets home, I'll greet him at the door with his drink to try to set the mood, in hopes of enjoying a calm and relaxing evening. Since I'm fasting for the amelioration of my marriage and can't have a solid meal for another three days, I will serve my honey and wait on him hand and foot.

Speaking of my love, I just heard his car pull up, I think. I nervously walk toward the front door. I'm not sure what kind of mood he's in, so right about now all I can do is pray God has answered my prayers sooner than later.

"Hey, Sha," Bernard greets, then kisses me on the tip of my nose. As usual, he reeks of alcohol.

Lord, thank you for answering my prayers. He hasn't been in this type of mood and this affectionate since we first met, I say silently, thanking God.

"Good evening, my love," I reply, then smile, displaying all thirty-two of my pearly whites.

He heads to the kitchen, and I follow him. "Looks like you've been burning in this kitchen. You've made enough to feed an army."

"Anything for you, my love." I blush.

"Anything?"

"Of course, Bernard. Why? What do you have in mind?" I quiz seductively.

"Well, ever since I found out about you and Nae, I haven't been able to escape the thought of it. I want in on that kind of action, and since I wasn't able to have a bachelor party, I think my wife should make it happen."

"Bernard, stop playing. I was confused, jealous, and on some crazy mission when I did those awful things. I wasn't even in my right mind."

"So, you can carpet munch for that clown, but when it comes to your husband, the man you claim is the true love of your life, the man your Bible instructs you to be submissive to, you come up with every excuse in the book?"

"That's not it at all, Bernard, and you know it."

"Then what is it, Sharon? Either you're tasting some cat for me or you're not. What's it going to be?"

"Bernard?"

"What, Sharon? I can go out and get it elsewhere if I want to, but because I honor our vows—something you clearly don't—I came to you like a real man. It's cool, though. Just remember that what you won't do, the next woman will, and I have a list of *nexts* waiting in line. So, what's it going to be, Sharon?"

I can't believe he would put me under this type of pressure and threaten me with what the next female will do.

Lord, I need your help on this one. I don't want to fail at another marriage. I want to honor you by being submissive to my husband. Please lead and guide me in this. I pray that after tonight, he won't bring it up again, I pray silently.

"Earth to Sharon," Bernard taunts, clapping his hands together in my face.

"I'll think about it, my love."

"Well, think fast! We're expecting company within an hour or so," he spits.

CHAPTER 84

BERNARD'S LUCKY DAY

My mental is all jacked up after I leave the hospital where I visited my boy D. I don't know how he's going to be able to live with himself and be completely fine, knowing his wife is knocked up by another dude. That is an outright slap in his face, if you ask me. I don't care what's going on with me and Sharon. I would snap her neck if she thought about stepping out on me. D claims he can't afford to lose anything else. Well, we will have to see how well that works out, because I would fuck Latavia up if it were me.

What I do know is I need a stiff one to relax my mental from all of this, and especially before heading home to the crazy-ass missus, I think as I pull up to O'Neill's.

"This parking lot is jam packed. What? Are they giving shit away in there?" I say loud enough that a woman exiting her car nearby overhears me.

"It really is, stranger," she says, her back facing me. Her voice sounds familiar.

"Stranger? Sweetheart, do I know you?"

"Not as well as I would like to get to know you, handsome."

"Nicole? Where the hell have you been? And what do you mean, not as well as you would like to get to know me?"

"You heard me. I know I was with your boy forever, but I've always wanted a piece of you—just to see what all the fuss was about—but I knew with me being with him, there wasn't a chance in hell. Well, he and I are history, so what's up?"

"Have you been drinking, Nicole? I don't eat after my boy, sweetheart."

"You don't have to eat anything. Better yet, you can watch me feast on your wife and join in on the fun, if you're up to it."

"Now you're speaking my language, sexy. The missus is at home, but I know she'll be down. Just give me a couple of hours and then come to this address," I reply, scribbling my home address on the back of my business card.

"Your wish is my command, Officer," she replies provocatively, licking her lips.

"Are your lips dry or something? Come wrap them around this fat stick right here and let me moisten them up for you real quick, so I have something to ponder on my way home," I taunt.

"Let's save that for later, handsome," she replies, then gets back in her car.

"Shit, I most definitely have to drink to that one. See you in a few, Nicole."

This has got to be the luckiest day of my life; I have always fantasized about being with two women at the same time, and that shit just magically came and found me. Now all I have to do is get Sharon on board. I know she will put up a fight at first, but I also know she will give in, especially if she knows what's good for her.

Real talk, I was a little caught off guard when Nicole said she'd always wanted to see what all the fuss was about. That's some shit. She was so in love with D for years—well, we thought she was. I guess she was thinking about me the whole time she was with my boy. One thing we don't do is eat after each other, but I know it's been a minute since he's seen, heard, or been with her, so that rule no longer applies. And this is different; I am not going to be with her alone. Sharon will be in on the action as well. So, technically, I will be performing my husbandly duties—no harm and no fuss, because a man has to do what he has to do sometimes. Plus, D's stuck on Latavia's nasty ass, and who in their right mind would turn down a threesome that jumped in their lap, anyway? Not me, that's for sure. So, on that note, enough said, because it's on.

CHAPTER 85

DARNELL'S LOVE FOR LATAVIA

Nard's words stung when they fled from his lips. I must have been allergic to the sting and in anaphylactic shock. Out of nowhere, I was feeling dizzy, nauseated, and as itchy as a dope fiend, and I couldn't breathe. If that shit wasn't an aversion or an allergic reaction, I don't know what is.

"Even with a baby on the way?" was the only thing I heard him say throughout our entire conversation. That question really struck a chord. For the first time in over ten years of knowing Nard, I wanted to lay his ass out. I know he doesn't have anything to do with me and Latavia's marriage woes, but that statement rubbed me the wrong way. I guess like the old lady used to say, "The truth hurts no matter where it comes from," and that shit beat me up really good.

I love Latavia with everything in me. I want our marriage to survive, to be resuscitated, and to get back on track to make up for lost time. She is the best thing that has happened to me, aside from joining the force. Seeing that my first love has been stripped from me, I can't imagine going on without my heartbeat, because I would probably stop breathing at that point. I love that woman! With that being said, I have to man up and accept the part

I played in not being straight up with her about Nariah. If I had, we wouldn't be here. So with that being said, I'm going to swallow my pride and accept this baby as if I'd planted the seed.

Latavia should be on her way up here to see me now, and I kind of feel like I felt the first time I met her in person at Victoria's Secret. That was one hell of a first date, and a brother has been in that same choke hold ever since. I have to keep reminding myself that, in our vows, we said for better or for worse, and in honoring what I said, I have to do whatever it takes—even if it hurts. I am a very loyal man, and if I am with you, I'm with you. Everything in me belongs to you.

"Darnell," Latavia sings, distracting me from my thoughts, as she enters the room.

"Yes, my love," I greet her, then give her a kiss on her forehead.

She looks so beautiful with that angelic glow to her face. I am assuming it's the pregnancy. *The old lady said pregnancy brings a glow to a woman, and I guess it has made its appearance*, I think, noticing fresh tears racing down her lovely face.

"It's okay, Latavia. I'm here, and I'm not going anywhere," I say, consoling her, whipping the tears from her eyes.

"I'm so sorry, Darnell," she mumbles, unable to get her words out clearly, struggling between trying to speak and crying.

"Baby, it's okay. We both have our faults, but it's nothing we can't work through together."

"Darnell, you don't understand. I'm—"

"I know, Latavia, and I will love both of you just the same," I reassure her, not allowing her to finish her sentence.

"I promise I will be the wife you need me to be, Darnell. I never stopped loving you. I will be the woman you fell in love with, I promise. Please give me a chance to make it up to you." She sobs as I pull her into my arms.

The hurt and shame displayed on her face and in her eyes confirm I am making the right decision by trusting in the betterment of our marriage and, most importantly, in our vows. Right now, there are no words left, just our tears, which are translating and verbalizing our innermost hurt and pain for us. I am not a crying, mushy man, but this shit right here has me acting like one. Like the old saying goes, the heart wants what it wants, and when the heart speaks, we must listen. It looks like my heart is listening, reacting, and responding all at the same damn time.

CHAPTER 86

SHARON HAS TO MAKE A DECISION

This can't be happening to me right now. What does he mean, we're expecting company within an hour or so? I never agreed to or signed up for this insanity. *Oh. My. God!* Is that the doorbell ringing already? Have I been stuck in this same spot for an entire hour?

"Bernard, is this really what you want your wife to do?" I say.

"Did the doorbell not just ring or what? Come down off your fucking high horse. I'm getting some of this pussy with or without you. So, either you're with it or you're not, Sharon," he scolds before opening the door.

As I continue to stand here, glued to the floor, my husband opens the door, greets and escorts in this five-eleven, soft-faced, ebony-complexioned woman with rounded cheekbones, a proportionally slim nose, high, trimmed brows, pouty, gentle lips, and a rounded chin that compliments her award-winning smile. Her body? Let's just say, I would be surprised if stripping isn't her profession of choice.

"Sharon, do you think you can stop praying, or what-ever you're over there doing, and join us?" Bernard calls.

Before I can answer or possible stab my husband to sleep at this point, the ebony goddess says, "How rude of you, B." Then she walks over to me and introduces herself. "I'm Nicole. I take it you're Sharon."

Lord, please forgive me for my thoughts, as they are far off right now.

"Where are my manners? I do apologize. Nice to meet you, Nicole. Would you like something to eat? I've prepared more than enough."

"I can see from right here you definitely have more than enough to eat, but what I'm craving ain't in that kitchen, Miss Sharon," Nicole replies seductively.

"Yes! That's what I'm talking about!" my other half exclaims.

I'm not sure how I'm supposed to feel right about now. I am intriguingly attracted to this woman. There is something about her, and I feel hypnotized and under her spell.

What in the world is going on? Lord, please intervene. Satan is trying to take control of my mind and my imagination. The God-fearing woman I am will not succumb to this satanic attack.

"It looks like the cat has her tongue, Nicole. We can most definitely get the show started until she comes to her senses."

"Bernard, can I please speak to you alone for a minute?" I beg.

"Make it fast, Sharon. We don't want to keep our houseguest waiting."

We step off to the side, and I say in a low voice, "Baby, I'm not up to this. Can we talk about it and possibly have her come over another time?"

"Look, Sharon, the way I see it, there isn't anything else to discuss. In fact, I am tired of talking. Go over there, stand in the corner, and face the wall until you're ready to come out and play fair. Until then, I don't want to see or hear from you," Bernard barks, rebuking me. Then he brushes past me and walks straight into Nicole's arms.

"B, you're going about this the wrong way. Please let me take it from here," Nicole pleads.

"All I know is both of you had better get your shit together, and somebody had better come and get this dick."

"Why are you doing this?" I say.

"Sharon, I'm not doing this with you right now."

"Sharon, I know this is difficult for you, but you don't have to do anything. Let me please you and show you how a lady is supposed to be treated," Nicole says.

"No, go ahead with that. I won't disgrace myself or my beliefs for a man ever again," I say firmly.

"Well, B, I guess it's me and you," Nicole notes. She zips his pants down with her teeth before taking a condom out of her bra.

I have no idea when she removed her shirt, but I love what I have seen so far. But hate the excitement in my husband's eyes as she slowly puts the condom on before having a seat on him in the chair, with her back facing him.

Dear God, I need you right now. Not another minute or hour, but right now, at this very moment. I have been placed in a very uncompromising position, and my back is up against the wall. Please give me a sign and lead me and guide me. I want to make my husband happy and please him, but I also need to be pleased. For years, in fact, all my life, I have placed everyone's feelings and needs before my own. That chapter in my life is over. It's time for me to be treated like the woman I am, like a lady. Dear God, please send me a sign or confirmation on how to handle this.

"Sharon, I know this is difficult for you, and B is a thorny man to deal with, but you don't have to do anything. This is all about you. Please allow me to please you and show you how a lady is supposed to be treated," Nicole says, evidently allowing God to use her to confirm and answer my prayers.

As the words escape her lips, my body becomes in sync with ever letter, word, syllable, and vowel floating in the air. I slowly turn to face her, and our eyes lock instantly as my hands begin to travel my own body, on a mission to remove every article of clothing off me that might stand in her way or prevent her from taking me to higher heights and deeper depths.

"Just lay back, sugariness, and allow me to get you acquainted with my clit annihilator, also known as my tongue," she whispers seductively.

I am in a trance. I usually close my eyes while making love, but I can't take my eyes off her. I need to prop myself up on my elbows to see her. She has to be an angel sent from God, because no one has ever made my body feel the way it feels right now.

"Shit, girl, you are taking this dick," Bernard blurts out.

Oh, my goodness, I forgot he was even here. I need to get it together, but I can't. I'm about to have the biggest orgasmic explosion of my life. It is taking over my entire body, starting from the tip of my toes, moving up slowly but aggressively, causing my body to tremble uncontrollably, to the point where I am now crying.

"Damn, girl, that shit was good! Where did you learn how to do all that? I know my boy ain't teach you none of this shit." My husband fumbles over his words.

"It's always been there. It just took the right man and situation to bring it out."

"We most definitely need to keep this three-ring circle we got going on in heavy rotation. Look what you did to my wife. She's passed the fuck out over there."

Nicole smirks, weary eyed, in response. "What can I say? I aim to please, and I please to aim."

"Is that right? Well, since you're in a pleasing mood, come on over here and put me to sleep. As you can see, I'm wide awake, at full attention."

"Not without the missus. It's only right."

"Fuck you talking about? Nothing we're doing is right, and now you want to be a Good Samaritan? Get the fuck out of here with that!"

"Shut up, B. I'm not Sharon, and you will not talk to me any kind of way."

"Calm down, girl. You know how I can get."

She must have special powers, since he backed down.

"So, anyway, to change the subject, how's your boy doing these days?"

"Shit's all fucked up. I'm sure you saw what went down on the news."

"Yes, I did, and I feel awful."

"You weren't feeling that awful the way you were taking this fat dick."

"Be quiet," she giggles. "So where is he now?"

"You know they have him secluded out East, under an alias, so no one can find him, which is a good thing, because he needs to get his shit all the way together. You know what I mean?"

"I can imagine. Well, it's getting late, and I need to be on my way. I really enjoyed myself. The three of us need to do this again."

"Indeed," I reply, and then I escort her to the door.

Once she is gone, Bernard says, "Damn. I see what 'pillow talk' can get you. Why the fuck did I answer any questions about my boy?"

"I don't know," I mumble.

"At least I didn't give her his alias or tell her exactly where he is, so I'm not worried. She was probably just being nosy, anyway, like a typical bitch."

CHAPTER 87

MARTINEZ'S LOVE AT FIRST SIGHT

Today marks a year since Cola marched into my life and made it complete, and now that I have temporary custody of my Gabby, it's even more complete. Right now, things couldn't get any better . . . unless Cola turned up pregnant. That would for sure make me the happiest man on earth. Unfortunately, it's highly unlikely to happen, considering Cola is on the pill and she makes sure I stay strapped up. Hell, she purchases more Trojans than I do. She said it is important for her to take things one day at a time, like she is in rehab or something. I will give her all the time she needs. Well, that's what my mouth says, because in my heart, I know she's the one.

The downside of things is Cola has never expressed her love for me verbally. She says she has never felt for a man the way she feels for me, and her actions speak louder than words. She can show me better than she can tell me, and to watch her work . . . Although her conversation, eyes, and actions do show and say she loves me, I just need to hear her verbalize it just once and my heart will be content. God forbid I bring it up to her or talk about marriage. I think the last time I did, she broke out in hives.

Back in the day, the old Gs I grew up around used to school me, saying, "Young blood, you will know when you have stumbled on the right one, and when you do, don't trip up over her and end up losing her. Do whatever it takes to keep her." I live by those words, and they are part of the reason I'm able to give Cola the time she needs. Hell, after my divorce, I was taking it easy, until the real love of my life strolled into the precinct.

If I'm not mistaken, the first day we met was the perfect coincidence, or fate, if you ask me. After the divorce, I took on more hours as a distraction and worked the graveyard shift. On this particular evening, I was retiring a little earlier than usual, and before I could walk out the door, in walked this chocolate-covered caramel kiss looking for Officer Carter, who she happened to have just missed by a matter of minutes. *Thank God!* I was instantly captivated by her prizewinning smile. Little did she know, I had every intention of making her mine at that very moment. You can say it was what we call love at first sight.

"Excuse me, Officer. I don't mean to bother you, but is Officer Carter available?"

"I'm sorry, but you just missed him. However, can I help you with something?"

"I was given his name because he usually patrols the area where my car was stolen, so I wanted to see if I could speak with him to see if he could help me out."

"Please come and have a seat, ma'am. My name is Officer Martinez, and if you don't mind, I can help you with that," I replied nervously.

I wasn't sure what it was about her, but I was starting to sweat as I talked to this woman, and all I was doing right then was my job. There was something about her, and I had to find out what it was and, most importantly, what it was she was doing to me.

This was looking to be a promising day for me, and her appearance was apparently more than a coincidence. She had been dropped off at the precinct, and she had the intention to catch a taxi home after she filed her report. However, as an officer of the law, there was no way I could or would allow that to happen, considering her purse was in the car when it was stolen. The assailant could possibly be at her place of residence, awaiting her arrival to finish the job he started, so of course, at this point, it was a no-brainer. I had to chauffeur her home to make sure the premises were secure, which they were.

Now it's a year later. This very day, I have been securing all her premises, if you know what I mean.

Cola's granny agreed to keep Gabby for the weekend since I have a special in-home getaway planned for Cola. When she gets in from work, there will be a car waiting to transport her to the spa, where she will receive a massage, a pedicure, and a manicure. I know women love those things, especially Cola. Plus, she deserves it. She is so good with Gabby—she is actually the mom my princess never had—which is why I always go out of my way for her. For instance, after her massage, she will be brought back to the house, where I'm having dinner catered and set up perfectly, just the way she likes it. Cola loves the Old Country Buffet, so I hired one of the chefs to cook at my place and bring the buffet to her. She always complains when we leave that they should give to-go bags; now she can have her to-go plate as many times as she'd like.

It's 7:00 p.m. She should be pulling up any minute; in fact, she should have been here about an hour ago. I'll give her a quick call to make sure she's all right.

"Hey, you, I was just thinking about you. I'm running a little late. I stopped by Granny's house before coming over, but I'm on my way now," Cola relays after picking up on the first ring.

"Good. How's Granny doing?" I ask, trying not to blow my surprise.

"Long story. You know how she is."

"Yes, I do know. See you in a few."

I have the car waiting for her, and the chef is preparing the dishes for the buffet now. Hopefully, she likes the buffet and enjoys her massage, because I am thinking about popping the question tonight. I've had this ring for six months now, and seeing that things have been going so good with us, I'm praying that, considering it's been a year, she will do me the honor of becoming Mrs. Martinez. Chopping it up with her granny motivated me to jump out the window on this one, being that, after Jessica, I vowed never to walk down another aisle. But Granny said Cola talks about me nonstop and says I am the best thing that has happened to her in a long time. With that, I am going to be a man about it and make it official. Granny has no need to give me false hope and is always blatantly honest about everything, which makes me feel really good about this.

While Cola is at the spa, I will have time to get Gabby situated and over to Granny's for the weekend. It almost amazes me how she took Gabby in as if Cola pushed her out herself. This is the family surrounding my princess and fulfilling her needs after all the stunts Jessica has pulled.

Speaking of Jessica, her tired behind didn't even bother to show up at the hearing on Monday. She pretty much forfeited her parental rights with that dumb move, and from the looks of things, my attorney strongly feels the court will award me full custody of my Gabby. I really have a lot to celebrate, now that I'm thinking about it, especially once Cola accepts my hand in marriage.

CHAPTER 88

DARNELL FACES REALITY

It feels so good and surreal to wake up with Latavia in my arms. I don't remember the last time I've felt like this or held her while she slept. She looks so peaceful right about now. The only thing missing is my hard-on. Without fail, for the five years we've been married, she has been my natural wake and bake. The boys in the hood get their high from illegal substances, but Latavia has been my drug of choice. I've been getting high off her love since we met. There was no way in hell she could lie next to me like this, and I would not want to pound her out. Maybe it's the head injury. Yeah, that's what it has to be, because when she's not around, the thought of her has my man on swole.

Looks like my Sleeping Beauty is waking up, and she's horny. How do I know, you ask? Well, I know my woman, and when she wants it or wants me to know she's awake, she backs that juicy booty up on my now nonexistent erection, or she calls herself stretching, if I let her tell it. Either way, that's what she's doing right now, and my man is sleeping like a fetus.

"Good morning, my love," Latavia says, turning over to face me.

"I hope you slept well, good looking," I tease.

"I'll feel a lot better after my husband makes love to me," she retorts, guiding her manicured fingers toward my flat tire.

Before things go somewhere they have no business going, and she thinks I am no longer attracted to her, I need to be straight up with her.

"Latavia, I want to make love to you and never stop, just to try to make up for the time we've lost. However, I don't think it's a good idea to do so until after you give birth to the baby, my love."

"I thought you said you accepted me and our baby, Darnell?"

"Latavia, please calm down. You know I'll love that child as if it were my own because of my love for you, but I am not sliding up in you while you're pregnant. As you see, I can't even get hard right now, no matter how bad I want you."

"So, you don't accept me or the baby, is that what you're saying?"

"Look, let's not act like things didn't go down the way they did at the end of the day and you're not pregnant by the next man. Which, in actuality, means no matter what happened between us, you were fucking around on me."

"I am sorry, Darnell."

"I know you are, and I forgive you. I just need time, baby girl. We will get back to what we were. It's just not going to happen overnight."

"Where can we go from here?"

"We can go wherever we need to go until we get to the place we need to be, no matter how long it takes, Latavia."

"But I messed up, and now you're not even attracted to me anymore."

"Latavia, are you serious? You're more concerned about sex than anything else? Were you worried about me or us while you were making love to another man?"

"Why are you talking to me like this? You aren't the only one hurting. I've been through so much, and I made a mistake. But because you can't see past being a cop, you don't believe people make mistakes. Well, news flash, Darnell, no one's perfect!"

"You have got to be kidding me! A mistake? Really? For a month or longer, you didn't realize you were making the same mistake over and over again without protection? And now you want me to go up in you raw while you're carrying his child?"

"I have condoms in my purse. I know how you are and don't want you to feel uncomfortable, Darnell."

"If you knew who I was or who I am, Latavia, we wouldn't be having this conversation right now. Now please let it be before one of us says something in anger we will regret."

"I see nothing I do is right anymore."

"Don't play the victim with me right now, Latavia! You know what? We are done talking about this."

"Fine. If that's what you want, fine, Darnell! I'll make it even better and leave you be. I am tired of fighting, being angry, and crying. Maybe we both need time to think and can figure things out when we go and see the marriage counselor, if that's still an option."

Sigh.

"So, you're just going to ignore me, Darnell?"

"I said I was done talking, woman!"

"Fine!" she snaps and storms out of the room.

***

"It looks like I am not the only one who feels this way," a familiar voice says from the doorway.

"What are you doing here? Better yet, why are you here, and how the fuck did you know where to find me?"

"I ran into B and asked about you. He is really distraught over you being here. What's going on with you?"

"He had no business telling you shit."

"Why are you so upset? Why can't we be friends? Wait a minute, from the looks of things, it appears you want to be more than just friends and *with* benefits. I guess little mama's still got it. That's really too bad for Little Miss Perfect. I saw her having a temper tantrum and running out of here."

"Keep my wife's name out of your mouth, Nicole."

"I have no problem with that. I am sure we can find other things to put in my mouth, just the way you like it, Daddy."

"Please leave, Nicole. I'm asking you nicely."

"Are you sure that's what you want? Because from the look of things, it appears you are currently having an R. Kelly moment. Your mind is telling you no. However, the way your pants are progressively growing, your body is telling you yes. So what's it going to be, big daddy?"

"Goodbye, Nicole," I scold and proceed to close the door to show her I'm serious.

"Well, it was good seeing you. Until next time, and trust me, sexy, there will be a next time, sweet thang," she mocks, then blows a kiss at me when she finishes her sentence.

What the fuck just happened? I cannot believe my boy gave me up like that. He knows better than that to do some shit like that; that's not how we get down. Nicole is old news. Why the hell did he feel the need to bring her up to speed on where I am or what I'm doing? Now is not the time for a blast from the past. I'm trying to get my head straight and figure shit out with Latavia.

After seeing Nicole off my property I make my way to the bedroom."I have a headache now from messing around with these women," I grumble right before sleep consumes me.

"Damn, Latavia. I see you missed Daddy. You ain't never sucked on me like this before," I moan from being sucked nearly out of my sleep.

"Don't nobody give it up like I do, baby," says a familiar voice, one not belonging to Latavia.

"What the fuck are you doing, Nicole?" I yell, jumping from the bed, only to realize I was having a crazy-ass dream. Some might call it a dream, but I know better—it was a damn nightmare!

Nicole puts the *t* in *trouble*. She comes off as a sweet, innocent person, but she is sneaky and fucked up. I think this woman actually gets off from hurting people. Of course, I had to learn the hard way; I didn't see it at first. Maybe I didn't want to see it. Now that I think about it, the signs were always there. For instance, I was seeing this female I met at the academy, and things between us couldn't get any better. It really was too good to be true. Well, long story short, she wanted me to wait until marriage to get the box. Now, I didn't have a problem with taking my time before we smashed, but marriage? Get the fuck out of here. I need to know what I'm getting into beforehand.

Nicole was friends with ole girl and put me on to the whole "no sex before walking down the aisle" rule. She said, and I quote, "Stacia doesn't believe in sex before marriage. Since all of us have become so close and are friends, I've taken a liking to you. I don't want you to set yourself up for failure." If I recall correctly, Nicole polished me off shortly after breaking the news to me. Usually, I don't fall for shit like that, but it had been a minute since I'd had some, so she caught a brother off guard. That was a red flag right there, but my man was thinking for me.

You wouldn't believe the shit that fucked-up bitch pulled on me. I'm not a fan of calling a female out of her name, but Nicole is on a whole other level. We had been going at it hard body for about five years before I was sucker punched. Listen to this fucked-up shit.

She worked as an executive assistant to the CEO of a not-for-profit agency, so all she really did was attend a lot of meetings and shit. If you ask me, she didn't do much of anything. She texted and called me during the majority of her day at work, because she had too much time on her hands. I am assuming boredom introduced her to the website Plenty of Dates. From what I pieced together when shit went left, she was the poster child for the site and went on dates frequently, including while we were together. With the crazy schedule I had with the PD, you could say I handed her to the site. This woman would fuck men, tell them she was pregnant, have them pay for a fake abortion, and keep it moving. She wasn't even pressed for cash like that, so I don't know what the fuck was wrong with her. As I think back, she had me real fucked up when I found out about her little scheme.

"Hey, babe, what are you doing drinking when my baby is in your stomach?" I scolded.

"I'm sorry, baby. I forgot to tell you I lost the baby and am now on bed rest. I was in desperate need of a drink after all of that and needed to clear my head."

"What the fuck you mean, you lost the baby and forgot to tell me?"

"I am sorry, Darnell. I know how much you wanted a child, and the last thing I wanted to do is hurt you."

"So, you thought forgetting to tell me was going to make things better?"

"See? This is why I didn't want to say anything to you, because you take everything the wrong way."

I am getting mad recapping that shit. But after getting into a full-blown argument, she charged out of the house. And forgot her laptop, which she'd left open, with Plenty of Dates front and center on the screen. I took that fortunate opportunity to read every email she had in which she discussed abortions, dates, and money for the abortions. This woman was pimping pregnancies, and to make shit even more fucked up, I was next on the chopping block.

She'd sworn she loved me and had never felt for another man the way she did for me. If that's love, I would hate to see what hate looks like. In all honesty, I guess I knew all along that the *signs* were present, but when you call yourself being in love with someone, you don't want to believe they're a bad person. You convince yourself they're not or they'll change. The joke was on my ass, evidently.

CHAPTER 89

NARIAH HAS A PLAN

I have been going at it with Officer Michaels on a regular now, and if I were on the outside, looking in, I would think we were in a relationship. Thank God I know better than that. However, I think he is right where I want him to be. He just can't be talking about he's thinking about leaving his wife for me. Yes, you heard me right—this crazy man is singing that same tired-ass song, talking about he has never felt for a woman the way he feels for me. *I know you haven't, because ain't no pussy like the one I got,* I think. Shit, who the hell does he think he's fooling with? It is quite comical, if you ask me. Situations like this are the things that keep my mind occupied while I'm in my cell and can't sleep at night. That's one of the reasons I'm lying here, recapping our last rendezvous.

"Nariah, I think it's time that you let me make love to you."

"People in love do shit like that, and all we're doing in here is getting our Bobby Brown on and humping around, Officer."

"Stop playing. I'm serious."

"That right there proves you aren't in love, but in lust. You clearly don't know me. If you did, you would know good and well I am serious right about now," I say.

"I think you're saying that because of my situation."

"You don't have to speak in riddles with me, Officer. You can say what it is—your marriage or your wife—and to be clear, I don't have a problem with any of the above. I know this is just a fuck for both of us while I am here."

"Is that all you think of me?"

"Wait? What? For one, you must have been watching too much of Harlem Nights *and my sunshine done ruined you. Please hear me, and hear me loud and clear. We, you and I, are nothing more than sex buddies. We get turned on more and stimulated from the rush of sneaking around. So yes, it's an unusual feeling, but you are confusing it with something that it isn't, Officer."*

"You are just a broken woman who's been hurt repeatedly and don't know a good thing when you see it. That's your problem."

"Now you're talking my language. Please hurt me, Mr. Officer. I've been a very bad girl." I slide down to my knees.

"I love you, inmate," he groans as I extract the balance of his unborn children.

"If I got paid every time I heard that, I would be able to hire the best attorney money can buy to get out of this shithole."

"You're not happy here? After all we've shared?"

"Happy? No. Sexually satisfied? Yes. There's a difference."

I know you're probably wondering why we aren't on a first-name basis, but that's too personal, and as you can see, homeboy can't handle anything of the sort.

Changing the subject, he inquires, "So, you've opted for Legal Aid because you're strapped for cash? I thought you had a successful business?"

"I never told you that. How do you know that?

"You are incarcerated, and we do have files on everyone. Let's just say I've done my homework on you, because I needed to know more about the woman behind the body snatching."

"Body snatching? What does that mean? I'm nobody's serial killer," I snap.

"Simmer down. Body snatching is the only phrase I could come up with to explain what you do to me when you get ahold of all this," he replies, grabbing his cock.

"Anyway, since we are on the subject, I've been meaning to talk to you about something."

"What? You are falling in love with me, inmate? Aren't you?"

"Hell no! Love don't live here anymore. No offense."

"That's what your mouth says."

"You know what my mouth says and can do to make those knees buckle. But, seriously, you know I'm in here because I was framed, right?"

"That's what everyone in here says, and if I got paid every time I heard that, I'd be the richest man in the world right about now."

"Well, if you play your cards right and help me out when I get done suing the NYPD, we can and will be some rich bastards. I promise to make it worth your while—monetarily, orally, and sexually, however you want it."

"So, fill me in. What's going on? I will do anything to help you, Nariah. You know how I feel about you."

"Inmate, will do just fine. However, I was framed, and I can prove it."

"You do know you're being charged with murder and your fingerprints are on the gun? Let's not forget the fact *that you were arrested for holding someone at gunpoint with the same gun in your possession. That doesn't look too good from where I'm standing."*

"I hate to burst your investigative Inspector Gadget bubble, but I have it all recorded, and the tape will show you I didn't pull that trigger."

"Are you shitting me?"

"No, I'm not," I wept.

"So why the hell are you just talking about the tape if you're innocent?"

"Because my life is on the line, and I can't trust anyone right now." I sob uncontrollably.

This was the first time I'd cried since my arrest. I guess not talking about it, and occupying my mind with any and everything else, helped me mask the pain. Bernard set me up, and most importantly, Tae betrayed me. They'd better get ready, because I have something in store for both of their asses.

I fill Officer Michaels in on everything. He promises to take care of things and put me in touch with his cousin, who happens to be one of the best attorneys money can buy. As you can see, I threw this good pussy on the right one this time and will be a free woman in no time.

CHAPTER 90

LATAVIA'S ULTIMATE BETRAYAL

A bath usually aids in settling my galloping mind. I'm uncertain if it's this song or everything compiled together, but what I do know is, the more Babyface harmonizes the words to "Never Keeping Secrets," the harder I cry. *Right about now, I hate everyone involved with putting this song together, because secrets are the catalyst to what destroyed my marriage. I promise from here on out, I'm going to do whatever it takes to make things right*, I think before slamming the remote to the radio down prior to turning it off.

"Oh my God! Bernard! What are you doing in here?" I screech when I open my eyes and see him staring down at my exposed flesh.

"I came to make sure you're on your best behavior until my boy gets back."

"I take it you don't believe in knocking?" I scold him, reaching for a towel to cover my naked frame.

"Not when I have a key," he retorts, snatching the towel away from me.

"You need to leave now. This isn't funny!"

"Who's laughing?"

"Get the fuck out of my house, Bernard."

"When I get ready to go, I'll do just that. You still don't run shit, Latavia. Haven't you figured that out already? I must admit, pregnancy looks good on you. You actually look better pregnant."

"Leave now, you disrespectful bastard."

"Didn't I say, when I'm ready?" He retaliates by circling his finger around my uncovered breast.

"*Stop*! How can you do this to Darnell?" I sob.

"Now you want to be holy fucking Mary and worry about his feelings?"

"Please don't do this. I'm pregnant."

"What the fuck do I care about you carrying another man's seed? It isn't my boy's, and now that I'm thinking about it, I've never tapped pregnant pussy before, and the thought of it is making my dick hard."

"You sick bastard," I shout, shoving him hard enough that he almost loses his balance.

"Keep your hands to yourself, bitch, before I put my hands all over you. But, knowing your nasty ass, you would like it."

"Please leave now!"

"For now, but we will pick up where we left off, sexy pregnant lady. By the way, you know if you go crying to my boy, it will only make things very unpleasant for you, and to add to that, there's no way he'll take your word over mine, anyway," He smirks as he retraces the tracks that led him into my master bath.

What have I done to deserve all of this? How in the world can he profess to love Darnell and have Darnell's back and in the next breath violate his wife? I did profess to love him and screwed that up, so who am I to question someone else's loyalty? I know what I need to do quick, fast, and in a hurry. That is to change all the locks in my house. I really feel like the scum of the earth right now, and to think I loved Bernard like a brother. I will admit he's probably right, and Darnell would more than likely take his word over mine, considering my track record. Either way, I have to find a way to tell him, because Nard can't and won't get away with violating me.

CHAPTER 91

SHARON PLEADS FOR FORGIVENESS

Dear God, please forgive me, for I have sinned. I thought and felt in my spirit that it was in your plan for my life that I be submissive to my husband and exchange fluids with Nicole. I am unsure now, because I keep having dreams and images of my own Sodom and Gomorrah. Lord, I plead for your mercy and forgiveness. I know I was wrong and ask that you extend your grace and your mercy. Amen.

All of this is completely insane, and the bizarre thing about it all is that things have been great between Bernard and me ever since Nicole made me cry. Just thinking about that woman makes my pearl tingle and sends chills up and down my spine. I can't shake her or the way she made me feel. Hopefully, now that I have fulfilled my husband's fantasy, we can both get her out of our system and move past this. I would like to work on us and possibly begin planning a family of our own. We're not getting any younger, and considering we are the happiest we've been in a long time, right about now, meaning over dinner, would be the perfect time to bring it up. He should be coming down to join me any minute now.

"How was your day, my love?" I inquire when he is seated at the dinner table.

"Not too bad, beautiful."

"You still know how to make a girl blush, baby."

"I can make you do a lot of things, I see," he says and snickers.

"Your wish is my command, my love."

"I'm sure I'll think of something, since you put it that way."

"Baby, I was thinking we should plan for an addition to our family."

"What? You want Nicole to move in with us?"

"Are you crazy, Bernard? Stop playing!"

"If that wasn't a joke, what the hell are you talking about? There's no way in hell we're bringing another man in my goddamn bedroom, Sharon, so cancel that shit, if that's what you're thinking about."

"No, silly. I'm talking about us having a baby."

"You're pregnant? How, when we have a lifetime supply of Magnums in the nightstand? Are you fucking around on me? Trying to pull a Latavia will get your muthafuckin' neck snapped."

"Bernard, do you hear yourself? You know I would never step outside of my marriage. That is the ultimate sin that God frowns upon."

"Then what the fuck are you talking about? Because I'm frowning right about now."

"I want us to have a baby."

"You have me, and I'll pick up one of those baby dolls Martinez's daughter has. I think it's called Baby Be Alive, because it looks real, and it even has a bottle, so you'll be all set. You know good and well I don't fuck with kids, and you knew that from the gate."

"Can you at least reconsider and think about it, considering I did something for you I was totally against?"

"What the fuck are you talking about?"

"Bringing another woman into our bed. Did you forget?"

"No, you done forgot you wanted it as much as I did. I saw the way you responded to her voice and touch. Now all I need is to see how good you are at munching on her carpet. Damn, that shit has my dick hard at the thought of it."

"That's not going to happen ever again, and I mean it."

"Shut the fuck up, woman, and bring me my food before it gets cold. You sure know how to ruin a good mood. Go eat in the bathroom or something. Just please do us both a favor and get out of my sight."

CHAPTER 92

BERNARD'S EXCITED

Latavia is always on that victim bullshit, with all this crying. She knows good and well she's been craving this dick. I know my boy ain't hitting it right; that's why she's out of line now. She needs to be taught a lesson to get her ass on the straight and narrow before D gets home, and who better to teach her than me? Her ass is lucky my phone vibrated, alerting me of the call I've been expecting, I think as I hurry to the car to accept the call.

"Hey, man, anything, or are you still living up in that pussy? I warned you she has some sweet, addictive shit."

"That she does. It's gotten so bad, I've stopped pressuring my wife for sex."

"You can't do that. You're violating all the man codes. Taking care of home always comes first. Think of it as foreplay. I just hope you didn't fuck around and fall in love with that ho?"

"Hell no! It isn't like that at all."

"I'm assuming you got all caught the fuck up and you neglected the real task at hand."

"Man, shut the fuck up! Where is my money? I've got some shit for that ass."

"Spill it and the cash is yours."

"Your girl has everything recorded on tape, and she asked me to help her out. She even told me where to find it and where to find the spare key."

"Get the fuck out of here!"

"I kid you not. I'll text you all the information after you deposit those dividends."

"Done deal. It's on the way now. Good looking, man," I say before disconnecting the call.

Nae's nasty ass had a video recorder set up for her and that old-ass man? Get the fuck out of here. Why the fuck would she want a recorded visual of old-ass balls? Either way, I've got her ass now. She thought she had one over on me. That explains why she has been so quiet and didn't get the best attorney she could fuckin' find. It looks like I'll have to shut this bitch up for good. I can't afford for her to get me and Michaels jammed the fuck up.

I call him back.

"I need you to stall her and act like you're working on things until I get another plan in place," I blurt out as soon as he picks up.

"Don't worry about that, man. Just do your part and get me my money."

"It's on the way now."

"Yeah, you said that shit a minute ago."

I end the call without saying another word and transfer the agreed amount of cash from one of my accounts into a prepaid account I set up under an alias for him. Now I'll wait for the information and head home in the meantime. Shit, all this excitement has me ready to poke a hole in something. Sharon had better be ready to receive this dick in all her holes.

"Damn, something smells good," I say, complimenting her, as I walk into the house.

"Good evening, my love," Sharon greets as I enter.

"Hey, baby girl, what you got cooking? I'm starved."

"Steak, potatoes, lobster tails, and salad for my king."

"Damn, girl, that's what I'm talking about! You're taking care of Daddy," I acknowledge, slapping her on that fat ass.

"Cut it out. Go upstairs and get freshened up while I put the finishing touches on dinner, handsome."

I don't know what it is, but Sharon has been a whole new person, and I can deal with her ass much better now. Things are good between us, just the way I like it, without the extra bullshit. What am I talking about? She's been over the top since Nicole fucked her clit up. Her turned-out ass doesn't know how to act now, which is good for me. It means Daddy gets to have playtime whenever he wants to now. Damn, my dick is smiling at the thought of that shit!

As soon as I get into the kitchen, I have to deal with the bullshit. This fucking woman sure knows how to ruin a goddamn good mood, talking about having a baby as soon as I get to the table. Sharon's done bumped her goddamn head.

CHAPTER 93

DARNELL'S AT A LOSS FOR WORDS

Like a deer in the headlights, I'm stuck here, staring into space. Did Martinez just say Nicole? It can't be the same person I believe it to be, but the Coca-Cola bottle shape is a dead ringer. The marriage part is what makes me leery. That woman gave me more ultimatums than I can count, threatening me into marrying her before I finally popped the question.

"Where did you just go?" Martinez asks, snatching me from my thoughts.

"My bad, man. I lost my train of thought for a minute. What were you saying?"

"I'm sorry. Is this too much for you?"

"No need to apologize. You're good."

"Are you sure, man?"

"Yes, trust me, I'm good."

"So what do you think I should do? What would you do?"

"Talk to her when she comes around or to her senses, and give her more time if she's frightened. There has to be an underlying cause. Every woman grows up looking forward to marriage, so there has to be more to her situation than she's giving off."

"You know what, you're right and you have a point. I didn't think that far into things."

"No problem. Now that I've heard so much about this Nicole, can we put a face to this mystery woman of yours?"

"Of course. This is my Cola." Martinez gloats as he shows me a photo in his phone of my ex-fiancée. You know the *same woman* who was up here trying to fuck the other day? Yeah, her.

Damn, this is some Jerry Springer–type mess! But I can't tell him about us right now; I don't think he'd be able to handle it right now. She is definitely up to no good. I know good and well her ass knows my connection with Martinez. I am really at a loss for words right now. I can't believe this shit.

What is that woman up to? Eventually, I know I'll have to break it down to him, but then again, that was the past, so I will let it be what it is. Hell no, I have to let him know, because that woman right there is toxic. Wait until I fill my boy in on this trifling shit. Speaking of my boy, I haven't heard from him or seen him in a minute. That's not like him at all.

"Sharon must have his ass on lockdown," I chuckle to myself.

CHAPTER 94

LATAVIA FORGIVES

Ever since the trial and everything in between, believe it or not, Sharon and I have become a little closer. I have confided in her about some things, as she has with me. I just can't tell her about her bastard husband right now, especially after everything that has gone down with BK. I don't want to hurt her feelings any more than I have.

She was very sincere and heartfelt with her apology and confessed an obsession with me over BK. That whole conversation was awkward at first, but I understood where she was coming from, ironically. Then there's our mutual newfound hatred for Nae, which joined us together at the hip.

"Good afternoon, Latavia. I am so sorry for your loss. I will keep you in my prayers."

"Get the hell out of my face, Sharon. You're the same Bible-talking, crazy bitch who's been stalking me over a man who clearly never wanted you."

"I guess I deserved that. I really thought that's what God ordained in order for me to show I wanted my marriage. As you know, I live by the Word, and the Bible says faith without works is dead, so I did what I thought I was supposed to do."

You're out of your 'faith without works'-quoting, rabbit-ass mind."

"I see why Braxton was so obsessed with you."

"What the hell is that supposed to mean? Because I can't see a damn reason why he wifed your deranged ass up."

"You are very outspoken, while I, on the other hand, would prefer to pray and turn it over to God in order to avoid confrontation."

"Well, you turned him right back over to me while you were praying."

"He was never mine in the first place. I've moved on and found my real love, or he has found me."

"Who would that be exactly? Nae or Nard? Because I am confused at this point. However, not as confused as you appear to be, gumdrop."

"I guess I deserved that as well, but what I've learned is hurt people hurt people, and when you have unresolved issues, it spills over into your everyday life. Let's just say I clearly had a leakage."

"So, you sucking on Nae's nasty twat was your unresolved issues spilling over? Is that what you're telling me, Sister Sharon?"

"Again, Latavia, I apologize for not getting a chance to get to know you first, and despising you based off my own insecurities. I come in peace in hopes that we can put the past behind us and, hopefully, become friends, considering we are going to see a lot of each other all the time."

That conversation really caught me off guard. I was very defensive and angry when speaking to her because I was hurt at the time. After learning that she went through Nae and Nard to get close to me, to possibly hurt me,

I was furious. I did my own research on her, and she appears to be a good woman deep down inside. She was just caught up on BK and that enormous hole-puncher cock of his. That alone would have the sanest woman going cuckoo for Cocoa Puffs.

After deep thought and reflection, I decided to let bygones be bygones, and like in any relationship, Sharon and I are taking things slow. I am now growing fond of our newfound friendship. I just hope I don't regret accepting her apology, because I will lose all my self-discipline and tap that ass again—of course, after my little one is born.

CHAPTER 95

NARIAH'S FATE

This is easier than I had imagined it would be. Officer Michaels said things are going well and his cousin will touch base with me after the trial he is currently working on concludes. Now all I have to do is sit back and wait for shit to get real, along with ignoring these crazy-ass women up in here. I do sympathize with their frustration about being cooped up in this place for however long they've been here, but that's no reason to be salty. We are all dealing with the same thing at the end of the day, but then again, they have to look at my fine ass every day, and that could cause friction, so I do understand their disgruntlement.

All this excitement has me horny as all hell. My sexy officer should be waiting for me in our favorite spot, I think, speed walking so I can release all my excitement all over his big dick.

What the hell? Where is Officer Michaels? He's usually here before me. Maybe he's running late, so I'll give him a little time to get down here.

Well, that was fifteen minutes ago, and I have no idea where he is. *Shit, I need some right about now. Where is he*? I think, sneaking out of the utility closet unnoticed.

"Excuse me, Officer Timmons. Would you happen to know if Officer Michaels is on today?"

"What concern is that of yours, inmate?"

"I apologize. I was just making conversation, Officer Dyke Bitch," I mumble under my breath.

Guess I'll do what I do best, and that's sleep this shit off. I'm not going to attempt to persuade one of these females in here to take a swig of my Nae juice. I need a nice, thick slong right now; a tongue won't do it today.

"What the fuck are you doing?" I sputter. I try to scream and remove the hand that is covering my mouth.

"Shut the fuck up, yellow bitch," an unknown woman's voice demands.

I try to wiggle and get her off me, but I'm unsuccessful because there is another woman holding my legs now. These bitches are raggedy; it takes two of them for little ole me.

This is clearly a fight I can't win right now, but when I am loose, they will pay for this shit, you better believe that, I think.

"Shut the fuck up, yellow bitch," is the last thing I recall hearing as she punctures me over and over with a jailhouse knife before everything in front of me goes blacker than her chubby oval face.

The End